A LITTLE
Magic

LINDSEY LANZA

"For my part I know nothing with any certainty, but the sight of the stars makes me dream."
Vincent Van Gogh

I wrote this one for the dreamers;
for all the little boys and girls who wish upon the stars,
for all the penguins with their heads in the clouds,
for anyone who could use a little magic in their life.

And for Erik, my winter person, the man who taught me that
kindness is sexy.

A Little Magic Soundtrack

Evermore - Taylor Swift, Bon Iver
Fly Away - Tones And I
Keeping Your Head Up - Birdy
We Were Raised Under Gray Skies - JP Cooper
All Too Well (10 Minute Version) - Taylor Swift
This Is the Day - The The
Lovefool - The Cardigans
Dancing in the Moonlight - Jubël, NEIMY
Beneath the Streetlights and the Moon - JP Cooper
Any Love - Dermot Kennedy
Oh My God - Adele
Sound of Your Heart - Shawn Hook
Something to Someone - Dermot Kennedy
Fire for You - Cannons
Hey Brother - Avicii
Hold My Hand - Lady Gaga
Stand By Me - Florence + The Machine

Scan to view full list on Spotify

Author's Note

A Little Magic is a romantic and cozy winter read that I hope leaves you with a smile. It also includes a main character living with lupus.

Lupus is a chronic autoimmune disease, and like any chronic illness, it looks wildly different for each person it affects.

The goal of this book is not to be an exhaustive account of life with lupus—that would truly be an impossible feat—but rather to shine a light on what it can be like to grow up with a chronic condition that affects all facets of your life, including relationships with family, friends, romantic partners, and most importantly, yourself.

Many settings depicted in this book are real. New England is a magical place all on its own. Also, my husband went to boarding school which has forever fascinated me, so I wrote about it.

Many places are also completely fabricated. Reality is over-rated, and I wanted to make up my own collegiate mascot.

Go Ice Bears.

Part One:

Sugar Valley

"Once, very long ago, time fell in love with fate."

Erin Morgenstern

Chapter One

Ellie

Now - December 1, 2023

WHEN DOES A HEART STOP BREAKING?

People are too quick to use the past tense. He *broke* her heart. They *were* heartbroken. It sounds so final, the last note in a song, the period at the end of a sentence. But a heart doesn't shatter like an egg, a small mess to be cleaned up and forgotten. No, a breaking heart merely cracks, opening old and new fissures over time.

It is a level-one earthquake, almost undetectable to the world around you, with aftershocks that come about so surprisingly they feel like an entirely new seismic event.

Can we end the breaking? Speed it up? Do anything to alleviate the ache? Or are we just left with painful memories to shove as far back in our mind as we can, in the hope that nothing sparks them?

I have been sparked.

My computer screen, normally my place of calm and happy, has turned on me. *Sugar Valley Village*. The words blur in my unblinking gaze, turning my vision hazy. I don't need sight right now. All my other senses have been lit, stoked, and are burning bright around me. *The taste of rich cocoa and peppermint, air scented by snow and spruce, sweetened with a little magic.*

"Hello? Earth to El?"

Midnight snow angels, kissing in the cold, flying across the ice until I'm breathless and...

"Ellie!" Fingers snap in front of the screen, dragging my attention back to the now. My gaze tilts and I look out the window, finding a crystal blue sky hovering over my favorite orange bridge. It's the first day of December, but you wouldn't know it here in San Francisco. Just another sixty-five-degree day with a bit of fog that's already burned off. I love this view from our little office in the Marina District, but when December hits, I just miss snow. "Are you okay?" Maya peers down at me and slides a finger across my cheek. I didn't realize I had let a tear slip.

"Sorry. Yeah, I'm fine. Just—" Dealing with a flood of memories I am completely unprepared for. Dr. Green will have a field day with this at our next session.

"El?"

"Yes," I finally answer her original question. *Have you heard of this place?* "I've been there. Years ago. It was shut down when I was a kid."

I stare back at the screen, at the article Maya found from some local Vermont news site, at the photo of the entrance sign for Sugar Valley Village, at the arrow pointing to Fox Family Tree Farm and the second photo of a man standing in the trees who can only be described as jolly. I blink away the next tear and hand the computer back to Maya.

"This article says it was closed for over a decade but apparently this new owner brought it back to life and he's turning it into an all-season resort. And he looks like freaking Santa Claus!" She barely pauses to take a breath, her excitement growing as quickly as her words. "It's perfect for *Wander*'s December newsletter, don't you think? A Vermont winter village revival story? We have to go check it out. And based on your face right now, I'm thinking the job is yours. When's the last time you were home?"

Maya is not only my business partner, but my best friend in the world. And she knows exactly how long it's been since I was home. Because it was right before I moved to the bay area six and a half years ago and met her. I give her a look that reminds her as much.

"Okay, so I know you have this aversion to home and seeing your family, but I really think this would be a great opportunity for us." She's probably right. We started *Wander* while we were still in college together at UC-Berkeley. What began as her local sight-seeing blog has now become one of the top boutique travel sites in the US. We've started getting acquisition offers from major travel sites as well as interests in substantial funding. But we don't want to make any decisions until we've hit all the goals we initially set out to achieve.

We specialize in finding the hidden gems, destinations that are off the beaten path, places that most often require a guide—us!—to make the most of it. Highlighting a place as magical and truly hidden like Sugar Valley, well, it could have a bigger impact than I care to admit.

"You're right, Maya. It's a great idea, but I'm not going. I'm the developer, remember?" Technically, I am the head developer. But I scout new destinations almost as much as she does. Part of the appeal of working together was having the opportunity to explore the world after nineteen years of staying in one place. And of course, the flexible hours of being my own boss, making it a no-brainer compared to other engineering jobs in the bay. The ability to work from bed whenever I need is what inevitably made the decision for me. "You should go."

"Oh, you know I would. But Greg and I are leaving on Saturday for Mallorca, remember? This article says the grand opening for Sugar Valley Village is on New Year's Eve. There's no way I could get there in time to cover it before then."

"Can't one of the interns—" Maya's death stare stops me from finishing the outlandish question. Last time we sent one— Alicia—on a scouting trip, she never came back. You wouldn't think to be worried about a Stanford grad getting swept up in rural Montana life, but I should have learned from years of reading romance novels that a sexy ranch hand was bound to appear and win her heart in under a week.

"El, please don't hate me for saying this, but don't you think it'd be good for you to go back? You wouldn't even have to see your family. But maybe it would be healthy to just be there, to know that you can do it."

"You sound like Dr. Green. When did you get so wise?" I quip, avoiding the heaviness in my chest. And she's right. It's ridiculous that I'm afraid of being back in Vermont, the state I spent most of my life in.

I am twenty-five years old, and I'm not the same person I was when I left home. I have grown up, experienced life. I've experienced *freedom*. Maya is my rock, but I am dependent on no one but myself.

I see my rheumatologist, endocrinologist, dietician and therapist regularly; without anyone else reminding me to do it. I have been to a rave, done ecstasy, surprisingly not at the same time. I walked the length of the Golden Gate bridge, climbed Twin Peaks, got drunk in Napa and went home with the sommelier. I have had sex with three different men, one who said he loved me just before I ended things a few months back.

I'm an adult now. Everything has changed.

And yet, it also hasn't.

The truth is, Maya doesn't know everything about my past. She doesn't know the real reason I fled Vermont and never looked back, because it had everything to do with those three words: *Sugar Valley Village.*

Chapter Two

Ellie

December 24, 2006

AFTER ALMOST TWO weeks of bed rest and way too many hours flipping between *Jeopardy* and *Food Network*, my morning finally started without any pain.

I woke up to the smell of my favorite blueberry pancakes and maple syrup, still feeling the high from last night's Hanukkah gift—a puppy! I'd asked if he could sleep with me last night, but Mom said he had to stay in his crate until we could train him.

I raced downstairs, excited for my special breakfast and to play with Noodle, but stopped when I got halfway.

"Why can't I go skating?" Ezra's voice traveled up the steps as my smile fell. My brother was not happy. "Theo invited me to his family's skating rink, his *own* rink! And it's not just ice-skating. They have a farm with goats and stuff, and pizza."

"Morning, Ellie! How's my birthday girl?" Mom found me walking into the kitchen.

"It's not even her birthday today! Midnight doesn't count. It's tomorrow. *Ugh!*"

"Ezra," scolded my mom. "Be nice to your sister. And you know why we celebrate today. Everything is closed on Christmas."

"Morning sweet pea," Dad said, finally looking up from his newspaper. "And stop playing dumb, Ez. It's Ellie's special day and we're spending it as a family. So stop asking."

As with most family conversations, I let them duke it out while I stayed quiet. I knew Ezra was annoyed with me. I made him miss hockey practice twice last week. I had been at the hospital a lot lately, and sometimes he had to come with us. I felt bad that he missed practice, but I also wished he liked spending time with me once in a while.

"Sweetie, how are you feeling this morning? Does anything hurt today?" Mom rested her hand on my forehead and then my cheek, checking my temperature like she did multiple times a day.

"I feel fine," I said, pushing her away so I could get back to the pancakes. I risked a glance at my big brother, wondering if he would speak to me today. He was wearing the permanent scowl reserved specifically for me, the only acknowledgment I would be receiving. I hated that he never smiled around me. When his friends were over, he was like a completely different person.

Dad walked over to the crate we set up last night and grabbed my new furry friend. When my parents presented the Bernedoodle to me yesterday, Ezra screamed and ran to his room. I knew why he was so upset, because he'd been begging for a dog since forever. But my parents always said they didn't have time for one. My dad was the dean at the local college and worked long hours, and Mom recently quit her job at a big law firm to teach classes there part-time. She only made the switch so she could have more time to take care of me.

It was my fault they were so busy, their schedules filled with doctors' appointments and sudden trips to the emergency room. It made sense why we couldn't have a dog. Then, a few weeks ago I heard my doctor telling Mom another pet might be good for me. *Therapeutic* was the word he used. I remembered because I asked him how to spell it. It was right after he said I had something called lupus.

Mom's cousin had the same disease, but it took years to get diagnosed. When I started getting sick all the time and never had energy to play, mom was convinced I had the same thing. She argued with a lot of doctors, because they said I was too young to test for lupus, but my mom was scary when she wanted to be. She used her trial lawyer voice, and eventually they gave in.

I couldn't tell if she was happy when they told her she was right.

"Are you sure you don't want to think a little harder on his name, sweet pea?" Dad placed the puppy in my arms, and he licked my nose. It tickled in the best way.

"Of course not. Noodle Kugel is the perfect name for him! And I can call him Noods for short."

"Judy, a little help?"

"You didn't have a problem letting her name the cat Latke."

"I like the name Latke. It suits her. But I can't have my eight-year-old running after the pup yelling 'Noods!'."

"Oh, I think it's a great name. Kugel's her favorite food, and now he will be her favorite furry friend."

"Thanks Mom," I said. Then I turned and crossed my arms. "And I'm gonna be nine tomorrow, Dad. I'm not a little kid anymore."

"Oh, don't I know it, my little mastermind." Dad sighed.

"Well, since you're such a big girl, are you going to help me walk Noodle here?"

"Yes!" I ran to the mud room and grabbed my coat. But before I could put it on, Mom bombarded me with a tube of sunscreen to slather all over my face. "Mom! It's snowing outside. I think I'll be okay."

"There's still sun peeking through those clouds, baby. There, done! Oh wait, before you go. What do you want to do today? If you feel up for it, we can go get ice cream, or see a movie? Anything you want, sweetie."

"Umm..." I did feel good enough to go out, which wasn't always the case. Some days I was too tired to get out of bed, especially the past few weeks. I really wanted to make a snowman, but I knew Ez would make fun of me and say it's just for little kids. He turned eleven in August but acted like our two-year age gap was an entire decade. I wished I could play sports like he did, but I was sick too often and didn't have the energy. I wasn't tired today though, and all I really wanted for my birthday was for my big brother to like me. "I want to go ice-skating."

Mom placed a hand on my shoulder. "Really? We've never gone skating before. It might be too much for you. I don't want you to push yourself, honey."

Ezra finally tore his gaze from the stack of pancakes, his eyes lit up like fireworks. "She doesn't even have to skate; she can just go look at the goats or something."

I looked back at my parents. "Yeah, I like goats. If it's too hard I'm sure there will be other things I can do."

I saw them have some silent conversation, before asking a few more times if I was sure. But there was no way I could change my mind after seeing my big brother smile at me.

Finally.

Sugar Valley was an hour drive from where we lived in Burlington. Dad decided Noodle should come with us, so I got to hold him in my lap the whole way there. He was the cutest thing I had ever seen in my whole life. There was a white stripe down the middle of his face, chest and belly, but both sides of him were brown and black. He was so soft and fluffy I just wanted to bury my face in him.

I had never been to an ice-skating rink before. I hadn't been to many places actually. Mom barely even let me go to school last year. She was always so worried about me wearing myself out. I had no idea what this place would be like, so I was surprised by how sparkly everything was. We pulled through a gate that was wrapped in fairy lights, just shy of twinkling in the midday sun. The words "Sugar Valley Village" flared to life, beckoning us through the main gate, and then we stopped at a large sign that had arrows pointing in every direction.

Mom said I was a really good reader and that I was already at a fifth-grade level, probably from how much time I spent alone with my books or watching game shows like *Jeopardy* and *Wheel of Fortune*—so I caught all the words on the sign. The arrow that pointed to the left said "Moon River Rescue & Sanctuary," while the one to the right said "Fox Family Tree Farm."

"Reindeer Rink!" Ezra exclaimed. "Go straight." *Reindeer rink.* It sounded like something from a storybook.

Ezra practically flew out of the SUV as soon as we parked. I had heard of his friend Theo before, but he'd never been to our house, so I didn't know much about him. He introduced himself at the village entrance and surprised my whole family by giving each of us a hug.

"Is that a *puppy?*" Theo pointed to my arms, his eyes wide and sparkling.

"This is Noodle Kugel the Bernedoodle," I announced proudly, holding him up Simba-style. "And I'm Eliana, but you can call me Ellie."

"Cool. Is he gonna come skating too?"

"Oh no," Dad murmured, swooping in and taking the pup out of my arms. "He'll stay with me while you kids go."

Ezra chose this moment to step in front of me. "Actually, Ellie can't skate, so she'll just stay with the dog. But we can go now."

I knew I shouldn't have gotten my hopes up. Ezra never wanted to hang out with me. Just because I used my birthday card to get him to the rink never meant he would actually consider including me. I turned my face down, hoping no one would notice my disappointment, but of course I could see my parents' frowns.

"Ezra, it's her special day. Why don't you at least take her with you to try it out," Mom scolded. "We'll be watching incase anything happens. She shouldn't be out there for more than a few minutes anyway."

"Mom, jeez. I don't wanna babysit. She said she would just look at the goats, remember? Right, Ellie?"

"Sure, that's fine. I don't have to skate." But even as I said it, I couldn't look away from the rink ahead of us. It was glittering in the afternoon sunlight, people gliding in wide circles with their arms in the air. It looked like freedom, and I desperately wanted a taste of it.

"I'll teach her."

Four heads snapped to Theo, shocked by his offer. For me, it was shock and awe. He was being nice to me under no obligation, something I didn't have much experience with.

"Really?" I said as my brother interrupted with, "No way."

"Dude, it's no problem. I've spent so much time helping out with the lessons they run here, I feel like an actual instructor."

After a few words of advice from my parents—*not too fast, please be careful, stay close to the rail*—we got fitted for skates and made our way to the ice. It was a little embarrassing how differently I was dressed than the boys. Mom made me wear a huge puffy coat that went down to my knees and wrapped a thick scarf around my neck that hid the entirety of my long brown hair. My mittens were just as thick and had elastic ties around the wrist to keep them from getting loose. I knew I was younger than Ezra and Theo, but I *really* looked like a child next to them.

"All right. Don't be scared, Ellie. I'll hold on to you the whole time, okay?" Theo took each of my mittened hands in his and showed me how to balance-walk toward the ice. "Bend your knees a little more. It'll make it easier. Yeah, that's perfect."

Once we stepped onto the ice, I felt a chill run through me, not from the cold, but adrenaline. It was like a cool breeze settling over my skin even though I was covered head to toe in winter wear. Theo skated backwards while he pulled me along like cargo. I knew I looked silly, but I didn't care. I loved every second of it.

"Are we gonna have to go this slow the whole time?" my brother whined.

"You go ahead, Ez. I need to show her how to stop and slow down before I let her go on her own."

"Fine. See ya." Ezra zipped past us, causing a few gasps from nearby skaters. He was trying to show off, but he was pretty good on the ice. According to him though, Theo was actually the best skater and hockey player he knew. I felt kind of embarrassed, keeping Theo from racing down the rink with my brother. But he didn't seem annoyed with me, not like Ezra, so I decided to enjoy it.

"This is fun."

"Yeah? Want to start skating on your own? I'll still hold your hands, but can you move your feet like mine? It's kind of like you're running but you never pick up your legs."

I mimicked his movements until I could feel us propelling forward. He let go of one of my hands and came around to skate beside me. There were a few times I lost my footing, but he was always there to right me before I went down. He gave me a few tips on how to balance better and then how to slow down and stop. Skating wasn't so hard after all.

After two laps of us skating side by side, Theo let go of my hand. I was so lost in my excitement that I didn't notice my brother fly by us and clip my shoulder until it was too late. Theo slid to a stop, a spray of ice almost reaching me as he called out, "Ellie!" and extended his arm for me to grab on to. But I wasn't fast enough. I catapulted, all nine years of my life flashing before my eyes as I lost control and went down hard.

Goodbye moon. Goodbye stars. Goodbye Latke and Noods. It was great while it lasted.

I lived, but the ice burned the skin on my face, and my elbows screamed after taking the brunt of my fall. And still, the only thing I could think about was trying not to cry.

"Ellie, I'm so sorry. I shouldn't have let go," Theo apologized. "You were just doing so well. Can you stand up? Here, take my hand."

Swallowing the pain, I let Theo help me up and drag me off the ice. My parents met us at the entrance, and of course were overreacting.

"Baby, where does it hurt?" Mom started scanning me for bruises, pulling at all the layers she wrapped me in earlier like she was attacking a pile of presents.

"I'm so sorry, Mrs. Klein. I promise I wouldn't have let go if I didn't think she was fine on her own. I've fallen a million times though, so I'm sure she's okay."

Mom acknowledged him with a grunt, but I could hear exactly what was going on in her head. *I'm sure* you're *okay when* you *fall, but that doesn't mean my precious, fragile Ellie will be.*

"Mom, I'm fine. It hurt a little at first but I'm all better. Can I please go back?"

"Back? I don't think so, birthday girl. Let's take a break and find a better activity for you."

"Ellie, you good?" I looked up at Ezra, surprised he was even talking to me, and gave him a quick nod. "Cool. Now we can actually skate." He patted Theo's arm.

But Theo was still looking at me, concern reaching every corner of his face. "It's your birthday?"

"Yeah. Well, tomorrow actually. I'm really fine. You can go back out there."

"Why don't we go get some birthday pizza?" Dad cut in. "I saw a sign for a place on the other side of the rink."

"The Pizza Emporium. It's really good," Theo offered. "The crust looks weird, but I promise it doesn't actually taste like peppermint."

Dad looked a little puzzled at that but grabbed my hand to pull me along with him and the dog. Then he looked pointedly at Ezra. "Go skate and meet us there in twenty minutes. I mean it. One second later and you're grounded." He reached for his phone to pull up a timer for dramatic effect and Ezra bee-lined back to the ice.

Our pizza came out as Dad's timer hit minute seventeen. And Theo was right about the weird crust. It looked like a candy cane. Ezra burst through the doors as I took my first bite of cheesy goodness, his face the shade of a tomato. I wasn't sure if he made me fall on purpose, but I was glad he made it back in time. I knew he'd just blame me if he actually got grounded.

And then the disappointment set in when I didn't see Theo

with him. I wasn't sad, exactly. But I was hoping he would be there for the rest of the day. I didn't really have friends, not like Ezra did. The closest thing I had to one was Miss Sue, the school nurse. I was absent a lot for hospital visits and "re-charge time" as mom liked to call the days I stayed in bed. At school, the other kids made fun of me when I couldn't join in on activities like dodgeball or relay races. It didn't help my popularity when I ended up spending that time talking to teachers instead.

Dad said I was too mature for my own good, but I didn't know how to be anything else. I spent all my time with adults.

"Glad you could join us, son. Your friend didn't want to come?" Dad asked.

"He went somewhere with his dad and said he would meet us here. Or did he have a twenty-minute limit too?"

"Be careful, Ez." Dad and Ezra were having some sort of unspoken standoff which happened a lot these days. I happily ate my not-peppermint-flavored pizza in silence while slipping little bits of cheese to Noodle. Dad put him in a backpack so we could carry him around without anyone really noticing. I kind of hoped he'd stay a puppy forever.

"Ellie, umm—" Ezra sat across from me, his features guarded. "I'm really sorry. I swear I didn't mean to make you fall. I shouldn't have been going so fast."

Ezra and I weren't close, at least not like I wanted us to be. He never wanted to be around me when I was feeling sick, which was often. It was frustrating how much he avoided me when I was stuck in bed for days at a time. We both loved trivia, but even watching game shows was something we only did together when I was healthy.

But looking at his face right now, I could tell he felt bad. Whether he meant to hurt me or not, he was sorry.

"It's okay, I'll be fine."

"I know you will. You're the toughest girl I know." His

words came out soft, but tears welled in my eyes anyway. He thought I was tough?

"Ezra." Mom came back from the restroom and sat down next to Ez. She spoke quietly but her lawyer voice still came through. "Don't think we won't be discussing what you did when we get home. I have never been so disappointed in—"

"Hey, everyone." I turned toward the voice and found Theo walking through the door with an older man. Mom stayed silent as they came up to our table. "This is my dad, Steve Fox. Dad, that's Ezra from my hockey team and his parents, and that's his sister, Ellie." I wasn't sure why, but I liked hearing the way he said my name. Something about it lit me up like a Christmas tree.

Everyone exchanged hellos and then my mom gestured at the table with a, "Why don't you join us for some pizza? We have plenty," her scolding of my brother seemingly forgotten. They flagged someone down to bring over extra chairs, and Mr. Fox went right into telling us all about Sugar Valley Village and what they did here. How the tree farm went back three genera-tions in his family, and when he and his wife took over, they slowly expanded it to include more small businesses.

"Sugar Valley's just a small town, about fifteen minutes from here. It's where I grew up," he explained. "The village really brings it to life in the winter though. All my wife's idea."

"Don't be so modest, Steve." A man in a chef's uniform walked over to our table from the kitchen. "If it weren't for you, my other restaurant would have been out of business years ago. But when are you going to open this village year-round?"

Theo nudged my shoulder from beside me, taking me away from the boring adult conversation. "I'm really sorry about letting you fall. Are you okay?"

"I promise I'm fine. It barely hurt." Lie. I could already feel the bruises that were sure to send Mom into a tailspin tomorrow. "Thanks for teaching me. It was so fun. I hope I can go again sometime."

"You should. Skating's the best. Anyway, umm...happy birthday." A glass orb was placed in my hand while my brain short-circuited. Theo was giving me a *present?* I couldn't remember getting a gift from anyone in my whole life besides Mom and Dad. I felt like I couldn't breathe. "It's a snow globe." Theo must have taken my silence for confusion, and proceeded to grab it by the base and shake it to show me how it worked.

"It's so pretty." I watched the glittering snow float down over a bunch of reindeer trapped in the glass, completely transfixed. *Theo got me a present.*

"Sorry it's sort of Christmas-y. I know you're Jewish, but they didn't have any for Hanukkah."

"I love it." I couldn't take my eyes off of Theo. Suddenly I started noticing all sorts of little things about him: his eyes that kept changing from green to gold, his sandy blonde hair as he pushed it to the side, the dimples that peeked out, giving away his smile when he was trying to hide it. I had never studied someone's face like that before, but I found myself trying to memorize it, wondering if I would ever see him again after this.

I wondered what he saw when he looked at me. A little girl smaller than others my age who didn't know how to skate. Boring brown hair and boring brown eyes, pale skin that never saw the sun. Would he even think of me after today?

"Ellie, what do you think?" Theo's dad looked pointedly at me, and I scrambled. Did he catch me staring at Theo? *Just say something, anything.*

"Huh?" *Smooth, Ellie.*

"I was just saying we usually get hot chocolate after pizza, a little tradition of ours. Unfortunately, Theo's mom is busy tending the horses, but we'd love for you all to join us. Fox in the Snow is right next door."

"It's the best. There's a whole marshmallow bar with candy and whipped cream so you can add all your own toppings." Theo added, like I needed to be persuaded to get hot chocolate.

"Fox in the Snow?" Mom inquired. I was curious too.

"The café," Mr. Fox said. "It's named after this guy." He gave Theo one of those proud-dad shoulder pats and ruffled his hair. "It's run by my wife's best friend, Cindy. When she opened it, Theo was around four and was always bobbing around in the snow. She and Carol used to joke about mistaking him for an actual 'fox' in the snow. Sort of a family name inside joke." He laughed.

"How sweet," Mom replied.

Mr. Fox looked back at me again and grinned. "Do you want to try the best hot chocolate in the whole state of Vermont?"

"Yes, please."

"Are you sure you're not too tired, honey?" Mom interrupted. "We can head home any time you want. You don't have to impress anyone."

"*Mom*. I'm fine. And I want hot chocolate."

THE SKY HAD CHANGED DRAMATICALLY by the time we left The Pizza Emporium. What was fluffy swirls of lilac had become a deep navy of crushed velvet, fat stars sparkling like diamonds above us. There were never this many stars in the sky at home.

And I had looked.

One major side effect of my new medication was insomnia. Sometimes when I couldn't sleep, I would take all my pillows and blankets into our sunroom, lie under the skylight and just stare. I didn't know what exactly I was looking for, but something about gazing at the stars always made my head quiet, like knowing there was more out there in the great big world. Like one day I could escape the confines of over-protective parents and weekly blood tests, and a brother who never wanted me around.

But today felt different, better than any birthday I'd had before. It felt like maybe there was a little magic in the world, and maybe I could catch a small piece of it if I wanted it badly enough.

"What do you think?" Theo asked after I took a few sips of the biggest hot chocolate ever.

"You were right. It's so good."

The marshmallows were all shaped like tiny snowflakes, and they had peppermint whipped cream which Theo convinced me and Ezra to try. We drank the delicious cocoa as Mr. Fox showed us around the rest of the village. There was so much to see I felt overwhelmed with this new sense of adventure. Words that didn't even make sense to me—magic carpet, tubing, duckpin bowling—it was meaningless, yet I wanted to do it all and all at once.

"I'm sure you folks already have a tree but if you want to grab one it's on the house," he said, pointing toward the tree farm.

"Dad, they're actually—"

"Is it six-forty-five already?" Mr. Fox interrupted, looking at his watch. "Theo, we were supposed to meet your mom thirty minutes ago." He said it like they were in trouble, but he was grinning. He turned to my parents. "Do you want to come with us to the animal sanctuary? Pony rides start at seven."

Ever since Ezra mentioned goats earlier, I was excited to see the animals. Theo said his mom was in charge of them which sounded so cool. What kind of job puts you in charge of animals? Because I wanted it.

"You've been very gracious hosts, but Ellie doesn't do well

with this much excitement. She really needs her rest," Mom replied. I glared at her but didn't say anything. I knew a lost cause when I saw one. This was probably the longest I had been away from our house since I was diagnosed, and I didn't want to ruin my chances of it happening again.

"I hope you guys can come back again," Theo said as he hugged me goodbye. He leaned down to kiss Noodle who was sleeping in my arms and my hands got all clammy in my mittens.

"Can we, Mom?" I tried to create my most angelic, hopeful, *healthy* face.

"Of course. It's a beautiful place."

I looked around, taking in all the lights one last time, inhaling the air that I could have sworn smelled like frosting. I wondered if that's how they got the name Sugar Valley. And as we walked back to the car, our footsteps crunching and Noodle's soft snores echoing in the night, I repeated one thought again and again.

I'll be back.

Chapter Three

Ellie

Now

"AND YOU'RE NOT PLANNING on letting anyone know you'll be there?"

"My family? Umm, no. I don't think so." I watch Dr. Green scribble in his leather-bound notebook while I search for any hint of disapproval on his face. "Does that make me a bad person?"

"A bad person?" He sets down his pen and uncrosses his legs so he faces me directly. "Ellie, absolutely not. I understand why you're hesitant to see them. I know there's a lot of tension there, and if you're not ready, then you're not ready." He gives me one of his warm smiles that always alleviates a bit of stress and picks up his pen again. "Tell me what kind of feelings you have when you think about seeing them."

"Fear? Maybe?" Is that the right word? I don't know if I'm exactly scared to see Ezra or my parents. I talk to my brother regularly enough, usually getting updates about how his residency program is going. Dad and I catch up a few times a year.

He loves hearing about *Wander* and I like sharing all my life updates with him, but Mom...

I let my gaze fall around the room while I search for the right words. I've always loved this office. Dr. Green likes to say he has a "green" thumb—his dad-humor is exceptional—and must have at least twenty different plants scattered through the office. The whole room feels alive. "I think I feel...*uneasy*. I'm not scared of seeing them. I'm...I don't know what I am. There's just so much space between us now. I wouldn't know where to start. There was all this tension before I left, and it was all because of *me*. And I guess I'm worried they all expect me to make things right but I'm still not sorry for leaving. Nor for staying away."

I pause, but Dr. Green just nods encouragingly. Sometimes I wish he would give me all the answers, but I know his job is to let me find them on my own. "The thing is," I continue, "I've changed. I grew up in this bubble. Small town, small family, small life. Not many close friends." *Do not think about Theo.* "But now, these last seven years...I've traveled the world and had all these new experiences that have made me into a different person. I don't know how to merge the old Ellie with the new. I don't think I want to."

"Why do you think you'd have to do that?"

"I'm not sure." He always asks the tough questions. "I just know that every time I've considered going home my anxiety gets so bad that I flare. How am I supposed to fix that."

"Try not to think of it as a fix. Nothing is broken. All you need to know is what is best for *Ellie*. Maybe that's staying away. Maybe it's confronting these feelings."

"But what's the right answer?"

"Ellie." He sighs. "No one has all the answers. I'm just here to help you ask the right questions." This time his smile looks sad, defeated. His eyes crinkle together like he's unsure if he should say what he's thinking. "Last time we talked about your mom, you got fairly upset. Do you still feel anger when you think of your family?"

I hate to admit it but... "Yeah. I do. At least with Mom. Not as much as before, but it hasn't completely gone away. She made things really difficult for me. I know it was never her intention, I know that. But she refused to ever see me as a whole person. Like my lupus defined me. And these years I've been away from home, it hasn't." My life isn't perfect, not even close. But I'm not my illness anymore, and I want to keep it that way.

"It's okay to say it, Ellie. You're allowed to be angry." He leans forward, bracing his hands on his knees. "Think about this. Let's say you wrote down the perfect apology. Every word you want to hear from each of them. Now imagine they spoke those exact words to you. Would it help? Would it be enough to let your anger go?"

His question jostles around in my head as I try and formulate the perfect apology from my mother. I'm not even sure what it would be. There are still so many secrets, things I never had the courage to tell her. Can I really ask someone to apologize for something they never understood?

But then I feel the anger start to simmer a little more, because there would have never been secrets if not for the way she treated me.

"I don't know. I don't think it would matter. Too much has happened that can't be undone. An apology doesn't change anything."

"All right. Realizing that makes things easier for you. Because now all you have to decide is what you want. You can go to Vermont, avoid seeing any of them, and keep to the boundaries of your current relationship." I open my mouth to speak but he holds up a hand. "I'm not judging you. I understand why you feel this way. There is no right or wrong answer, remember? I just want to help you come up with the solution that benefits *you*. That's why we're here. For you, no one else."

"Okay." This is a common topic in my therapy sessions. How to prioritize my *own* feelings, my *own* health, my *own* wants and needs. It's been challenging for me to do this after spending so much of my life making myself fit into the lives of those around me. Hiding my illness, downplaying the symptoms I was feeling, never wanting to make anyone who fell into my orbit uncomfortable. "What's my other option?"

"Well, you can decide you want more. You said an apology wouldn't matter, but do you want to try having a relationship with your mother again anyway?"

I don't relish the fact that I no longer have a relationship with her. Actually, I think I do want more, but I always wanted more with her. She was just never open to having the type of relationship I wanted, to being the kind of mom I needed—the kind I used to watch every night on TV. To being my *friend*.

"I don't know."

"That's okay. Why don't you think about this some more, and we'll pick it up again next time. If you change your mind and want to talk while you're away, you can always give me a call."

THERAPY ALWAYS DRAINS me of a full day's worth of energy. Just like my yoga and Pilates classes, I need a long bath and a nap when I'm done.

I lie in bed, reading over the notes from yesterday's meeting with my dietician, and pull open my Calm app to start my afternoon meditation.

This routine has been solid for months now, but I can't get my brain to shut off today.

What's wearing on me is that I know Dr. Green is right. Seeing my family, showing them who I am now, it's the validation I need to put the past behind me. But I am scared, scared that it won't go the way I see it in my head, scared that I will never have the respect I want from them, scared that everyone's been better off without me.

After a quick nap I decide it's time to start packing for my flight tomorrow. And that's when I realize my biggest issue isn't my mental or physical health, but the fact that I have lived in California for six and a half years and have nothing appropriate to wear for winter in Vermont.

I frantically call an Uber to chariot me over the bridge to Corte Madera, praying Nordstrom has some extra tall, waterproof boots in my size. If there is one thing I can be certain of, it's that Sugar Valley is never lacking in snow. I make a list on the drive of everything else I'll need: a knee-length coat, mittens, a fleece-lined hat since wool irritates my skin, and leggings as thick as I can find.

The temperate San Francisco weather has been a godsend for my joint pain. I miss real winters with a passion, but if I'm not well and bundled, I know I'll be hurting the whole time.

ELLIE

I hope you're happy. I just charged over $1,000 to our account for winter gear. This scouting trip isn't cheap

MAYA

Worth it! You'll be the cutest little snow bunny! *bunny emoji* *skier emoji*

The owner finally emailed me back. He said he's still working on some of the final touches, so he'll be pretty busy, but that you're welcome to explore on your own and take as many photos as you'd like

> Send lots of selfies!

ELLIE

> <<scowling selfie>>

MAYA

> Cute! Maybe it's finally time to get on Instagram so you can show off that sexy frown of yours

ELLIE

> Not a chance

MAYA

> No more negativity! Also, please try to get some pics with the owner if you see him. He's got seriously lovable grandpa vibes *santa emoji* *hugging emoji*

Two planes, eight hours of flying and a frantic and rushed layover in Detroit later, I step into the Burlington airport filled with anxiety. Logically, I know I won't run into anyone here, but my heartbeat refuses to catch up with my brain.

Theo's still in Boston from what I can tell from his Bruins profile. He retired at the end of last season, and there have been no new updates of what he's doing now. My parents have always had an irrational fear of flying—a gene they passed on to Ezra—and Dad hasn't been on a plane since he escorted me to college over six years ago. I'm not sure why I'm the only family member who enjoys traveling by sky, but I have a feeling there's some saying about a caged bird that explains it.

And yet, even though I know they won't be here, I zip through the terminal in stealth mode, pulling my hat down and sunglasses on until I reach the car rental desk.

ELLIE

Made it to the green mountains. Pray for me

MAYA

I'm so proud of you, El. I know it wasn't easy

ELLIE

Says the girl who basically forced me to go

MAYA

Best friends are honest with each other. And you need this

Best friends. A smile immediately finds its way onto my lips as I remember how lucky I am to have her, of how patient she's been with me over the years. I had always hoped for a friend like her, even though I never expected one.

Maya and I met just two weeks after I moved to California. After getting accepted at UC-Berkeley, I found her blog while researching the campus and surrounding areas. The day Dad left, I visited her favorite spot, Ti-Bear. I had never even heard of boba tea and had definitely never sat at a café by myself before, but after that first sip, I was addicted.

After devouring every single tapioca pearl—even the ones I had to scrape off the bottom of the cup—I decided I should leave a comment on the blog post, saying how much I enjoyed it. But when I attempted to log on to the site, it wouldn't load. It only took me a few minutes to track down the domain info and get the owner's email address. Before I talked myself out of it, I was messaging Maya Bloom, offering my web services. Sure, I was a first year and had yet to even step foot on campus, but there was a reason Berkeley accepted me, and I was proud of my self-taught coding skills.

I had no idea the blogger would be another Cal student only a year ahead of me, and after our first meeting—over boba of course—we were a done deal: friends, business partners, and a few months later, roommates.

It's hard to pinpoint why we have always worked so well together. Maybe there's a Jewish connection, even though neither of us is very religious. It could be the whole "girls in tech need to stick together" thing, but we come a dime a dozen in Silicon Valley. Really, we both just needed an anchor, someone to be our person.

While I grew up feeling both isolated and suffocated at times, Maya spent her childhood traveling the world. We were complete opposites, aside from our mutual love of romance novels. Her dad owns a boutique hotel chain and when he met Maya's mom during a trip to Brazil, he found his match. They refused to stay in one place, deciding instead to relocate with every new property acquisition. Maya has lived in nine states and seven different countries. Their current home base is in Barcelona, hence Maya and her boyfriend's upcoming trip for the holidays.

Even though our childhoods couldn't have been more different, we both grew up lonely. We both know what it's like to have no one to confide in, no one to understand us, and now we both know that will never be the case again. Ezra and I may be blood related, but Maya is my soul sister, the sibling I always dreamed of having.

ELLIE

Miss you already. Please don't fall in love with Spain and decide to move there. I won't survive with that much sunshine

MAYA

No promises. What if I buy you one of those fancy silk parasols to carry around like an Austen leading lady?

ELLIE

My arm will get sore

MAYA

Fine. We'll stay with the fog. Anything for my
Ellie Belly

ELLIE

heart emoji

IT'S ALMOST dark by the time I make it to Sugar Valley, but instead of heading to my hotel in town I find myself turning toward the village.

The welcome sign comes into focus, and a waterfall of tears break free.

Each arrow pointing to my most cherished memories has me in a chokehold, little flashes of history clouding my sight. Visibility is already mediocre at best from the snow that started five minutes after leaving the airport. If I can't get my emotions in check, I won't be able to drive at all.

Flickers of mini horses and marshmallows shaped like snowflakes dance through the wind outside. I can see everything: my first time on skates, that ridiculous gimmicky pizza crust, Noodle bobbing through the untouched powder. The visions refract while each memory sparkles like sunlit snow. I see it and I don't, because Theo's face eclipses it all. Green-gold eyes and soft lips, the smile meant only for me. It's impossible to see anything here without him in it. Even the man running toward my car looks like him in my current state.

Wait. Why is there a man running toward my car? And why is he waving his arms around like that? I give my head a little shake, trying to focus on what's real and now. I blink a few times to clear my vision but he's still there and getting closer. I think he's yelling something, but I can't hear him from inside the car.

I catch a faint, "Look out!" but my tires are already spinning. I grip the wheel but realize I completely lost control. Shit. Why does it feel like I'm skidding on ice? I don't think I turned off the main road, but it's impossible to tell with how thick the snow is now falling, blanketing the ground.

The skidding stops as soon as I feel my car begin to tip forward, just slightly. I throw it in reverse and hit the gas, but everything just spins. My heart races to a new level, and then I'm really panicking. I've never lost control while driving before, and I have no idea what to do. I look over my left shoulder and see the running man right outside my window, still looking like some mythical adult Theo. And now he's angry.

He's yelling words that hang like the wind in the thick flurry outside, inaudible to my ears inside the car. His exasperation is on display while he screams and points. What is he pointing at?

And then I see it. The sign I hadn't noticed before. The one announcing exactly where my car has ended up: Fox Pond.

Chapter Four

Ellie

December 24, 2008

I OFFICIALLY HAD A BIRTHDAY TRADITION. The best part? My brother loved it.

Christmas Eve slash my early birthday was now spent at Sugar Valley Village. Two years ago—after my embarrassing fall—I'd begged and pleaded for my parents to get me ice-skating lessons. I got them over the line by bringing it up during a visit to my rheumatologist so they couldn't use my lupus as an excuse. And finally, a few months before birthday number ten, they gave in.

Theo was totally impressed last year when he saw me doing one-foot glides. "Are you sure you've only been taking lessons for a few months?" he'd said. I knew he was just being nice, but I still felt a jolt of pride at his words.

It wasn't fair that I only got to see him on my birthday. He and Ez were together all the time for hockey, and Dad went to some of their games, but no matter how much I begged, Mom never let me join. Even when they just went skating for practice I was banned.

So this was my chance to show everyone—mainly Theo—that I wasn't just an average skater. I had finally perfected my crossovers and I was turning eleven at Midnight. Practically a teenager. I felt unstoppable.

LAST YEAR, after skating, Theo had offered to take us tubing. He must have remembered how protective Mom was, because he promised her that he'd keep me safe and take us down the slower path. The minute she had turned her back, Ezra booked it to the fast and curvy one, but still Theo stayed by me.

"You ready to try something new, Adventure Girl?" It had taken me a second to realize he was talking to me. *Adventure Girl?* I wish.

He took my hand as we trekked through the snow to the magic carpet, and I let out a deep sigh at the flat, sturdy-looking walkway. It meant we didn't have to climb.

We hopped off at the top and he helped tuck my scarf into my coat before he showed me how to sit comfortably on the tube.

"I'll be right behind you, okay? I'll never take my eyes off you."

I'd looked around, embarrassed. There were kids much younger than me diving headfirst onto the tube. I was trying to stop myself from shaking, and I knew Theo could tell.

"Adventure time, right?" He smiled at me, in a way that was so encouraging I would have probably jumped out of a plane if he'd asked.

"Adventure time." I smiled back and got in the tube.

We went down seven more times.

. . .

"For the last time, Ellie, you're not going tubing this year!"

Ezra and Dad both kept their headphones in while Mom and I fought the entire drive to Sugar Valley. November had been a month of flare-ups, so she was getting even stricter about physical activity. I had hoped she might change her mind after skating, but I was out of luck.

"Your cheeks are red," she murmured, placing her hands around my face. "I should have never let you skate today. Tubing is out of the question, baby."

"I feel fine, Mom! It's cold. Everyone's cheeks are red."

She just huffed in response. I wasn't sure why I even tried —she never listened to me. It was like it didn't matter when I was feeling good, all she could see were the bad days.

My doctors were optimistic, but I didn't understand half the words they said. All I knew was that most of the time I felt good, and if things were really going to get worse for me as I got older, then shouldn't I take advantage of my current healthier self?

No matter how hard I tried to reason with her, she could never see it that way.

So while the guys went tubing, I went to the animal sanctuary with her and Dad instead.

As much as I hated missing tubing with the guys, the mini horses were amazing. Three of them were out trotting through the snow, but it was the gray one that immediately caught my eye, and I ran toward it to get a better look.

"This one's Tinkerbell. She's very friendly." The nice woman tending the animals didn't seem to mind me practically hanging over the fence to get a closer look. In fact, she reached out her hand. "Want to hop over here? You're welcome to pet her, just let me show you how."

After a quick glance at Mom to make sure I wasn't banned

from climbing a three-foot log fence, I hopped over and let the woman direct me.

"Flatten your hand like this," she said, showing me the best angle for Tinkerbell to smell me, and then where to touch her neck so that she was comfortable with me.

Her coat was soft and silky under my fingertips, but I pulled my hand away and whispered, "You should go play with your friends now." As if she understood me, the mini horse nudged my shoulder, looking for more attention.

I giggled just as Mom yelled, "Ellie, be careful!"

"Ellie? Are you Theo's friend?" The woman looked at me like she just found out Santa Claus was real. She was younger than Mom—at least I thought so—and she had pretty blonde hair that was tied into a braid. I examined it so I could copy the style later.

"Yeah. Well, my brother's his friend, but—"

"Oh, don't be silly!" She reached out her arms to wrap me in a hug. "He told me all about you. The snow globe girl." She *winked*. "I'm Carol, Theo's mom." She squeezed me again before moving toward the fence and introducing herself to my parents.

Carol made small talk with my parents—mostly about how the animals ended up here—as she toured us around the sanctuary. It was massive and they had tons of different animals. The horses were just closest to the rest of the village because they were the big attraction.

"You'll have to come back in the Spring, Ellie. Most of our animals are tucked away when it's this cold."

But not all of them. I got to see geese, an albino peacock, and an *actual* baby moose. Though the gray mini horse still had the biggest slice of my heart.

"Can I come back and visit Tinkerbell?"

"Any time. You know we're always looking for volunteers to

help out here. We get lots of kids your age in the summer. You seem like a natural with the animals."

Volunteering at an animal sanctuary sounded like a dream. One that Mom's expression killed before it had a chance to bloom.

"That's very nice of you to offer," she voiced to Carol. "Ellie isn't well, so..." She trailed off like that was an actual answer. "But we'll try and come back for a visit. It's good for her to be with animals. They seem to relax her."

Carol flashed me a puzzled expression that I could have sworn said "is she for real?" But then she actually said, "Nothing's better for the soul than falling in love with animals. You better come visit Tinkerbell. She'll be very disappointed if you don't."

"Hey sweet pea," Dad said, wrapping an around my shoulders. "Ez just texted that they're done. Want to go get some hot chocolate?"

I had been dreaming about Fox in the Snow for days—especially those adorable snowflake marshmallows—so it wasn't that difficult to drag me away from the animals. I was also excited to see Theo again after spending time with Carol. *He told me all about you.* Maybe he wasn't just my brother's friend, after all.

"Happy Birthday, Ellie." I tried to slyly wipe the melted marshmallow from my lip as Theo handed me my gift. Last year he'd given me another snow globe, a polar bear in place of the reindeers from the year before. I figured that if he got me one this year, I could officially count it as a tradition too.

"Penguins!" I took the globe from his hands and shook, watching three penguins in scarves get caught under the flurry.

"They're my favorite bird. They're so cool. Did you know a group of penguins is called a waddle?"

I giggled. Waddle was such a funny word. "Why are they your favorite?"

"I don't know. They're just cool. Like, they're birds but they have flippers instead of wings so they can't fly. But they can swim super fast, and no other bird can do that."

"They're so cute." I eyed each little penguin in the globe. "I'm going to name them. Cherry." I pointed to the one in a red scarf. "Berry." The one in blue. "And...Larry." The one in green.

"Great names. Perfect, actually. I know you said owls were your favorite, but I still haven't been able to find one. Maybe next year." *Maybe next year.* Theo didn't realize those words were the best gift he could have given me. Everything about today confirmed one thing: Theo was my friend.

I thought back to how much better the past year had been with my lupus. I didn't miss as much school, and the medication I took was helping. It still kept me up at night, but it was manageable, and gave me ample opportunities to read. Making friends at school was a different story, especially after being held back a year for missing so much of third grade. And I always felt awkward trying to join in conversations, like I just didn't fit in, like I wasn't *meant* to.

The worst part was that everyone at school knew about my illness. But no one actually understood it. Having an invisible disease that was sometimes really bad and sometimes completely fine was not something kids my age could wrap their heads around. Most of the time they avoided me. Sometimes they would ask weird questions. Google was my enemy, listing tons of symptoms I never had and others that weren't as clear cut as they may have seemed on the internet.

So many words stuck, words that I didn't want anywhere near me, words that couldn't tell anyone who I actually was.

A few months ago, Mom convinced me to invite some girls to our house for a sleepover. It was going well, if maybe a little awkward, but when I left the room to go make popcorn, I over-

heard them talking about me. Bella giggled and said how
"weird" I was, then Kirsten agreed and said she couldn't believe
their moms made them come. I bit my lip so hard it bled, just to
stop myself from crying when Kirsten asked, "Are we gonna
catch her lupus?"

Maybe I was destined to be a loner. I couldn't really
imagine what it would be like to blend in with the masses, all
the ways I would have to alter myself to fit the mold. The kids
in my class were ignorant. They thought books weren't "cool."
They ranked friends by the quantity of T-shirts someone had
from Abercrombie. Why would I want to be like them instead
of me?

And Theo liked me as I was, so I didn't feel like changing
for everyone else.

"I love it. Thank you for always remembering my birthday."

"It's sort of hard to forget." Duh Ellie, it was *Christmas*.
"My mom helped picked this one out actually. I'm sorry you
still haven't met her. She's always busiest on Christmas Eve."

"Hey dude, you ready?" Ezra interrupted before I could
correct him.

"Yep. See you later, birthday girl!"

I spent the rest of number eleven with Mom and Dad. Theo
invited Ez to sleepover at his family's cabin. They were going to
spend Christmas day practicing on the ice while the rink was
closed to everyone else. I clutched my new snow globe to my
chest the entire ride home, wondering what kind he might get
me for birthday number twelve.

Chapter Five

Theo

February 22, 2010

"Happy birthday, Theo." Mom smiled at me, before her eyes widened. "My god, I cannot believe I have a fourteen-year-old son. I do not feel old enough to have a fourteen-year-old!"

"Stop spiraling, Carol. Theo's birthday is about him, remember?" Dad quipped, smirking.

My mother was anything but vain, but she hated getting older. I grinned at her before saying, "I'm sure everyone here thinks you're my older sister."

"I knew you were my favorite kid."

"Only kid."

"Semantics." She took my arm and tugged me up the spiral walkway that wrapped around the largest fish tank I had ever scene. Turning back, she yelled behind us, "Come on, Steve. Keep up."

Last night, my parents surprised me with a road trip to Boston. We arrived just after midnight, then got up bright and early to spend the day at the New England Aquarium. We had tickets to my first professional hockey game tonight—Bruins versus Blackhawks—and I had never been more excited.

"Aren't the stingrays just beautiful?" My gaze followed Mom's finger as she pointed to one gliding by us behind the glass. "They have cartilage rather than bone. I think that's why all their movements are so impossibly graceful," she said. "They don't swim like anything else in the sea."

Coming here with her was a dream. She knew so much about each creature that I wondered how it was possible to keep all those facts stored in her head. The only conclusion I could come up with was that Carol Fox was the smartest person in the world.

Earlier, when we were checking out the seahorses, she told me she had wanted to study marine biology originally. She loved everything that lived in the ocean. But after college she knew she'd never want to leave Vermont, so she stuck to being a vet. Dad helped her open the sanctuary so she would have the opportunity to work with all sorts of animals. House pets would never have been enough for her.

"Do you know what a group of stingrays is called?" I asked. She almost always knew the answer.

Her eyes gleamed as she replied, "A fever."

I repeated the words "a fever of stingrays" in my head several times. I had to tell Ellie the next time I saw her, and I didn't want to forget. We celebrated her twelfth birthday less than two months ago, so I knew it'd be a while before I saw her again. Ezra and I hung out all the time, but I had still never been to their house. He said it was boring over there, so he always got a ride to my house, or we'd meet somewhere in the middle.

"I don't know much about all these animals. Nothing like

your mother. But I gotta say, this is pretty cool," Dad said to me as we got to the top of the walkway. The main attraction at the aquarium was a massive cylindrical tank that viewers could watch from all sides. The spiral walkway took us from the bottom to the very top of the tank, where there were now trainers feeding the fish, dropping different types of food into the opening while they ran off facts about each species.

"It's awesome. Thanks for bringing me here, Dad."

He wrapped an arm around my shoulders, giving me a just-manly-enough side squeeze. And then he leaned in to whisper, "But you're more excited about the game tonight, right?"

Dad loved hockey. He played in high school but told me he was never that good, nothing like me. He said with my natural talent, he thought I could go all the way, and I was starting to believe him. Being on the ice was more a part of me than breathing. Skating always made me feel invincible, like absolutely anything was possible. Even the miniscule chance that I could play professionally had me training harder than anyone else I knew.

Dad threw me a wink before sneaking up behind Mom and wrapping his arms around her.

"Steve!" she squealed. "Can't I admire the fever in peace?" She threw me a wink. She and I both knew not to let our guards down around Dad. He loved making us jump.

She turned in his arms and I looked away when I saw their goofy smiles, knowing they'd be kissing soon enough. They were annoying at home, but even in public, they would never be mistaken for anything but happily in love. It was embarrassing sometimes, but I wanted to hate it more than I actually did.

"Hey guys, can we go see the penguins again?" I brought my hands up to cover my mouth and pretended to gag. I was being ridiculous, but hello? It was my birthday.

Mom regaled us with hundreds of more animal facts as we swept through the rest of the aquarium, visiting my favorite penguins for the third time, and they kept their PDA to a minimum.

And before heading to the game, she finally gave in to my dad's requests to get Italian pastries from the North End. Dad and I both shared a love of dessert. I had never had a cannoli before, but I knew I would be requesting them for every future birthday.

Most of the guys I knew, or anyone my age really, would probably think it was lame to spend my birthday with my parents. Mom even joked how I was probably days away from hating them now that I was fourteen. That was never going to happen though. I loved my parents. They were my best friends, and I wouldn't trade them for anything.

THE BRUINS WERE UP two-to-one in the third period and the whole crowd at the Garden was on their feet.

I had played in hundreds of hockey games, but never had I felt electric energy like this. It was addictive, crawling its way into my bloodstream until my ambition grew legs. The lights, the music, the chanting; I wanted it all.

"Do you really think that could be me one day?" I shouted into my dad's ear.

He leaned over and said, "Abso-*fucking*-lutely." His eyes quickly darted to my other side. "Don't tell your mother I said that."

The crowd cheered as our goalie made another save, but once the sounds died down, Dad continued. "I have no doubt you'll play on that ice one day, if that's what you want. You've got the talent, and you've definitely got the discipline. Just promise me one thing."

He paused to look at me, expecting my assurance before he even told me what the promise was. But I trusted him with my life, so I replied, "Yeah, I promise. Anything."

"You go to college. You *finish* college. Don't be like your old man. Once you get that degree, you do whatever the hell you want."

I soaked in his words as I jumped along with the crowd when my favorite player, Zdeno Chára scored another goal. I cheered until my lungs gave out, completely under the spell of this current hockey high. Three-to-one with less than five minutes left had me feeling pretty good about a Bruins victory.

Dad nudged me and said, "Promise me. I'm serious. I don't care how good you are, or what offers you get. You're going to college and graduating."

I had never thought much about college. My mom went and my dad didn't; that was what I knew. And there wasn't anyone I respected more than my father, so college never felt like something I *had* to do. But if it was important to him, it was important to me.

"I'll keep that promise if you give me one in return."

"Always the negotiator." One of his eyebrows went up, waiting for my proposition.

"When I go to college, and play hockey on their team, you have to come to every game."

The serious look on his face vanished as a wide grin spread slowly enough to look villainous.

He clapped my back hard. "Try to fucking stop me."

The buzzer sounded the end of the game and the cheering started again. The din of the crowd was hard to hear over, but I could clearly make out my mom shouting behind me, "I'm bringing back the swear jar."

❄

"WE SHOULD PROBABLY GET TO SLEEP."

Ezra gave me his usual "yeah, okay" look and I chuckled. He might be relaxed about our game tomorrow, but I knew if I didn't try to force my eyes closed soon, I'd be tossing and turning all night. Sure, we were playing the youth league and most of the guys just learned to body-check last year, but it was a *state championship.*

Ever since I saw the Bruins play two months ago, there was this new fire burning within me. A flame that wouldn't accept defeat. We had to win tomorrow.

And I was going to skate alongside Ezra, who always had my back.

"Think we're gonna win?" He asked from the trundle bed next to me. His parents let him stay over tonight since we wanted to practice drills at the rink by my house earlier today. I also lived an hour closer to Brattleboro, where we'd be playing tomorrow.

"Hell yes. I won't *let* us lose." I replied. "Just keep Johansen out of my way and I'll take care of the rest. He's the only one on their team who likes to play dirty."

"If you weren't so good, you'd be annoying as fuck," Ez commented. "You know that, right?"

"Better keep scoring goals then," I quipped, a wide smile pointed back at him.

"If he even stick-checks you once, I'll take him out." Ezra threw on his serious face, the one that made him look more seventeen than fourteen. We weren't beyond using the power of intimidation.

"Thanks, brother."

It was just after nine, but we said goodnight to my parents and came to my room right after dinner, hoping to get a decent sleep.

Instead, we were playing Super Mario on my Wii.

Ezra's phone rang and I paused the game. He answered on speaker, like always. We never had any secrets from each other.

"Hey Mom, what's up," he muttered toward the phone.

Her voice came through different than normal. She sounded stressed. "Hi honey, I hope you're having fun with Theo. I just wanted to talk about tomorrow."

"Yeah, game starts at 11:30," he replied. "We're supposed to get there an hour early though."

"Please thank Theo's parents for me. It's wonderful they're able to take you. Your dad will be there at eleven; he's going straight from golf. I umm...I'm not going to be able make it. I'm so sorry, Ez."

Ezra's face fell as his jaw clenched hard. He was pissed. His mom hadn't come to many of our games, and Ellie never did. It was usually just his dad, and even he missed a lot of them. I had no idea what that felt like. My parents never missed a game, no matter what.

"Why?" He answered back to the phone. That one word felt deadly coming through his mouth, his anger on full display.

"It's just too far, Ez. I can't leave Ellie alone all day. It's two and a half hours each way. I really am sorry. You know I'd love to watch you play."

"Just bring Ellie," he pleaded. "She always says she wants to come watch."

"You know I can't do that. There are way too many people at these events. We can't risk her getting sick from someone who wasn't smart enough to stay home."

"Mom—" His voice cracked this time and I looked away. Ezra was the closest thing I had to a brother, but I still didn't think I shouldn't be listening to this conversation. "She's not a baby. You really can't leave her alone for one day? This is a big deal to me." Mrs. Klein started to interrupt but her tone was placating from the start and Ezra continued over her. "You never care about anything I do. You know I love Ellie, but why does everything have to be about her? Just one time, you can't put me first?"

"Ez..." She sighed. The exhaustion was heavy in her voice, like she barely had the energy to respond. "I'm trying my best. Just give me a break, okay? I promise if—"

"Mom, just go. I'll be *fine*." The sound of Ellie's voice coming through the phone shocked me a little. I hadn't seen her since we celebrated her birthday last December and I sort of wished she were coming tomorrow too. I bet she would love hockey.

"Ellie, what are you doing?" her mom questioned suddenly. "This conversation has nothing to do with you. How's your—"

"All right. Sounds like you're busy," Ezra interrupted. "Thanks for nothing." He hung up the phone and I waited nervously to hear what he had to say to me. I wasn't sure how to make him feel better. I guessed Ellie wasn't feeling well, but it sucked that his mom couldn't come. I knew how badly he wanted her to.

I held my breath, waiting for him to talk, but he just grabbed the controller and started our game back up.

"Watch out Luigi," he said, breaking the tense silence. "My Bowzer's gonna demolish you."

WE WON THE GAME, three-to-two. I scored every goal.

Dad took me and Ezra to my favorite pizza place after the game. He even let us have our own table by the arcade while he sat at the bar, probably because he'd had enough hockey talk on the ride.

Mr. Klein never made it; something about being needed at home.

It was obvious Ezra didn't enjoy the win like I did. Of course, he didn't. It wasn't the same without your people cheering for you and as we sat here, going over the plays, I hated his parents almost as much as he did. Why couldn't have at least one of them showed up for him?

"I never would have scored those last two without you, Z. You bulldozed Johansen," I mentioned between bites of pizza, grease dripping down my chin. It was already my fourth slice, and I was still starving.

"Yeah, shoulder's gonna hurt tomorrow," he replied, rubbing behind his neck. He grinned back at me. "Worth it though."

We laughed, talking through all the big moments of the game; times we messed up, times we surprised ourselves with how well we actually played, time spent in the penalty box. We would both be starting high school in the fall, and with that came trading in the youth league for our school teams. It wasn't going to be the same playing without my best friend.

"I can't believe this was our last time playing together. It sucks," I muttered.

"I know. And I'll be down in Connecticut. Then they'll never come watch."

Shit. I hadn't even thought about that. Once Ezra went to boarding school, I'd be seeing him even less. No more sharing a hockey team, and soon we'd be a three-hour drive from each other too. But I had only been thinking about *me*. His parents would be even farther from him. I wondered if he was right— would they ever visit? Go to his games? Were they really that strict with Ellie to never leave her alone? Ez never explained what that was all about, and I was hesitant to ask.

"I'm really sorry they couldn't come today, Z."

"Yeah. I'm used to it. Ellie has it worse. She's stuck in that house. At least I get to be here with you."

"What do you mean? Why is she stuck there?"

"Nevermind," he mumbled. "Wanna go play skeeball?" With that, he got up from the table and headed toward the arcade room. I grabbed one more slice, stuffed it in my mouth, and trailed after him.

Chapter Six

Ellie

.

Now

THEO.

Theo, Theo, Theo.

Why can't I stop seeing Theo? I jump out of the car in case it sinks any deeper into the partially frozen pond. But the man in front of me will not stop looking like *Theo.*

"Ellie?"

If I'm not imagining the utter shock stamped all over his face, he might actually be Theo, *my* Theo.

"Hi." Because what the hell else am I supposed to say to the man who tore my heart to pieces and has been devastatingly missing from my life for seven years?

"Hi? Ellie, wh—"An ugly groaning sound coming from my car cuts off his next words. I'm pretty sure it's about to take a very cold swim if we don't do something, and fast. "I'll go grab my truck and tow you out. Stay away from the ice." He physically moves me over about ten feet and I try not to think about how it feels to have his hands on me. "Don't move!"

I watch Theo run through the snow until he's no longer visible. For a minute I wonder if the entire thing was a mirage. Did being back here make me conjure some image of my first love? A white knight to save me from my poor driving? My car is still definitively taking a dip in the pond, but there's no trace of the man. I look down and even his footsteps have vanished.

It takes a moment for me to realize how cold I am out here in what's turning in to an actual snowstorm. I zip up my coat and wrap my chunky scarf over my face, only letting my eyes peek through. And then I see it, a silver truck heading toward me, and I can't decide if Theo being real is the outcome I was hoping for.

"Hey!" He jumps out of the truck, yelling over the storm. "Get back in and throw it in neutral."

I follow his order, and maybe I watch him intently through the rearview mirror as he attaches a chain from his truck to my rental. Theo was always strong, but he's bigger, taller now, a *man*. At twenty-seven, his face doesn't look too different from when he was twenty, except that he's sporting some major scruff he couldn't grow back then, and his hockey-hair has been trimmed shorter. But his body has definitely changed. Even through a winter coat I can't stop staring.

My car starts moving—thankfully backward—and I'm jolted out of my lust-filled reverie. He tugs me out of the pond and back to the road, which I apparently veered off from quite a way back.

I'm safe. My car's okay.

Shit.

Now I have to face the white knight.

I'm not sure how long I sit in my car, frozen in place. My initial plan was to drive out of here without another word to the man who haunts every one of my dreams, but now I can't actually see a single road anymore as the snowfall has morphed into a real-life blizzard.

A loud knock on my window startles me as I hear, "What the hell are you doing?" yelled at me from across the glass.

I shrug. The anxiety has officially made me stupid.

"Get out of the damn car, Ellie!"

I do as I'm told. I think following orders right now is much more desirable than trying to think for myself in any real capacity. Theo tilts his head to the passenger side of his truck, and I climb in.

"Were you really just gonna sit in your car and wait for me to leave you there?"

"Umm, I'm not sure." I reach for the stone in my pocket, giving it a quick rub to calm my nerves. Unfortunately, I think I need something stronger. "I wasn't—I wasn't expecting to see you here."

I might have been a mature kid, but at twenty-five, I've never felt more like a child. I suddenly wish I had something to suck on.

He gapes at me. "Well, I wasn't expecting to see you either. What are you doing here?"

"My company...*Wander*..." Apparently those are the only words I know right now.

"*Wander*? The woman I emailed with was Maya. Do you go by Maya now?" I can't help but laugh at his incredulity.

"Nope, still Ellie. She's my partner, and she's in Spain. So here I am." I lift my hands to waggle my fingers, only to realize I'm still wearing my mittens. *This is going well.* "I had no idea you'd be here though. She said a new owner decided to fix it up."

"New owner." He points both thumbs toward his chest, and I can't help the swell of pride I feel. He finally got it back. How did I not see this coming? *Of course,* he got it back.

But Maya kept saying the new owner was a sweet old man, and Theo is supposed to be in Boston. What happened to the Santa Claus I was meant to get selfies with?

Theo starts driving, apparently feeling as though that short conversation was sufficient. A few minutes later, we pull up in front of a large cabin and he jumps out of the car. Why is everything adult Theo does worth watching? He's just moving through a blizzard, but his strength is somehow on full display. It's my turn to get out next, and he swings an arm out for me to grab onto. "Hold on. It's slippery as fuck out here and your boots are worthless."

I ignore his insult but take the hand and let him pull me up the steps and through the front door. My boots are warm, and cute. I didn't realize they would need to have an iron grip on the soles.

"Wow." It's the only word that comes to me as I step inside the cabin, a place I can immediately feel as Theo's home. I always wondered what his house would be like. The dark wood and shades of green scream Theo, while the impressive fireplace beckons me further inside. "Is this?"

"No. Our old cabin's gone. There was a fire; no one was around," he offers quickly. "I started building this about two years ago, still a work in progress though."

"I love it." A small smile tugs at his lips but he tries not to let it show. His smiles aren't mine anymore, a fact that I know, yet makes me inexplicably sad. "So, Sugar Valley. I can't believe you actually got it back. That's...incredible." Theo has barely taken his eyes off of me since we stepped inside. He's looking at me like I might crack open or vanish at any moment.

"Yeah. I told you I would. It never changed for me." The weight of his gaze settles heavily on me, daring me to question him, but I won't take the bait.

"They would be so happy."

His throat moves but he's still staring at me, his eyes fixed on my face like he's trying to work out a riddle. But then his stare turns soft, melty. It's how he used to look at me. Before it all disappeared.

"What are you doing here, El?" The question is pleading, searching for an answer that's anything but simple.

But it is simple. "I told you. *Wander...*" His face falls, finding my response insufficient. "In fact, I should probably try to get some photos outside before the storm gets wor—"

"It's been seven fucking years."

"I know." My voice is meek compared to the depth of his own. I can barely look at him.

"Are you real? Are you really here right now?" he murmurs softly this time.

My voice fails me, completely unprepared for this encounter. Both sets of our eyes grow glassy but no matter how hard I search, I can't find any words that are big enough for this moment. And before I'm successful in my hunt, Theo strides toward me and wraps me in his arms.

We're both teary-eyed now, caught in this tight embrace between friends, lovers and strangers all at once. The heat of his hand on my back warms my entire body, coaxing me to sink into his comfort. His arms move up and down, like he's actually checking to make sure I'm not some apparition, squeezing gently when he reaches my shoulders, my hands, my waist. I squeeze him back, unable to stop myself from chasing his touch, his woodsy scent, his *everything*.

It is not just a hug. It is my first friend and skating lessons and peppermint whipped cream. It is snow globes and stolen kisses and the warmth of three blankets. It is New Year's Eves and birthdays and dancing under the stars.

It is the greatest hug of my fucking life.

Chapter Seven

Ellie

December 21, 2010

THE VILLAGE WAS CLOSED this year.

Over the summer, Theo's parents were in a car accident. They didn't make it.

Mom wouldn't let me go to the funeral. "You know what these things can be like," she'd said. "There are just too many people. Too many chances you'll get sick." Like that was more important than my friend who lost both of his parents. Not being there made me feel sick anyway.

She stayed home with me while Dad took Ezra. They told me there were hundreds of people there, practically the whole town of Sugar Valley. Ezra had come home with red-rimmed eyes and didn't leave his room for days. It was the first time I had ever seen him cry.

Things got worse from there. When he got the news that Theo had to move all the way to Rochester to live with his uncle, his sadness turned to anger. Nothing I said could make him feel better. Every attempt was met with a brusque, "just leave me alone, Ellie."

I wasn't sure where Rochester was, but I heard my brother talk about it all the time. It was far enough that they wouldn't see much of each other, and definitely too far to share a hockey team.

Last year's birthday had been full of nothing but joy. Ezra and I got along, mom let me tube, Theo got me another snow globe to add to my collection, one with a pirate ship that I was obsessed with. Sometimes I even slept with it next to my pillow.

Now all our traditions were gone. Four years of blissfully perfect birthdays I knew I would always remember. I overheard my parents discussing how unfortunate it was that Theo's uncle was given the property when they passed. Apparently, he sold it right away and the new owners had already terminated every lease agreement with the local businesses. They just wanted the surrounding land and had no plans to re-open the village.

It didn't matter to me. It never would have been the same without Theo anyway.

My magical birthday wonderland was now nothing but twinkling memories.

"Hey, Ellie. Can I come in?" Ezra tapped on the doorframe before stepping inside my room. He was rarely this polite, so I figured he had a favor to ask of me. He got home from boarding school this morning, but this was the first we'd spoken.

"What's up?"

"So, I know your birthday is this week, and I'm really excited to celebrate with you. But I was wondering if you would mind if Theo came to stay with us over the break." I tried to will my face to stay neutral. My brother wasn't allowed to see how much this prospect excited me. "His uncle sucks and doesn't do anything for Christmas and... well, Theo really hates it there."

"He does?" My chest ached with this knowledge I wish I had already known. Without his parents, did Theo have anyone else to count on? Sometimes I really hated Mom and Dad, but I didn't know what I would do without them either.

"Yeah. His uncle's like really private, I guess. He lives in the middle of the woods and like never leaves. He won't even drive Theo to school. He has to take the bus everywhere."

"He should absolutely come here then. But...it's not really my decision. Don't you have to ask Mom and Dad?"

"I did, and they were fine with it, as long as they talk to his uncle and everything. But they said I had to ask you since it's your birthday," he sulked. Okay, so maybe he only asked out of obligation, but it was still an opportunity to make my brother happy, and I rarely turned those down.

"Of course, he can come. I know how much you miss him, Ez." I missed him too. How could the only family he had left not celebrate Christmas for him?

To me, Theo *was* Christmas.

Sure, there was the whole Jesus thing. Not that I knew much about it, never having stepped foot in a church. But people were always talking about Christmas *spirit*. That spirit was Theo. I was sure of it.

"Thanks, Ellie. I'll make sure we all do something fun together." My bones filled with warmth at the idea that Ezra planned to include me in whatever the guys would be doing. "I mean, on your birthday, obviously." Well, I would take that too.

THEO'S ARRIVAL had my whole family in a whirlwind.

While Ezra and I were mostly excited to see our friend, Mom and Dad were frantically trying to find Christmas decorations and festive recipes. We had never celebrated Christmas in our house before. Hosting an orphan on his first Christmas without his parents, one whose parents had literally run a Christmas tree farm and winter village for a living? No one wanted to let him down.

Dad and Ezra spent most of the twenty-third hanging lights around the house and setting up a fairly pitiful plastic tree in the sunroom. I remembered watching Rory and Lorelai string cranberries and popcorn around their tree in *Gilmore Girls*, so that was my big project. I wasn't sure why anyone would want popcorn on the tree instead of in a bowl to snack on, but I wasn't about to question anything I learned from my favorite TV show.

It looked like a sugar cookie factory in our kitchen (this last batch was shaped like candy canes) when the guys got home from the airport. I desperately wanted to hide my enthusiasm about seeing Theo, but the second I heard his signature "Hey, birthday girl," I ran directly into his hug.

"I'm so happy you're here. And I'm so sorry about your parents." I knew I should say something else, but nothing sounded right when I'd practiced in my room earlier. Dealing with grief like his was something I hadn't experienced in my life.

Theo hadn't lost his sparkle, but it was significantly dulled. He was the constant that made my birthday come alive every year. But that adventurous spirit he so generously shared with me was lost from his eyes. Now it was my chance to return the favor, I just had to figure out how.

"Thanks, El. It's really nice to see you."

"Come on, I'll show you my room!" Ezra lasted a whole minute before whisking him off to form their twosome. I didn't care. He was staying with us for *ten whole days*.

· · ·

"THIS IS DELICIOUS, MRS. KLEIN," Theo murmured through a mouthful of potato pancakes and my mom's signature brisket. "My parents never cooked on Christmas. They were always so busy working, so we just ate pizza every night. What's this called again?" He pointed to the beef smothered in juicy onions and carrots.

"Brisket. It's what we usually make for our holidays, so I figured why not give it a try?"

"Cool. I like trying new things." After a few more huge bites he turned to me. "Are we having birthday cake too?"

Mom and I exchanged wide-eyed looks before breaking out in a fit of laughter. We had been completely heads down planning for Theo's arrival and trying to Christmas-ify our house, we'd sort of forgotten about my birthday.

"We have lots of Christmas cookies." I offered with a shrug. Mom had been really strict about my sugar intake this year anyway. Sugar, dairy, gluten, nightshades, alfalfa sprouts, apparently. Every food was a potential lupus-amplifier. It was very possible it wasn't just an honest mistake. I enjoyed cookies enough, but I would only have one or two. Frosting was my kryptonite.

After dinner, Mom asked me to go make sure everything was set up in the basement for Theo. We didn't have a real extra bedroom, but we had a huge basement and on one side of it was a bed, bathroom and miniature kitchen.

Ezra used to comment that it would be his apartment once he was in high school, and my parents would remind him that he was being sent to boarding school. I could never tell which of them were joking until he started at Avon Old Farms last fall. Having Ezra in Connecticut for most of the year was a big change, and unfortunately it only made Mom fuss over me more.

The other side of the basement was our main family room.

We had a big sectional, a couple of recliners and a mounted TV big enough to make it feel like a theater. When Ezra had friends over, they always hung out down here, but I was never invited.

I loved this room. The dark jewel-toned colors on the walls, the scent of the well-worn leather couch, the plush carpet I loved sinking my toes into, everything about it was inviting. No matter the season, being in the basement felt like a cozy hide-away during a winter storm.

"Are you gonna watch with us?" Theo asked, as I placed the cookies on the table.

"Umm..." I wasn't planning on it. I rocked back on my heels and looked to Ezra, where he was sprawled on the couch flipping through channels, not sure what to say.

He sighed. "Yeah, you can stay. But we're not watching some dumb girly movie, okay?" I nodded my agreement ferociously.

"Ellie, where are you?" *Here we go.*

"Down here, Mom," I yelled, groaning inwardly. The guys settled into the couch, already discussing what to watch, and it provided the perfect cover to inch toward the stairs. Ezra was firmly in his action movie era and pushing for *Die Hard* while Theo offered up *Avatar*. I really hoped our guest would win. I liked action movies, but I had seen enough of *Die Hard* for a lifetime.

"Ellie, shouldn't you be getting ready for bed? It's after eight." Mom was in the basement, fussing over me like she did every night. She held her hand up to my forehead, something that felt like a subconscious tick of hers by now.

"I'm fine," I said, pushing her hand away and taking a step back. "And I'm not tired. Can't I just watch a movie with them?" I tried keeping my voice low. The guys were on the sectional ten feet away, and I did not want this conversation overheard. I didn't have many friends, but I was pretty sure eight-thirty was a pathetic bedtime for anyone my age. And it was my thirteenth birthday at midnight. If there was any day I should get to stay up, it was this one.

"Okay, sweetie. Just make sure you don't stay up too long." Before she went back up the stairs she shouted, "Ez, keep an eye on your sister, will you? Make sure she has enough blankets. It's chilly down here."

"*Mom.*" Ezra and I both whisper-shouted to our mother in annoyance, but it did the trick.

I unclenched my fists and sat on sofa under my favorite fleece throw, hoping Theo hadn't been listening.

"Are you sick or something?" Of course, he heard. But his tone wasn't accusatory, just curious.

"She has lupus, it's no big deal. Mom's just kind of a psycho about it." Ezra's explanation felt somehow condescending while also extremely accurate. I shrugged in agreement, loving how easily he summed up my entire life. No need for further discussion. My brother might have been a genius.

"Here." Theo handed me his blanket. Then he got up to grab another from the basket on the floor and handed me that one. It felt like a cozy bookend to his question. "Do you like sci-fi?" He asked. "We were talking about watching *Avatar* if that's cool with you."

"I love that movie. I actually got to see it in the theater. Remember, Ez?" My brother huffed in response. Looking back, I think he had asked to go see it with friends. Mom and Dad made him go with us instead, at some weird time when the theater would be empty. Oops.

"Yeah, we saw it when it first came out, too. Mom was refusing to go because she absolutely hated the movie *Alien*, but Dad kept promising her it wasn't like that. We had to beg her to go with us." Theo started to laugh at the memory, but in seconds his amusement soured and his chin got all wobbly. I couldn't even imagine how hard it would be to lose your parents, to have every fond memory tainted and tarnished with the reminder of losing them.

I turned toward Theo fully. "Do you miss them? Your parents?"

"Ellie, you can't fucking say that." Ezra yelled.

"Why? If you were gone, I'd miss you. I would tell everyone how much I missed you."

"Sometimes it's better if you just don't talk, okay?" The harshness of his words hit me in the gut. It felt like any progress we made recently was just in my head.

"It's okay, actually," Theo offered. "I don't mind. And yeah, Ellie. I miss them a lot, every day."

"I'm sorry I didn't come to the funeral. I really wanted to be there, but I wasn't allowed to go."

"That's okay. There were so many people there. It was kind of overwhelming." His throat bobbed a few times as his eyes cast down, but I nudged a little closer, showing I was here. I was listening.

"What do you miss the most? Right now?"

"Ellie!"

"It's fine, Z. Chill." Theo defending me warmed my skin like sunshine. A sad smile crept over his face, and he looked back at me. "I miss everything, but I think, since it's Christmas, I'm really missing our traditions, ya know?"

"What kind of traditions?" I asked. Theo was speaking my language now.

"Well, you guys were part of it too. Every Christmas Eve we had to work the village. It was the busiest day of the year. So, we'd go skating, get pizza, hang out with the horses. I can't remember a year we didn't end the night with hot chocolate at Fox in the Snow." His eyes were shining a tiny bit, but a smile was peeking out too. I nodded, never looking away, and he kept going. "And then Christmas day was our big day off since everything was closed. We'd stay at home and my dad would make a huge pillow fort so we could all lie down together and watch Christmas movies. We never had a couch this big or anything"—his eyes wandered around the room—"our house was pretty small."

It was the first time I ever considered what it would be like to live somewhere else. I didn't have friends to invite me to their homes, so I never even thought about ours not being the standard.

"I love pillow forts," I said, even though I'd only ever seen one on TV. "What else?"

"My mom would make waffles and we'd load them up like ice cream sundaes..." Emotion poured from Theo's voice, and the hugeness of what he'd shared settled over me. Even though he was smiling, I wanted to cry for him. He would never get to do any of those things again, at least not with his parents. "It's stupid, I guess. Just stuff I got used to because we did it every year."

"It's not stupid at all," I offered. "Theo Fox, we're gonna have the best Christmas ever."

I wasn't sure if he responded. I was already running up the stairs yelling, "Mom!"

BIRTHDAY NUMBER THIRTEEN—THE actual day of—was spent inside of the most amazing pillow fort covering half the basement. We all cuddled with Noodle and slipped him way too many treats, I let Latke sleep on my toes, and we watched every Christmas movie we could find.

Dad helped me scrounge up extra blankets, pillows and

cushions, and he even strung up lights, creating the perfect holiday ambiance. Mom and I made pizza from scratch so everyone could have their favorite toppings—and so mine could have a gluten-free crust.

Our waffle iron was broken, but I promised Theo that if he came back next year, we would have the full experience.

"Ellie, you've done enough. This is awesome. You're a really good friend."

Friend. I loved hearing that word now.

"What do you wanna watch next?" I asked. Ezra had fallen asleep a while ago, even though it was just after two in the afternoon. My brother could nap harder than the dog. But Theo and I kept watching with Noodle and Latke in between us in the fort.

"Why don't you pick?" Theo offered.

"Actually, I heard about this new penguin documentary on Netflix, *Penguin Parade*. It's about this little island in Australia totally inhabited by penguins. Have you seen it?"

"No, but that sounds awesome. Let's watch it."

Theo really did love penguins. He kept pausing the TV to share random facts with me. "Did you know there are eighteen different types of penguins?" and, "Did you know some can leap nine feet high in the air?" and—this time he was talking specifically to Noodle—"Did you know there were prehistoric penguins that were as heavy as gorillas?"

Honestly, I was starting to fall in love with penguins myself. In a weird way I related to them, birds that couldn't fly. What I would give for a pair of wings, to not feel trapped in this house all the time. And I liked their resourcefulness, how hard they worked to take care of each other. The show said how some penguins would spend an entire day swimming hundreds of miles to find fish to eat. They risked predators from sky and sea, but made the trek every day, just to bring food back to their family. It was kind of beautiful, and it filled me with that same sense of adventure I felt whenever I was with Theo.

"Sorry if I'm being annoying." He cleared his throat. "My mom loved sharing this stuff with me. It's sort of ingrained in me now."

"It's not annoying at all. I want all the animal facts. Please, give me more. Actually, give me your best one."

"That's way too much pressure," he replied. And then, "Okay, let me think."

Watching Theo think was my new favorite activity. His nose and eyes were scrunched, and his jaw popped back and forth. He tilted his head from side to side, using one hand to pet Noodle, resting the other on Latke. It was mesmerizing.

"All right. I think I got one. Do you like seahorses?"

"Maybe? I don't know any personally. Are they nice?"

"Brat."

"Of course I love seahorses. They're adorable."

"Well, I was at the New England aquarium last year for my birthday, and Mom told me about this secret seahorse obsession she used to have." His words stopped abruptly, and I caught his grin dropping. Each time Theo mentioned his parents I saw the ache written all over his face. I knew he liked talking about them, but I wished I could take away his pain. He cleared his throat. "Anyway, she told me they're the only animal where the male gets pregnant instead of the female. Pretty cool, right?"

"Weird. But you're right. That's a pretty good fact." I focused back on the screen and watched three penguins slide down a hill on their stomach. It almost looked like they were mid-flight. Like they had this blind faith that their bodies were meant for the sky. "I feel kind of bad for them. That they can't fly."

"Don't be sad." He smiled at me. "They're happy on the

ground and in the water. Wings are just a state of mind anyway. That's what my mom always said."

Wings are just a state of mind. I liked that.

We went back to watching the documentary, the back half all about mating patterns, a topic we somehow kept coming back to. But I was fascinated by the penguins, how they built their little families and were known to mate for life, or at least extended periods of time compared to most animals. Some of the rituals were pretty interesting too. At one point they talked about male penguins gathering rocks to gift to females to woo them.

"Ellie, promise me you'll never let a guy get away with gifting you a rock." He popped up to rest on his elbows. "You gotta make them work harder than that." I laughed. Only crystal balls filled with fake snow for this girl.

Not that Theo was trying to woo me. Not that anyone was ever trying to woo *me*.

"I don't know. The rocks are nice. It's their way of showing commitment," I offered.

"Yeah but, come on. Here's a pebble, now mate with me for life? It's kind of weak."

"It's sweet! And once they mate, he brings her food."

Theo glanced at me with narrowed eyes, a thoughtful look floating over his features.

"All right, you can accept a pebble." He lay back down on the pillows. "As long as he feeds you."

Chapter Eight

Theo

Now

I DON'T WANT to let go of Ellie.

If I do, will I lose her again? It still doesn't feel real that she's here, in my home, in my *arms*.

The last seven years unspool behind my eyes, memories I've tried locking away in the far recesses of my brain. Years one and two, when I still had faith that our separation was a minor blip; the three after that when I put every ounce of energy I had into hockey, only thinking about Ellie at Christmastime when I rehearsed what I'd say when I saw her—*if* I saw her; the last two when I all but gave up hope, not wanting to let myself dwell on the Ellie-sized hole in my life.

It's now I realize what I've been doing building this cabin. How foolish to think it wasn't always about her. Is there anything I do that isn't about her?

Ellie isn't in a rush to let go of me either. I can feel the way she breathes me in, the way we're both fueled by memories. But this hug has already lasted too long, and we reluctantly peel away from each other.

"I should go," she mumbles.

I stare at her in bewilderment as she takes three long strides away from me, opens the front door, and lets in a gust of wind that almost knocks her over. I immediately walk over and slam the door shut.

"Seriously, Ellie?" She gives me a sheepish look but doesn't move away. "All right. Look out the window." We both turn and watch the whiteout. The wind is so wild that snow floats in every single direction, resembling some alien-planet tornado. "If you can tell me what direction your car is in, I'll let you go."

She huffs at me. *Huffs.*

"Let me? I can leave here whenever I damn well please." She reaches for the door again, but I grab her hand.

"It's not my fault that you've somehow lost your mind. You know you cannot drive in that. You can barely walk in it. You're staying here until the storm passes, even if I have to tie you up in here."

We both go a little wide-eyed at my statement. I didn't mean anything sexual but my mind went there, and I can tell hers did too. Shit.

In all the millions of times I have thought about seeing Ellie again, this is so not how it's gone. I have practiced this conversation, considered all the angles of when and where we would find ourselves together again. But I never considered she would risk frostbite over spending more than five minutes with me.

How did she get to this point? I have only ever seen the loving side of Ellie. The kid who wanted nothing but to make her brother happy. The girl who brought back Christmas for me. The woman who told me she loved me, and fucking *meant* it. Where did she go? Because this Ellie, she's looking at me like she's still considering taking her chances in the storm.

"Can you come sit down? Please?" My voice softens like I'm trying not to spook a wild animal, but I guess it works because she follows me to the couch.

"Ellie, it's really great to see you. I'm not sure if I've had a chance to say that yet." Great might be the biggest understatement of the century. Seeing Ellie after all this time doesn't feel great. It feels like a fucking miracle.

"You too." She finally sinks down on the cushion instead of staying perched on the edge. "I'm just in shock, I think. I wasn't prepared for this."

"It's me. What do you need to prepare for?" She *flinches*. What the hell? I know it's not the right move, but I don't give a damn, so I move closer and place both hands on the sides of her face. It feels so good to touch her, natural even. And she seems more relaxed too. Like my words were scary but my embrace is not. "I'm really happy you're here. I wish it wasn't because you're trapped and can't leave, but honestly, I'll take it."

I release her and walk to the kitchen, needing some distance before I fucking kiss her. Her eyes follow me, but she still doesn't say anything. It's not like Ellie to be quiet, but I'm wondering if I even know her anymore. Right now, I just want to make her comfortable. One look outside tells me she's going to be here for a while yet.

"Want an omelet?"

She perks up at that. "You can cook?"

I deadpan, holding my arms out at my sides. Does she really think I'm a twenty-seven-year-old man who never learned how to cook eggs?

"Sorry. An omelet sounds great, actually."

"Happy Hanukkah, by the way," I offer, grabbing a few things from the fridge.

"Oh yeah, it's the first night." She gets up and joins me in the kitchen. "Got any candles?"

. . .

ONCE WE'VE EATEN—AND formed a makeshift menorah out of
eight votives and anything else she could find in my hardware
box—Ellie seems much more relaxed. It's killing me inside not
asking her a million questions. I want to know every second of
her life since she left Vermont.

Since she left *me*.

But I push that thought aside and focus on the easy stuff:
work, travel, friends. It doesn't feel natural, but it feels safe.
Safe is good, for now.

"The site looks amazing. I can't believe I didn't know it was
yours. I spent a couple hours looking through it after Maya
emailed me. Honestly, I was really excited to do this feature. I
hope you'll still—"

"Of course, we will. You should have seen my face when
she showed me the article about the reopening. I was so excited,
but I also think I went into shock for a minute. Like every
memory I had here came buzzing into my head."

"I feel like that every day." She sucks in a breath at my
statement, but it's the truth; she knows how many of my memories include her. And just like that, we've left safe territory. So
screw it. "Are you still seeing someone?"

"Still?"

"Yeah, Ez said you had a boyfriend last time you talked. He
thought it was pretty serious."

There's a long pause before she admits, "No. We broke up
a few months ago." Hmm, no mention about the serious part.

"Why'd you break up?"

"Wow, you're just really diving in, aren't you?"

"Yeah." I'm not going to apologize for wanting to know her.
We've never pussyfooted around each other, and I don't plan
to now. And seven years apart or not, I need to know if the

door is open. If she still holds on to even a sliver of the past like I do.

"Well, if you must know, he told me he loved me." She looks to the mugs on the coffee table, the pictures hanging on my walls—anywhere but me.

"Isn't that usually a good thing?"

Her sad eyes find mine and she shrugs. "I don't know. I guess it just didn't feel right anymore." I'm not going to argue with her. Of course it didn't feel right. Just like no other woman has ever felt right to me. I might have been a kid when I fell for Ellie, but I know what we had was special. It was never the kind of love we could replicate with someone else.

"Are you tired?" I haven't missed the few yawns she's been trying to hide, or the numerous glances toward the window to check the weather. It's dark now but I can tell the snow has gotten worse. The wind sounds like a wolf howling after its lost mate.

"A little. Do you think—"

"Nope. You're not driving anywhere. Did you even check the weather before you came? They've been predicting a white out for days. I was planning on driving down to the city today to wait it out."

Her face looks sheepish. "I didn't even think about it. I knew I needed winter clothes but—well, honestly, I don't think I've checked the weather once since I moved to California."

I scoff. "You've gotten soft out there in the sunshine, El. Look, I'm sorry but I'm gonna have to kidnap you for the night." I smile, making it clear that I'm joking, and luckily she grins back. "I've only got one bed, but—"

"Seriously? Of course, you do." Her words are muttered under her breath and I can barely make them out.

"What'd you say?"

"You're ruining my favorite trope." She pouts.

"I have no idea what that means, but I was going to say that I'll sleep down here."

More muttering, more pouting. Finally she gives in and I walk her upstairs. I point out the two rooms that are yet to be furnished before showing her the bedroom. She had to abandon her luggage in the car that's currently sitting under at least three feet of snow, so I grab some sweatpants and a shirt for her to sleep in.

"Were you able to grab your medicine?" I just remembered she only had a small purse around her arm when she came in.

"Yeah, I just have one pill I take daily now. Going the holistic route mainly," she mumbles.

"Really? That's awesome. You look great by the way." And she does. Her long brown hair falls in loose waves down her back begging me to run my fingers through it. Those glittering dark eyes are as captivating as I remember. I can barely look away, but I remind myself she's not going anywhere. At least for the night.

I watch as she shifts from foot to foot, anxious energy pouring from every inch of her. I still don't get why everything I do is making her uncomfortable, but she's acting meek. It's throwing me off in the worst way that I don't know how to communicate with her.

"Will you be okay up here? I can sleep on the floor if you want."

"No, I'm fine, just…I don't know. This is just so strange. Being here with you."

"Hey, it can't be that bad. You used to like me, remember?" Her smile doesn't reach her eyes and it feels like a gut punch. She didn't just used to like me. She *loved* me. She said she'd follow me anywhere. The way she's reacting to my presence physically hurts, a deep ache in my bones that feels something like grief.

I don't want to leave her alone up here. I want to talk, to get answers, to find out if I still mean anything to her like she does to me.

But I'm almost afraid of what she'll say if I push any harder, so I leave her with my bundled-up clothes in her lap, and head downstairs for the night.

ELLIE KLEIN IS *in my bed.*

I can't seem to get this impossible thought out of my head. Ellie is back, Ellie is *here.* Ellie is in my fucking bed and I'm not in it with her.

For seven years I've planned our reunion. Even the last two when I lied to myself, pretending I wasn't holding on to hope. I've planned it meticulously, every detail from my opening line of "Hey, birthday girl," to the way I would kiss her again the moment we were alone. But every scenario happened differently than this. Every scenario included her coming back to Vermont to see me.

She didn't even know I'd be here.

Does she realize what she did to me when she left for California? Does she realize losing her felt like losing my parents, my *family,* all over again? Does she know there's a massive hole in my chest that gets a little bigger, a little heavier with every year we're apart?

If she knew all this, would she even care?

I'm not sure how long I've been pacing in my kitchen, thoughts of Ellie relentlessly pummeling my heart. The decision has been made to go back upstairs, to ask for all the answers I need *now.*

I have one socked foot on the first step when the power clicks out.

Chapter Nine

Theo

December 31, 2010

THE FIRST CHRISTMAS without my parents was surprisingly okay.

I had spent the past six months—my first semester of high school—hating life, fighting with my uncle and not even trying to make friends at my new school. I missed Vermont. I missed my hockey team and my best friend. I missed Mom and Dad more than I thought was humanly possible. And fighting against the anger that followed me around was too hard sometimes. Because I was fucking *angry*.

I didn't even have hockey to let out my frustration anymore. All the bitterness just festered inside me until I felt like a shaken-up soda can full of rage.

Why me? Why *them*?

Mom and Dad were two of the most positive people I had ever known. They spent their lives caring for others; for animals, for their neighbors and all the local businesses they supported, for me.

Losing my parents was hard enough, but Carol and Steve Fox were so much more than that. They might have been Mom and Dad, but they were also Sugar Valley. They were laughter and joy and Christmas waffles. Without them it felt like every bit of sunshine was sucked out of the world and the rest of my life would be filled with nothing but gray skies.

Mr. and Mrs. Klein offering to have me for the holidays was so generous, but I wasn't even sure I wanted to go. Ezra had such a nice family, and I didn't want to bring them down with the gloom that surrounded me, especially during his sister's birthday.

Yet somehow, being there helped. Each day I spent with the Kleins, my anger receded bit by bit until I felt like a human again. They never treated me like some sad orphan while I was there, and they made me feel like I could actually be okay. Ellie was the first person to really ask me about Mom and Dad since they passed, letting me talk about my favorite memories. It was hard at first, but after a day of performing all our Christmas traditions, I felt the heaviness lift from me.

I really loved her for that.

"Theo, can we chat for a few minutes, just us?" Mr. Klein pulled me aside after breakfast. It was New Year's Eve and sadly, I would be heading back to Rochester in two days, back to the uncle who made it abundantly clear that he didn't want me there.

I followed Mr. Klein into his study, and he closed the door behind us. For a minute I wondered if I had done something wrong. The thought of upsetting them after how great they had been to me felt like a knife to the chest.

Mr. Klein was much more imposing than my dad had been. He was well over six feet tall and built like a linebacker. It was always weird seeing him with his wife, who wasn't much bigger than Ellie at thirteen.

"Is everything okay? Did I—"

"Nothing to worry about, son. Have a seat. I wanted to discuss something with you." I sat, intrigued, and still a little nervous. I hoped I hadn't overstayed my welcome.

"What's up? Umm, sir?"

"No need for the formalities. I just wanted to ask you about your new school. Are you happy there?"

"Umm, I guess?" The answer was a hard no, but he didn't want to hear that, right?

"Be honest with me. Ez told me you were the best player on your old hockey team, but he wasn't sure if you were on a new one yet. Have you joined the high school team there? Made friends?"

His eyes held no judgment, so I was honest. "No, sir. Honestly, I hate it there. My uncle said I can't play until I get my license because he won't drive me. I'm basically working on school bus hours only, and nothing is walking distance from his house. It's in the middle of nowhere." I would be fifteen in February, but wouldn't have any freedom until my next birthday. I was counting down the days.

"That's a damn shame. Your uncle, is he treating you all right?"

His eyes told me he was thinking the worst. "Yeah, he's fine. He's just kind of reclusive, I guess? He doesn't really like to be around other people. He and my dad were never close, so I barely knew him before I moved there."

"I see." He took in a long breath and readjusted in his chair. Placing both elbows on his knees, he continued, "Has Ez told you about his new school down in Connecticut?"

"Yeah. He, umm, well he loves it. Except for the no-girls part." I wondered if I crossed the line, but Mr. Klein just grinned at me.

"Yeah, that was no coincidence. My boy can get easily distracted."

We shared a knowing look. I definitely had crushes, and I knew a few guys with girlfriends, but no one talked about girls as much as Ezra.

"Well," Mr. Klein went on, his tone serious again. "Avon is one of the toughest schools in the country. They also have one of the best hockey programs, and they're currently in need of a center. From what Ez tells me, you're a damn good player, but you also get good grades, yes?

"I do. I had almost all As at my old school. This year's been tougher..."

"Don't worry about that. I want you to meet with their headmaster, if you're interested. They'll require placement exams and a few interviews, but I think you've got what it takes. How would you feel about going to boarding school?"

I wasn't sure how to respond. Boarding school sounded great. Anything to get away from my uncle sounded great. But I had no money. My parents didn't have much to begin with—most of it was tied up in the village—and the little cash set aside for me in the will wouldn't be mine until I turned sixteen. At least it would be enough for a car. If I knew one thing about boarding schools, they were expensive as hell.

"There's no way I could afford—"

"They have scholarships. You would qualify for financial aid, and I've already written a recommendation. I'm an Avon alumnus myself, and I know what kind of men the school looks for. You would do very well there."

"This all sounds amazing, but why?"

"Why?"

"I mean, why are you doing this? I'm not your responsibility. Why are you going out of your way to help me?"

A small, sad smile tugged at the corners of his lips. I had never seen him make that face before. "Because I can."

The rest of the conversation felt like a blur, Mr. Klein having an answer for every objection I came up with. I could see how he was the dean at Vermont University, completely taking charge of everything. Before I knew it, he was scheduling an interview and tour for me, even a time to meet with their hockey coach.

It wasn't hard for him to convince my uncle to let me stay in Vermont an extra week so we could do down to Avon together. Honestly, my uncle wouldn't care if I never came back at all.

Maybe I wouldn't.

Three weeks later I was officially a Winged Beaver—the weirdest mascot I had ever seen. I was free from my uncle, playing hockey again, and got to share a room with my best friend.

I knew things would never be the same as when my parents were here, but I liked to think they had some hand in helping turn things around for me. It was just so sudden, how things went from bad to worse to kind of amazing. As amazing as life could be without them.

I was never religious, especially after losing my mom and dad. I didn't think I could ever accept the idea of a higher power. But after that year, I started to feel like a believer.

ASPIRANDO ET PERSEVERANDO.

To aspire and persevere. It may have been the Avon motto I was taught my first day at school, but it quickly became my personal mantra, two words guiding me into adulthood.

My new school felt like a haven. Sure, the staff were stricter than anyone I had ever met before. I was pulled out of class twice in my first week after forgetting to make my bed in the morning. But being there gave me purpose. For the first time since the accident, I felt like there might be a future to look forward to.

Ezra loved to complain about the rigidity of boarding school. Too many rules, not enough freedom. For me, it was the opposite. The rules gave me a path to follow, guidance I could no longer get from my father. And as for freedom, I felt dizzy with it. I was playing hockey again, didn't have to rely on anyone else to drive me anywhere. Everything I could ever need was on campus.

Mr. Klein came to visit twice that spring. Ezra was always thrilled to get time with his dad away from the rest of their family. Sometimes it bothered me, the way he would talk about his sister. *Everything always has to be about her. They probably don't even notice I'm away at school.*

I never got that sense from Ellie, though I didn't say as much. All she ever wanted was to make her brother happy, to make everyone around her happy, even me. I had never met anyone as selfless as her before.

Ezra didn't seem to have the same problem sharing his dad with me. He included me in everything, and I was grateful for it. Whenever Mr. Klein would visit us, we'd all go out to dinner together. Each time, he would make a point to ask me about school, about hockey, about how I was handling life. That meant a lot to me. I knew he would always care more about Ezra; I knew I wasn't his kid. But I found myself starting to look at him as a father-figure anyway. Who else would have given me this kind of gift?

These were the thoughts rolling through my head as Ezra begged and pleaded with me to go along with his big Thursday-night plan.

Even though I was still a fifteen-year-old guy who didn't always follow the rules, there was no way in hell I was going to put this gift in jeopardy. Not even for my best friend.

"No way, Z. We could get expelled."

"Oh, come on. Don't be so dramatic. No one's getting *expelled*."

Yeah, he wouldn't. His dad was an alumnus. I was a nobody. I would definitely get expelled.

"You don't even have your license yet. Who the hell is letting you borrow their car when you can't legally drive?"

"TJ," he said matter-of-factly. And of course, he would. TJ was the A-team hockey captain and about to graduate with an NHL deal already in the works. Why would he give a shit what happened to his car?

"We're not allowed to leave campus. If anyone sees us, we're screwed. And how are you planning to sneak into Miss Porter's anyway?" Our sister school was only fifteen minutes away, but their rules were just as strict as our own, maybe worse.

"Marissa's taking care of it. She also told me Abby had a message for you."

I gulped. Abby and I hooked up at the last event our schools shared. She was a year older than me, stupid hot, and kind of scary.

"What message?"

Ezra's smile morphed into something devilish. "That she has a single."

Shit. Her own room? The only person I knew with their own room who wasn't a senior was my teammate, Raj. And that was because his original roommate was in rehab.

I was tempted, sure, but Ezra wasn't winning this one.

"Good for her. I'm not going. Feel free to go without me. I'll try my best to cover for you at lights out."

Ezra was definitely a bad influence, but no one could say he wasn't a good friend. He abandoned the plan as soon as he realized I wasn't budging. And then he came up with a new one.

"Are you serious? What did you say to get them to come *here?*" He shot me that cocky expression girls fell over themselves for. I had to give it to him...he was good at this.

Abby was sixteen and had a car, so their escape plan was a bit simpler, but still not easy. Both of our schools had strict policies about leaving campus or having guests. Fortunately for me and my fifteen-year-old hormones, Ezra and the girls had it all figured out.

"THEY'RE ALMOST HERE," Ezra chirped after checking his last text message. "You take the room. TJ told me about a spot I can use with Marissa."

I really didn't want to know any more details, but there were no complaints from me. Our room was so small it barely fit me and Ezra. I was happy to have Abby there without any awkward maneuvering of two couples.

And as soon as we were behind closed doors, I was even happier for the privacy. I had hooked up with a few girls at my old school, but none of them were like Abby. I was about to ask if she wanted to watch a movie when she grabbed my shoulder and kissed me. Both our shirts were off a few seconds later.

My second time getting to third base was a lot better than the first. Being in my room had its advantages over the coat closet from our last dance. But when we finished, I wasn't sure what to do with her. We weren't friends, exactly, so I had no idea what to talk to her about. The little time we'd spent together she never seemed that interested in learning much about me, but now that we were alone, I was nervous she'd start in with some basic getting-to-know-you questions like "so, where do your parents live?"

Ezra and Raj were the only guys at school who knew about my parents, and it was hard enough talking to them about it. No one ever knew what to say to me, how to *handle* me, so I kept it hidden whenever I could.

Abby's eyes flickered to mine from across the bed. *Yep.* All my least favorite topics were coming.

"Want to watch TV?" I asked, cutting her off just as she started to speak.

A few minutes later, I was knocking on Raj's door, begging for refuge.

"Dude, what did you *do*? She came all the way here to hook up with you and then kicked you out of your own room?" Raj was legitimately cackling. I was hiding out in his extra bed now, waiting for Ezra to send the girls home.

"Don't leave me hanging here, Foxy! I need to know how you fucked it up. If you can't get a girl, we're all screwed."

"Hilarious," I mumbled back. I loved Raj, but he enjoyed making fun of me a little too much. He also refused to call me anything but Foxy. "She wanted to watch this reality show, *Blind Dates* or something stupid like that."

"And you said no? Foxy, Foxy, *Foxy*. When a girl lets you see her boobs, you watch whatever she wants."

"How do you know I saw her boobs?"

"I didn't before." He winked at me like the creep he was. "Also, your shirt's on backwards. And inside out. Kind of assumed you got dressed in a hurry when you came over here."

"How observant," I muttered. "And I didn't tell her no, I just asked if we could watch something else instead."

"ESPN?"

"No. *Planet Earth*."

"*Dude*."

"What? What's wrong with that? I love nature documentaries," I argued.

"You're not even stoned." Raj's disappointment clouded his features. "But she really got that pissed just because you're a nerd?"

"No, her reaction was similar to yours. She just sort of dismissed me and took the remote to turn on her show."

"So what the hell happened, then?"

That's the embarrassing part. I wasn't sure what happened. What we watched on TV didn't actually matter, but the thought that popped into my head somehow escaped my mouth. I didn't even mean to say it. I didn't even know why I was *thinking* it.

"After she turned the dating show on, I sort of blurted out something like, 'I wish Ellie was here'."

Intrigue floated onto Raj's expression, his signature smirk starting to form. I bet he would have been happy to watch the reality show. The kid lived for drama.

He sat up to attention and looked at me pointedly, one eyebrow cocked high. "Who's Ellie?"

Chapter Ten

Ellie

Now

THE SOUND of chattering teeth pulls me from a listless sleep. Shit. They're mine.

Holy fuck, I'm freezing. Aches start announcing themselves in my wrists and shoulders, followed swiftly by my hips. Autoimmune diseases don't like the sun. They also hate the cold. So much fun for me.

I wrap myself in the comforter and head downstairs to find a thermostat.

"Fuck, fucking...shit!" Well, I've found Theo. When I reach the kitchen, he's bouncing on one foot, hopping around and searching for...something. He must have stubbed his toe. And he must be wearing at least three coats.

"Why is it so cold in here?" His body jolts at the sound of my voice.

"Power went out. I'm trying to find a flashlight so I can go check the generator."

I reach into my purse that's still in the kitchen and grab my phone, realizing I left it down here in last night's stupor. I see a string of texts from Maya.

MAYA

How is it? Where are all my snow bunny selfies?!

Did you meet santa? *santa emoji*

Pics or it didn't happen!

Hello? Bat signal to Ellie Belly, please respond!

If you turned into an Abominable Snowman I'm going to be SO MAD

Friend test! Call me back!

A quick pang of guilt hits me while I flip on the flashlight and hand the phone to Theo. I make a mental note to call her first thing in the morning.

"Thanks, El. Mine was dead. Sorry if I woke you up."

"Nope, hypothermia did. Go."

Theo's back inside moments after I hear the telltale signs of electricity humming through the house. Without meaning to, we huddle in a weird embrace, seeking warmth from another body. I find myself sinking a little too deeply and pull away. The man has always had an exceptional gravitational pull. His hugs are more addictive than candy.

"It's going to take a bit for the place to warm up. Why don't you take this extra blanket?" He picks up the quilt from his sofa, the one he was clearly using to sleep under down here. "It's only two-thirty. You should get some more sleep."

And that's when it hits me. I *am* actually living out the one-bed trope. Obviously, I have to offer him the bed. This cabin is currently no better than an ice box, and I'm the intruder. Am I really supposed to let him freeze down here? And sure, he'll offer to sleep on the floor, but when does that ever make sense? Especially when I have shared a bed with the man in question before. A man who I wish I would have shared a bed with a lot more than I ever had the chance to.

God-damn romance novels. I *love* this trope. It's when the characters who obviously like each other but refuse to admit it, are forced together. Where cuddling happens and they finally realize how they feel. A few weeks ago, I would have paid money to be in this situation, only with anyone other than Theo Fox.

Because there is no confusion about my feelings for Theo. I have loved him for most of my life. I don't need his warm body next me to have that epiphany. The only thing it will do is remind me of the actual distance between us these days. *Ugh.*

"Come upstairs and share the bed with me, okay? Until it heats up in here." I raise my palm when he opens his mouth to argue. "Just shut up and sleep with me, Theo."

Yeah, those were a poor choice of words. Especially considering it's not the first time I have propositioned him, or the second. He's trying his best not to react but there isn't a single emotion I can't read when it comes to Theo's face.

"Come on, don't make it weird," I grumble.

We trudge up the stairs wrapped in our respective quilts and immediately fall down on the bed. He has a king, so it's not like we actually need to touch each other. In fact, I have zero plans of allowing any skin-to-skin contact. The heat will kick in soon, and it won't be necessary at all.

I settle onto my side of the bed, grazing so close to the edge that I'm pretty sure two more adults could fit in between us. But the heat floating from his body to mine won't let me ignore our current closeness. Underneath all the blankets we're sharing, space is relative.

"This is weird," he mutters.

"It's not weird," I scoff. "We're adults. We can share a bed together and be mature about it." Right? At least, I think I can. It's not often I find myself in situations like these, especially since my typical nightly routine includes at least thirty minutes of mediation and a Korean face mask that has me resembling the killer from *Scream*. Inviting men into my bed isn't really my thing.

Minutes pass with no response and I wonder if he fell asleep. His breathing is shallow, not at all how I remember. Maybe he sleeps differently now. I'm not sure why that makes me sad, that the sound of Theo asleep might not be a part of my brain chemistry anymore.

Maybe this is weird, being so close and still so far away. Until my nineteenth birthday, I never wanted an inch of space from Theo. And now I've had three thousand miles for seven years, but the empty space on the mattress between us feels like oceans, maybe even worlds.

How will I ever be able to sleep like this when all I can think about is touching him? Time has done nothing to erase my memories. I know exactly how good he feels wrapped around me, how perfectly my cheek fits against the hollow of his chest, how warm I'll be the second we connect.

Calloused skin sizzles against me, his hand snaking across my waist. Was he thinking it too? At first, his touch is so gentle I wonder if I might be imagining it, conjuring all the images in my head. But then he grips my middle and tugs me to his side of the bed. He pulls me tightly against him, no room for mistaking what this is, more than just friends sharing heat. His arms envelop me as my body hums with the connection, synapses firing across every inch of my skin.

Exactly how I knew it would feel.

"This okay?" he whispers against my hair.

My response is a breathless "Mm-hmm." It's all I can choke out because I *want* to say no. I want to say nothing about this is okay. And yet maybe what I need isn't the same as what I want.

I can't remember the last time I was cuddled like this, a tight spoon, possessive and grounding all at once. Warmth and contentment seep into my bones, relaxing each and every muscle. His nose grazes the back of my neck, and I can feel him breathe me in as I follow his lead. He smells like snow.

"Now it's not weird," he whispers onto my shoulder.

He's right. It's a lot of things, but weird isn't one of them.

And still, I think about pulling away, think about telling him how inappropriate this is. I also think about rolling over, climbing on top of him, and kissing him senseless. Until I forget every reason why we have been apart for so long. I think about screaming and slapping his face, letting him know all the ways he broke me, has continued to chip away at my heart for the last seven years.

I think and think and think. But before I have any idea what I should do, his breathing starts to slow. It's the sound I know so well as Theo fast asleep, and a smile tugs at my lips with this knowledge. I shut off the war in my brain before it consumes me, and focus on nothing but Theo's arms around me, until sleep catches up with me too.

Part Two:

Ripples

"I am made of memories."

Madeline Miller

Chapter Eleven

Ellie

December 23, 2011

"I don't understand why you won't let me go. Ezra's at Avon. You even helped Theo get in there. Why can't I go to Miss Porter's?"

It was the same conversation for weeks, but I refused to give up. Going to boarding school was my one chance to fit in. To make new friends who didn't know me as "lupus girl." It was the only thing I wanted right now, and my parents refused to listen to me.

"Ellie, baby, you've gotta stop with this. You know we're not sending you away to school. I'd miss you too much, honey."

"So, you don't miss me?" Ezra piped up. He had been an unlikely champion of my request, even offering to visit and check in on me weekly. Avon was only fifteen minutes away from my dream-school, and he had his own car now.

I kind of felt bad for Ezra. My parents didn't even ask him if he wanted to go away for high school, the decision was just made for him. My dad went there, so I think he was proud to attend, but still, his question was valid.

"Ez, come on. Of course, we miss you. Your situation is different though. Ellie, your doctors are all here. There's just no way you could take care of yourself alone."

Finally. An argument I was prepared for. I still had my hopes on Miss Porter's, but I knew Connecticut was a long shot. And no matter how many times she said she would miss me, I knew the real reason came down to my lupus.

Fucking lupus. My doctors told us repeatedly that it was under control, *mild* even. Yet my parents treated me like I was completely disabled.

They were so hard on Ez to excel in school, in sports, in everything. Me? They figured public school would be easy enough that I could miss as many days as I wanted, that I wouldn't be obligated to participate in extracurricular activities like the private schools required.

How could they think so little of me? Sometimes it felt like the only thing they saw when they looked at me was my illness, like there was no other part of me worth knowing. Screw that. I was determined to be some*one*, some*thing* other than my shitty immune system.

"Fine. What about Champlain Academy? It's only twenty minutes from here."

Ezra's shit-eating grin reinforced my confidence in this plan. He knew I was getting somewhere now. And my mom's shocked expression matched perfectly with her inability to respond.

Champlain Academy had probably never even been on their radar. It wasn't exactly a top tier school like Avon Old Farms or Miss Porter's, but that was the last thing I cared about. All I wanted was out of this house. A second chance at making friends and having schooldays I didn't dread.

I brought it up again at dinner when Dad was home. It was our last night with just the four of us. Theo was getting here tomorrow for the holidays, so I needed to make traction now. I wondered if it would be easier or more difficult if Theo were here, but he had stayed at school a few days longer than Ezra for hockey stuff, and I had to take the chance now incase his presence was too distracting.

Mom said Champlain was a bad fit because it was co-ed, like I was somehow more fragile when boys were around. Dad was warming up to the idea but of course it was her decision in the end. I begged, and begged and *begged*.

"Just fucking let her go!"

"Ezra. *Language!*"

"Mom, seriously. Let. Her. Go. Don't you see how miserable she is? You can't trap her in this house forever. Do you really want your kid to hate you for the rest of your life because you wouldn't let her have friends?" He was officially my hero.

"Ezra, do *not* speak to your mother like that!"

"Come on Dad. You're no better. When are you going to stand up to Mom? You have an *intelligent* daughter." He stood up at the table and threw his napkin down on his plate. "Do you realize how smart Ellie is? She took an online coding course meant for college kids." Three sets of eyes shot to Ez. He was really going for it, and I was happy the secret was out. "Yeah, I paid for it because she was too scared to ask you. You know, because you won't let her do anything other than rest? And now you—two college professors—are denying her the chance for a better education? Why? Seriously, *why?*"

My parents and I were completely stunned. I had never heard Ezra yell at them like that, and I never realized he cared about me enough to fight for me this way. I couldn't stop myself from crying; this weird mixture of angry, sad, proud tears slipping down my face.

"Come on, Ellie. Let's get out of here."

Ezra took me to Panda Express. I had rarely driven with him since he turned sixteen last summer, so I jumped at the chance to go. He knew it was my favorite and that Mom almost never let me eat there. It was only reserved for when I was feeling my absolute worst and her guilt set in. Otherwise, the lupus diet reigned supreme.

"Thank you for standing up for me. It really means a lot." I could barely speak on the drive over, but with our steaming bowls of orange chicken on the table between us, I broached the subject.

"I needed to say it. And I'm sorry I haven't before. They're way too strict with you." I couldn't do much but smile. It felt so good for my feelings to be validated, by my brother of all people. "Also—" He paused and took a long sip of his fountain soda. "Look, I'm sorry we never hung out last summer. I know I acted like a dick."

I gaped at him, chopsticks hovering over my dinner, and fought the urge to look over my shoulder. Was he talking to me? It wasn't that his words weren't true: Ezra *had* avoided me all summer and pointedly told me to find my own friends. But I never imagined he would actually feel bad about it.

"It's okay."

"It's not okay. You don't deserve that, and I promise I'll do better. All right?"

I nodded, trying to keep my emotions in check. We'd never had a conversation like this before.

Does this mean things will actually change between us?

When we got home, Ezra was sent to his room and told he was grounded until he went back to school. I felt horrible, but at least Theo would be here soon to hang out with him.

And then the biggest surprise of the year came: Mom and Dad said I could apply to Champlain Academy. The catch? I had to go as a day student. Apparently, I missed that little detail in my research. Most boarding schools offered both options, so it wasn't that surprising, but I wished I'd had a plan to argue for boarding. I didn't.

Yet after the conversation with my brother, a future with a new school, and Theo coming back to visit tomorrow, nothing could bring me down.

SUGAR VALLEY WAS STILL CLOSED, but my birthday tradition held, with a few minor changes. Like last year, Theo spent winter break with us, two whole weeks to celebrate all our favorite traditions.

Ezra found a place nearby that had outdoor skating, and even though he was supposed to be grounded, Mom and Dad let us go on Christmas Eve "for Theo's sake." And since Ezra had a car now, we didn't have to deal with them tagging along. Of course, mom still fussed over me before we left, but after Ezra yelled at her last night, I could tell she was reeling it in a bit. Maybe his words had struck a chord.

The skating lessons were scrapped last year. No matter what I said, Mom deemed it too stressful on my body and reckless for me to take it any further. She had been paying close attention at the one moment when I fell practicing a jump, and that was the beginning of the end. I wasn't allowed to have bruises.

But I still loved skating with Theo and Ez. I kept up with them these days, and even learned a few tricks, like my one-foot spins that were fun to show off. Mom always let me go with the guys, trusting them to take care of me. I think I owed Ezra more than I realized for that one.

After skating, we picked up pizzas and all the ingredients

needed for an epic hot chocolate bar. And as soon as dinner was over, we got started on the blanket fort. I knew Theo's tradition was technically on Christmas Day, but with my birthday at midnight, the guys decided it made sense to set it up the night before.

Mom and Dad even said I could stay in the basement with the guys, at Ezra's urging. I'd all but glued my lips together to keep from squealing and changing his mind. It felt like we were finally friends, like he actually enjoyed being my brother for a change.

That week flew by. Ezra's grounding was basically forgotten. He and Theo spent most days training at the gym or the rink. They were all hockey, all the time. They were both on the A-team this year which I was told was impressive for sophomores. After listening to my dad, it sounded like Theo was already the star of their team. And he called Ezra the enforcer, which honestly just made me laugh. If only I could go to one of their games and see it for myself.

"Hey Ellie, you wanna play?"

It was New Year's Eve, and the guys had been playing NHL on Xbox for hours. I came down to the basement to bring them snacks when Theo popped the question.

"I don't know how."

"Here, you can play for me. I need to go call Marissa." Ezra stood up and handed me the controller right as Noodle plopped himself down on the sofa.

"I'll teach you. It's really easy," Theo offered, so I plopped myself down too.

"Who's Marissa?"

"Girl from Miss Porter's. They talk on the phone for hours. It's so annoying. Did you know your brother was one of those 'no, *you* hang up' people?" My laugh burst through my mouth. I loved when Theo confided in me like this. He was never mean but sharing Ezra stories like this was my favorite.

"So, is she like his girlfriend?" It checked out that Ezra wouldn't tell me or our parents if she was.

"Nah. They just hook up sometimes." Ew, whatever that meant, I did not want to know.

"Do you have a girlfriend?" Oh no. I didn't mean to say that; it just sort of popped in my head. I was never good at filtering myself, especially around Theo. He made me feel so comfortable, happy...carefree. And the thought of him having a relationship with another girl, one that he was closer to than me, it irked me. I had to know.

"Nope. No time. I've gotta focus on hockey. If I don't get a scholarship, I'll never go to college."

"Why do you think that? You seem smart to me."

He laughed. "I'm no idiot, but I'm definitely not a genius. Hockey's my only road to a scholarship. There's no way my uncle is planning to give me a dime for school, and, well—" He paused, clenching his jaw. Something like melancholy mixed with determination skated through his features. "It would have crushed my dad if I didn't go to college. I can't let him down."

"Oh." I was just filled with eloquence tonight. But I didn't know how to respond. I had this urge to offer my help, but what would that even look like?

"Ready to play?"

Theo walked me through the buttons on the controller while I chewed over his words. I felt for Theo, for the difficulties he was suddenly facing in life that no one prepared him for. And yet part of my selfish heart was happy. Happy that he didn't have a girlfriend, and somehow even happier that he had no plans for one. I wasn't delusional enough to think I could ever be his girlfriend. Guys like Theo would never date someone like me. But at least if he stayed single, our relationship would remain special, sacred, even if it was only me who felt that way.

"See, you're getting it. I'm still gonna crush you though." After almost an hour, I had picked up the game and was playing...relatively well. I wasn't a gamer, but I appreciated Theo's enthusiasm, even if he was going easy on me.

"I'll just have to practice for next year. Then we'll see who's crushing whom." Theo smiled at me then and I could swear I lost my breath for a second. I was used to spending time with him, but every so often I would get kicked in the face with how gorgeous he was, how sweet, how much I craved his smile when it was only us.

And this smile, it felt different.

It wasn't ending.

Our gazes held for what seemed like hours. It felt like something was snapping into place and my heart started beating uncontrollably as he kept looking at me, kept smiling at me...

"You guys are still playing?" The spell was broken as my brother bounded over the back of the couch to sit between us. "Happy New Year, sis." Ez ruffled my hair and I looked at the clock, realizing we just played through the new year.

"Happy New Year, *bro*," I mocked.

"Happy New Year, weirdos." We both laughed at Theo. I wasn't sure what was happening before Ezra interrupted us, but his face looked perfectly normal again. It was probably all in my head.

"Wanna watch a movie?" Ezra asked.

"Sure, you pick."

Ezra put on *Tron* and promptly passed out. He was snoring like a bulldog before the opening credits finished. Theo asked if I was tired, but I wasn't. And he moved next to me on the couch, so we didn't have to speak over my brother.

"I don't sleep much, actually. My medicine keeps me up.

That's why Mom is always on me about my bedtime. She thinks if I have a nightly routine, it'll help me sleep better."

"Do you think it helps?"

"Nope. I think the drugs do what the drugs wanna do." Theo offered a sad smile at my quip. Sometimes I forgot most people my age weren't taking a boatload of medication every day. They didn't find my drug jokes particularly funny. "Sorry. Sometimes it's easier to joke about it, ya know?"

"Can I ask you something?"

"Sure." Theo Fox could ask me anything.

"What's it like, having lupus? I tried to research it, but I couldn't really tell what it all meant." Theo researched lupus? To find out about me? This revelation caught me so off-guard I was speechless. "Sorry. If it's personal I totally get it. I was just trying to understand it more. I know your mom's super protective, but I want you to be safe with me too. I mean, not with me, but like, when we hang and stuff."

Theo's hands were fidgety between us, and his eyes tracked each movement. My heart melted at the revelation that he was nervous about this conversation. That it mattered. That he cared this much about me.

All I had ever known was a mom who treated me like a problem to be fixed, a dad who wasn't around enough to make a difference, a brother who ignored my illness completely, kids at school who were so ignorant that they thought I was contagious.

Not once in my life had someone asked me what it was like for *me*.

"I don't mind talking about it. Sometimes it makes other people uncomfortable." His eyes caught mine, and the way they didn't waiver—didn't even blink—made the words tumble out. "So, it's kind of like my body doesn't have a normal immune system. Before we knew what it was, they just thought I constantly had the flu or pneumonia. Now that I take medicine it's not so bad. Most days I feel fine, but I can get tired or worn out easily. And I get flares every so often, where it gets worse. It can be really painful. Like remember last New Year's?" He nods. "I said I couldn't go skating because I had plans, but I didn't. I was having really bad aches, like my whole body hurt."

"Why'd you lie about it?"

"I don't know. Sometimes it's just hard to explain. Like—okay. I know I look completely normal, but my head and my joints will be hurting so bad, or I'll feel so exhausted I can barely stand. It's really embarrassing."

Theo grabbed my hand and held it for a minute between us. "Ellie, that's stupid. Please don't ever feel embarrassed around me, okay? I would have stayed home and hung out with you."

"Really?"

"Of course." Those words hung between us, and the crush I pretended not to have on Theo snowballed out of control. I quickly turned my head toward the TV, to the movie we had never actually started watching. Ezra and Noodle were both snoring in time with each other, creating a relatively peaceful melody.

Latke—who must have jumped into Theo's lap at some point—started to purr, adding to the sounds around us.

"She really likes you. She never lets me pet her like that." She slept with me every night, and I loved that she picked me out of the rest of the family to share a bed with. Try to touch her, though, and she was gone like the wind.

"Yeah? My mom always loved cats." As soon as the M-word came out of his mouth, his demeanor shifted. Furrowed brows, tight lips, his chest and shoulders a bit more rigid than usual.

"What do you miss the most? Right now?"

His gaze shot to me. Catching Theo off guard might be a

new favorite hobby. A grin spread across his face, and his eyes lit up even in the dim light of the basement. "I kind of love that question." I smiled back. "You know, most people are afraid to even speak the words 'mom' or 'dad' around me. But you just go for it."

"Ezra says I have no filter. It's kind of a problem."

"He's wrong. Never change, El." Actual butterflies were at war and the battlefield was my chest cavity. *El.* No one ever called me that.

"So...? Tell me. What are you missing now?"

Nostalgia skated across his face as his smile changed, lost in a memory. He laughed quietly, shaking his head. "It's stupid."

"No, it's not. What is it? Tell me."

"Secret grilled cheese." A small laugh escaped me. I wasn't expecting that.

"Are you hungry?"

"I'm always hungry."

"Okay...I think you need to explain this one."

There was a twinkle in his eye as he sank further into the couch. "So, you know I, umm, eat a lot?" I nodded. Mom was always stressing about having enough food when he visited. "I guess I got my appetite from my dad. He was always hungry—like every minute of every day, that man could eat. But Mom was always on him to be healthier. She was so worried about his cholesterol, always telling him she wasn't going to let him die young of a heart attack and leave her all alo—" He scoffed, and I couldn't do anything but watch while every emotion washed over him. "I guess she should have let him eat whatever he wanted. Didn't matter anyway."

I was so out of my league here. I didn't know what to say to him or the right way to comfort him. I decided to go for distraction. It's what I turned to during my bad days.

"Tell me about the grilled cheese, please? The suspense is killing me."

The look he threw me was filled with gratitude. I tried petting Latke to distract myself from his perfect smile, but she bolted away. Surprise, surprise.

"Okay. So, Mom was really strict about how much we could have for dinner. Dad always complained about being hungry, and I was too sometimes, but she was hardcore. She controlled the food, and we had no say in the matter. It was always 'either have more broccoli or suffer'." I started to giggle, picturing Theo and his dad begging Carol for more lasagna and her sending them to bed hungry.

"My dad discovered that on nights when mom had a glass of wine, which was pretty frequent, she slept like the dead. Nothing could wake her up. So he'd sneak out of their room, come get me, and we'd make secret grilled cheeses."

I loved this story. I wanted to live in it.

"He was so stealth about it too. He was terrified of her finding out, so we had all these rules. Must be wearing socks, can't turn the stove above medium, open all packaging inside the pantry to muffle the noise. It was ridiculous, but they were the best grilled cheeses. We would each have like four." He tilted his head in a way that reminded me of how Noodle looked when I asked him a question. "I wonder how Mom never noticed the food that went missing."

Oh, poor Theo. His mom absolutely knew what was going on. Moms always knew what was in the kitchen. I didn't have the heart to tell him though.

"Is it bad that that's what I miss? I know there are so many other moments that are more important, but right now, that's all I can think about. That I miss those damn grilled cheeses."

"It's not bad. It sounds like a great memory." He wasn't looking at me anymore, lost in his own head. I really didn't want to make him sad, but I was trying to learn how to be there for him, how to be the kind of friend he needed. And there was one thing I was pretty sure I could do to cheer him up. "Theo?"

"Yeah?"

"Wanna go make some grilled cheeses?"

Chapter Twelve

Theo

January 1, 2012

You ARE SERIOUSLY BLOWING my mind right now."

I was sitting on the island, watching Ellie prep—her word—our grilled cheese sandwiches. Gourmet grilled cheese sandwiches, by the looks of things. She'd moved on to grating the second type of cheese.

"We just always used singles," I mumbled. Everything about the Klein's house was fancier than how I grew up, but I had no idea there was a better way to do grilled cheese.

"That's good too. Singles melt really well. But I promise you're going to love this. The white cheddar is so yummy, and the Havarti makes it extra melty." She continued grating while simultaneously shoving away every offer of mine to help.

"How'd you learn to cook like this?" I didn't know anyone our age who cooked. All I could use was a microwave and even that had turned out poorly a few times.

"I watch a lot of cooking shows. When I stay home from

school and I'm not feeling well, it's usually *Food Network* or *Jeopardy*. Not sure why, but they relax me."

"*Jeopardy*, huh? No wonder you're such a brainiac."

She tried to shove me with the spatula, but I caught her arm in my hand. Something glimmered between us, the hairs on her arm standing at attention, and I let go before I could chew on it.

"Almost done." She turned back to the stove where the sandwiches were sizzling. Watching her cook was sort of hypnotizing; it was hard to look away. Even as she slid the sandwiches onto a platter and sliced them into perfect triangles, my eyes were glued to her every movement.

We sat down on the stools under the island, each taking a sandwich from the platter in front of us.

"Shit, that's good," I said with a mouthful of hot cheese. Understatement. It was one of the best things I had ever tasted.

"It's the garlic butter. And the cheddar. It's from a local farm; so good."

"Nah, it's all you, El."

"Thanks," she tittered, tilting her eyes down and biting back a grin. "I'm glad you like it. I hope it keeps the memories intact." My sandwich was gone by the time she stopped talking and I was already reaching for a second.

My eyes shimmered at her thoughtfulness. I couldn't help thinking how happy I was to have someone like her in my life. An hour ago, it was all secret grilled cheeses, but now a million of my favorite memories swam through my head. I filtered through them while I ate, deciding which ones to share with her, which ones she'd enjoy the most.

"This one summer, at the sanctuary, someone brought my mom a raccoon."

"What?" Ellie asked, mid-bite. I shouldn't have been surprised my out-of-context storytelling startled her; I'd been having a conversation in my head after all.

"Yeah, I guess they found it injured in their yard and thought she'd want it. My dad was adamant about getting rid of it, but I fell in love."

"With a raccoon?" Her tone was sarcastic, but her eyes were smiling.

"I was like, seven. They're cute! And my mom refused to turn down any animal in need. We even named it—"

"What the hell are you guys doing?" I jumped off the barstool at Ezra's voice. I wasn't sure why, but it felt like I had just been caught. *Get your shit together, man. You're just eating sandwiches and talking about raccoons.*

"I made grilled cheese," Ellie announced. "Want one?"

"Sure," he responded, drawing out the word and trudging of the counter. He grabbed a sandwich, but his face was tight as his eyes bounced between us. "Why are you still up, Ellie? Mom would flip if she knew you weren't in bed."

"What, are you gonna tell on me?" she quipped. But her smile faltered when Ezra didn't crack. She looked confused, then disappointed, and finally, she said, "Okay, then. Night boys. You can clean up," before heading upstairs without another word.

"What was that about?" I asked Ezra. He looked annoyed and it made no sense.

"Nothing. Just didn't want her to get in trouble."

"Bullshit."

Our eyes met in a standoff, and I watched his jaw work. He was definitely pissed.

"Are you into my sister or something? You know she just turned fourteen."

My gut reaction was to mention that I was still fifteen for another month and a half, but luckily that's not what I responded with.

"We're just friends. Don't make it weird."

"You sure about that?"

No, I wasn't sure about that. I would never say it aloud, but I did like Ellie. Maybe not romantically, or maybe yes, I didn't know. But I liked being around her. I looked forward to seeing her every year, even more now that I didn't have my parents. She just made me feel good, like I could always be myself.

And yeah, maybe I found myself trying to find ways to make her laugh. Or smile. Why wouldn't I? The girl radiated joy. She was the kind of person that would see me sobbing on the fourth of July and start singing Christmas songs until I was happy again.

She was the only person I ever talked to about Mom and Dad, the only person who *encouraged* me to talk about them. She liked hearing about my memories as much as I liked telling her.

But again, I didn't say any of that.

"I'm sure," I replied.

It was the first lie I had ever told my best friend. I tried to promise myself it would be the last one too.

Ezra only grunted in response, so I changed the subject. "Did you try this grilled cheese though? It's unreal."

Chapter Thirteen

Ellie

Now

Went to shovel your car out.
Hot chocolate is waiting for you in the kitchen.
-T

THE NOTE LIES on the pillow next to me. It's cold to the touch but I can still feel the heat from Theo's body, the body that was wrapped around me half the night.

How I could I let this happen? Of all the wild ideas I'd had about what my time in Vermont would look like, this was one of the only scenarios I didn't see happening. Sure, the idea of seeing Theo popped into my head, the *horror* of it. But getting snowed in at his home, sleeping in bed with him, no imagination went that far.

I couldn't let myself get sucked in again. Not with him.

I had to stifle these feelings before they grew wings.

Theo didn't just tear my heart into tiny pieces, he humiliated me. And the fact that he doesn't seem to realize that makes it so much worse. Days of crying, weeks of trying to make sense of his lies, years of coming to terms with the fact that our relationship wasn't the same to him as it was to me. And less than twenty-four hours in his presence, I can barely stop myself from falling in love all over again.

Fuck.

I pad down the stairs, grateful for the warm air being filtered through the house and go in search of my hot chocolate. I would assume Theo drinks coffee like every other grown adult, but it was nice of him to think of me and my favorite winter beverage.

I ladle some cocoa into a mug. It's the real stuff made on the stove and smells decadent. My first sip and I am in chocolatey heaven. I barely take my lips off the mug as I move to sit in front of the fire and live out my coziest fantasy.

Snow falls heavily beyond the window, and I wonder how Theo is shoveling anything when it's still coming down so hard. Watching the storm from inside the warm cabin, sipping hot cocoa—from a hand-thrown ceramic mug, might I add—is magical, but guilt churns in my belly that he's out there suffering in this.

The front door flies open and the Abominable Snowman version of Theo bursts into the cabin. He sets down my suitcase and shakes like a dog, clearing clumps of snow from his head before his gaze finds me curled up on the floor.

"You look cozy."

"You look...like you could use this more than me." I extend my arm, offering him the mug.

"Thanks." He pulls off his hat, coat and boots and joins me on the floor, stealing one sip before handing the mug back to me. "So, your car..."

"Oh no. What happened to it?"

"It's fine, just buried. I tried, El, I really did. This storm is insane." He does look remorseful, like he failed me in some way. But the only person who failed is the girl who never thought to check the weather before going to Vermont in the middle of December.

"Shit. I better call Maya." I spring up from the floor to go grab my phone, but Theo's hand reaches out and stops me.

"Service is out." He gulps. "Sorry."

"There's no cell service?" I shout in horror. Theo shakes his head, eyes cast down. "Wi-Fi?" This time, my voice is meeker, a lot less angry and a little more hopeful. His reaction is the same.

What the fuck? How are there still places in the country that can be cut off from the grid like this? Maybe New Hampshire, but not *here*. Not the place where I need to be working, namely uploading content to our website. And no cell service? I have never needed to talk to Maya more than I do in this moment. Without her or Dr. Green, I'm not sure I'll survive another night with Theo.

"Please don't freak out. I promise it'll all be back soon. Nothing's gonna happen to you, okay? You're safe here. You're safe with me." Theo's words wash over me like a warm bubble bath; he's always been so damn sweet. But he doesn't realize why I'm panicking.

"Sorry, it's not that. I just don't know how to get my work done. I need to be out there getting photos, which—" I take another look outside and immediately picture the scene from *One Hundred and One Dalmatians* where the dogs are marching through a snowstorm. I can hear Lucky's voice, shaky and meek. *I'm tired, and I'm hungry. And my tail's froze, and my nose is froze.* That would be me after thirty seconds in this storm. "I don't think the weather is going to cooperate." I huff. "And I can't even call Maya to let her know what's going on. Or have the rest of the team find a different feature while this one's delayed. The whole thing is a disaster!"

"Ellie, take a deep breath." Begrudgingly, I do. It's exactly what I should be doing, and I know that. I can't let the stress get to me or my whole body will be suffering. "I can help you. I have tons of photos you can use. They've never been posted anywhere. All taken on my phone, right?"

He grabs a laptop and pulls up an image gallery for me to look at. Could Theo really save the day here? He's right about the phone. One of the draws to our website is that every photo we post was taken on a phone. A common complaint we discovered early on in our business was that people felt bamboozled when they saw professional photos online and were sorely disappointed with the reality. In the beginning, we just couldn't afford professionals, but it worked in our favor, people becoming loyal subscribers for the transparency we offered.

We still wanted our photos to look good, to capture the best of each destination we promoted, so every member of our team has taken photography classes to learn about lighting, angles, all the basics to help us get the most from our camera phones.

Theo's pictures aren't bad.

"You took all these?" I ask. I'm currently eyeing one of three mini horses standing outside the animal sanctuary's gate, the "Moon River" sign hanging overhead. The photo must have been taken right at sunrise and the light is nothing short of breathtaking.

"Yeah. This place has kind of been my obsession all year. Ever since I left the Bruins."

I really want to ask about hockey but I'm too scared to open up that Pandora's box.

"These are great. I can absolutely use them, if you're really okay with it."

"Of course. Anything I can do to help. You're doing me the favor by promoting the village, remember?"

It didn't feel like that anymore, but maybe we were helping each other.

"Could you help me with the write-up too? I want to make sure I don't miss anything."

"Hmmm." His lips are pursed together and he's tapping his chin. *Way to leave a girl hanging.* "I'll help you with all of it, but I've got one condition. Something you have to do before you go into full work-mode."

"Seriously?" He nods, his lips pulled taut. "Fine, what is it?"

"Snow angels."

Chapter Fourteen

Ellie

December 24, 2012

THEO

Are you awake?

ELLIE

Aren't I always?

THEO

Good. Come downstairs

Quietly

And dress warm!

I TIPTOED out of my room and down the stairs. It was Christmas Eve, but Ezra had the flu, so instead of us all crashing in the basement, the night was uneventful. Other than mom turning into an evil dictator, keeping him away from me and forcing him to wear a mask at all times. You know, the usual.

I found Theo in the kitchen, fully decked out in winter gear and a wicked smile plastered on his face.

"Come on, look." Theo directed me toward the window where I saw what was making him so happy.

Snow. A ton of it.

Somehow, it hadn't snowed this year at all. For Vermont, it was unheard of, and for Theo, well, snow was practically his love language.

"Put this on." He handed me a knit hat with a huge pompom on top. "And grab Noodle. We're gonna make snow angels."

If Ezra had been with us, he would have thrown a fit about how childish this was. He turned seventeen last summer and suddenly grew out of all things that didn't involve hockey, parties, or girls. He even warned me last week that he and Theo would be spending New Year's with friends "their own age," so I shouldn't get my hopes up.

But in an interesting turn of events, Ezra came down with the flu yesterday. He'd left the door open after he brought his stuff in from the car, giving Noods the perfect opportunity to bolt. Three hours searching for my precious Bernedoodle in the cold brought his immunity down to my level.

"Thanks," I said to Theo, pulling the hat over my messy hair and throwing on my tallest boots. Not wanting to go down like my brother, I wrapped a thick scarf around my neck and followed him outside, Noodle safely secured in his harness.

I felt...rebellious.

Sure, Mom would be happy with how bundled I was, but the truth was that I had never gone outside this late at night before. I checked my phone to see the time of eleven forty-eight. I was almost fifteen.

"How does it feel to be a year older, birthday girl?" Theo eyed my phone before I slid it back into my pocket.

"I don't know. The same, I guess. Nothing really changes at fifteen."

We stepped off the porch and into the snow, clearing a path as it fell like thick confetti over our heads. Noodle immediately flipped onto his back to perfume himself in his favorite substance. The sky was dark, but the moon hung high enough to glaze my yard in a faint inky glow.

"That's not true." He took my hand to help me get through what seemed like at least two feet of powder. "Have you looked in the mirror lately?"

I. Was. Deceased.

I could have sworn there was a moment when Theo got here yesterday, right after our welcome-home hug, when he looked at me. Like, really looked at me. The kind of top to bottom perusal I only saw in movies. The kind of look where the guy just couldn't help himself.

But I didn't believe it then. No one ever gave *me* those looks. Or if they did, I never noticed. I knew I wasn't ugly. I had clear skin, round eyes, a dimple that a few girls told me they were jealous of. A couple guys had even asked me out at my new school.

Of course, Mom had a strict, no-dating rule. Ezra had never been mandated when it came to girls, curfew, nothing. But me, I might as well apply to be the first Jewish nun.

Was Theo trying to tell me I got pretty?

My strict diet paired with my finicky immune system kept me skinnier than I would have liked. My new friends at Champlain Academy were all getting boobs, but not me. I barely needed a training bra. Kat and Livy were always telling me I had the best hair, and I enjoyed the compliment. I loved my long, thick brown locks. It probably had something to do with the plethora of supplements Mom forced on me. Maybe they worked. I would never let my friends in on this secret though. They were totally oblivious to my lupus.

It was nice having friends. Even if they didn't really know me. They were all boarding students, so I was already the odd one out who got picked up every day. I missed out on a lot of gossip, and the TV marathons, and sneaking out to the boys' dorms. That part didn't bother me so much.

The only boy I had ever felt anything for was right in front of me.

"You think I look different?" I didn't just want to be beautiful. I wanted a beautiful person like Theo to *think* I was beautiful. They were two completely different things.

"Yeah." That one word stretched and pulled into something auspicious. *Yeah, and I like it. Yeah, I see you differently. Yeah, and I'm feeling the same way that you are when we look at each other.* The possibilities were endless. "I mean, you look older, you know."

"Not too old to make snow angels, though?"

"Never." He pulled me down into the snow with him, our gloved hands still clasped together. Noodle started running in circles around us, overly excited by everyone being on the ground with him.

We sank into the fresh powder, swinging our limbs and never letting go of each other. Noodle made sure the angels were completely destroyed, but I knew my memory of them would be forever intact.

"Thanks for coming out here with me."

"Thanks for asking." We were still, just two people lying on their backs in the snow. His cheeks were pink, and I could see pieces of his golden-brown hair curling under his hat. He started growing it out long for hockey and I loved the way it looked. His hazel eyes glowed in the moonlight. "Sorry Ezra's sick."

"Come on. He would never do this with me. You're my adventure girl."

Adventure girl. I wished that was who I was. *Over my mom's dead body.*

Once we felt the snow start to seep through the weak points in our winter gear, we rushed back inside to get warm. Theo grabbed Noodle, who was over fifty pounds now, and carried him up to my room so we could dry him off, erasing the evidence of our midnight madness.

As soon as we entered my room and I closed the door, Theo froze.

"I've never been in here before."

"It's nothing special. I barely even sleep in here. I'm usually in the basement or the sunroom or just anywhere that..." I trailed off when it was clear Theo wasn't listening. I followed his gaze to my windowsill, the one lined with every snow globe he had ever gifted me.

My shelf of treasures.

"You kept them all?"

"Of course! Why wouldn't I?" Suddenly protective over my favorite gifts, I rushed over to the shelf. Did he expect me to throw them away?

"I don't know. I guess I just never expected to see them all together like this. Actually, I almost forgot." He sped out of my room and down the stairs before finishing the thought. When he returned, he was bent over and breathing heavy, one hand braced on his knee and the other holding something behind his back.

"Happy birthday, El." He shook the snow globe before handing it to me, so I could watch it transform right away.

"*Owls.*" I watched the faux snow descend over two winter white owls perched on a branch. Spots dusted like nutmeg accentuated each feather and their wide-eyed expressions matched my own. He always promised he would find me one with owls.

I was so moved by this gift it was hard to speak. I couldn't cry in front of Theo. I had to stay cool. This night was already turning into a favorite memory—I could feel it.

"Did you know a group of owls is called a parliament?" I blurted.

"Huh." He looked genuinely surprised. "I wonder why. Maybe because they work together or something? Or 'cause they look so serious? You already know, don't you."

I nodded but didn't say anything. Dad said I could be a smart aleck sometimes. I wasn't trying to show off, but I read a lot. I had a ton of random information in my head that most people wouldn't think twice about. And it was fun to teach people things. It was fun to teach *Theo* things.

"Come on, El. The suspense..."

"Did you ever read *The Lion, The Witch and The Wardrobe*?" He tipped his head up and down, urging me on. "C.S. Lewis—the author—he called them that in the book. I guess it stuck."

"Really?" I nodded again. "That's actually pretty cool. So, what are you gonna name them?"

"The owls?"

"Yeah. I love the names you come up with." That made me smile. And I did already have names for them.

"Butter and Scotch."

"Perfect."

"Thanks for this. I love it. I love all of them." I placed my new snowy bauble on the windowsill next to last year's Hanukkah-themed globe. I loved that he found one with a menorah in it for me.

"Shit. If I keep up the tradition, I might have to build you a new shelf. Looks like you only have space for two more." I grinned, maybe too enthusiastically. The idea of Theo spending more time in my room, *building* something for me? It was almost too much.

"I better head downstairs before we wake anyone up. Thanks for playing in the snow with me."

"Anytime."

"Goodnight, birthday girl." He hugged me before he left my room, and I could have sworn he kissed the top of my head. I replayed that moment over and over for the rest of the night.

My birthday felt different this year. With Ezra holed up in his room, Theo and I cycled through our traditions alone. I wasn't complaining. Every new time I spent with him alone felt momentous.

"I wanted to ask you something," Theo said on Christmas morning, just before we left for the movies. Mom agreed to let me go so Ezra could escape quarantine for a few hours.

"Okay."

"So that checklist I saw in the kitchen, those are all your symptoms?" His question caught me by surprise.

"Umm, it's more like *all* symptoms. I don't have most of the ones on it." I quickly read through the list in my head. They were embarrassing whether they were checked off or not. *Awesome.*

"Do you mind if I ask what you use it for? I promise I wasn't snooping. It was just lying out and I was curious and—"

"It's okay, really. I trust you." Our eyes met then, and I had to catch my breath for a minute. Every new moment with Theo was turning into something sticky and sweet, its taste always lingering long after it was over. "I'm supposed to fill it out every three months so I can take it to my doctors' appointments and show them how I'm doing. You can't cure a chronic illness or like, fix it, so all they try to do is manage my symptoms. Depending on how bad they are between visits, the doctors will change up my medicine or keep it the same. Stuff like that."

"It looked like a lot more than every three months, El."

"Yeah. Mom has me do it weekly. And there's a separate one to fill out during flares. Since it's all about dealing with my symptoms, if I'm not constantly telling the doctors what I'm feeling, they can't help me. She overdoes it, but I don't mind that part. It makes me feel in control of the illness. Even though sometimes it feels like I'm treating myself. The doctors just go on whatever I tell them."

"Really? What's the point of seeing the doctors so often then?" I loved how Theo had this fight behind his eyes, solely on my behalf. "It just seems like a lot if they're not helping you."

"They still run a lot of tests. Some people with lupus have issues with breathing or their kidneys and it can be really serious. They're always testing me for stuff to make sure I'm in the clear. It gets old but I like it. There's actual proof for Mom that I'm not dying, and she can relax. Like a physical report card with an A+ in survival."

He didn't like my joke. Not even a twitch of his lips.

"I wish I could do something to help you, El."

"Talking about it helps. It's kind of nice. No one ever wants to talk about it. Not like this."

To NO ONE'S SURPRISE, Ezra was back to perfect health only two days after Christmas. And then suddenly, I was the one falling ill.

The flare came on swiftly this time, with no warning other than a minor headache on the twenty-seventh. There was no fever, and the pain was minimal, but the exhaustion was all-consuming. I felt too weak to even hold up a paperback, so I turned on the Red album and threw my headphones in.

I was humming along to "All Too Well" when the song was interrupted by a familiar chime.

> **THEO**
>
> I keep wanting to ask how you're feeling. But I know if you were better you'd be hanging out with us. I don't know what to say, but I still wanted to check on you so...hi

Theo was thinking about me? I stretched out my limbs that hadn't seen movement in several hours and brought my pillows and phone with me to the floor. I leaned against the foot of the bed, trying to find a comfortable position as my thumbs hovered over the screen.

> **ELLIE**
>
> Hi

> **THEO**
>
> How bad is it?

> **ELLIE**
>
> Not so bad. I'm really bored and fidgety, but I'm too weak to do anything but lie here like a snuggle of sloths

> **THEO**
>
> Like how you slipped that in there. Did you know they're also called a slumber?

ELLIE

Snuggle feels more on-brand at the moment, considering the meds I'm on won't let me sleep

THEO

That sucks. Ez said we couldn't visit you. Are you really not allowed to be around anyone? I thought your mom checked on you a lot

ELLIE

He just doesn't like to be around me when I'm like this. I think it makes him uncomfortable

Less than a minute later, there was a knock on my door. I tossed my phone to the pillow and choked out a garbled "come in," and then Theo was there, in the flesh.

"Hi," I mumbled, still sitting on the floor. I didn't have the strength to rise up to his level.

"Hi." He sat down next to me. "How—" He scoffed. "Do you know how hard it is not to ask how you're feeling?"

"Go ahead. Get it out of your system."

"Nope, not gonna do it. Reminds me of when Mom and Dad died. Everyone kept asking how I was. It took everything in me not to scream at them, 'How the fuck do you think I am, you idiot?'" Laughter bubbled out of me, but he kept going. "I know you feel like shit. I can see it in your face, so I don't need to ask."

"I'll be fine. I'm used to it, remember?" I tucked my hands underneath my thighs. Anxiety was an old friend of mine, but right now, I wasn't sure if Theo's closeness was the cause.

"Yeah. You're tough as nails, El." Tough. My brother told me I was tough once too, but I hadn't truly believed it. Maybe I should start.

"I know you need to rest, but I just wanted to give you something." He reached into his pocket.

"You already got me a birthday present, Theo. No more gifts."

"It's not a gift, not really. Here." He held up a small, smooth stone along with a folded piece of paper. When I unfolded it, the words "rub me" winked back at me.

"Rub me?" I asked, a blush quickly creeping over my skin. He looked at me expectantly for a moment before his eyes dropped to the floor.

"Shit, I thought you'd get the joke. I saw you had all those copies of *Alice in Wonderland* when I was in here the other night." He nodded to the bookshelf above my bed, lined with all my favorite classics. "Sorry if that was really creepy. It's a worry stone. You rub it and it's supposed help you relax."

"It's pretty." The stone was warm, probably from the time spent in his pocket. It was white but slightly translucent, with a sheen that resembled saturated moonlight. It felt like silk between my fingers, much softer than it looked.

"It was my mom's actually. She always had one in her pocket, said it helped with her anxiety. I thought it could help you too."

"Theo..." My words died on my tongue at the thoughtfulness of this boy. "I can't take something that was your mom's."

"It's cool. She had a bunch. And I think it'll help. You just hold it like this." He took the stone back from me, our fingers brushing, and made a show of rubbing his thumb up and down. Then he handed it back and I mimicked his motions. It *was* sort of relaxing. "It's nice, right?"

"Yeah, it is. Thank you for this. It's so sweet of you."

"Anything to help my adventure girl get back to adventuring."

. . .

By New Year's Eve I was moving around a bit more, but not much else seemed feasible. At least it was enough for Mom to let me out of bed.

"Hey, baby girl, are you feeling better this morning?" I stood next to the kitchen island, waiting for her to come check my temperature as always. Luckily, there was no fever this time, but still she checked twice a day and took diligent notes with each ninety-seven-point-nine result. "What do you want for breakfast, sweetie?"

"Whatever the guys are having is fine."

"French Toast. Thanks for finally joining us, sis." Ezra pulled the chair out next to him for me. It should have been embarrassing to have Theo directly across from me. I knew I looked horrible, and he hadn't seen me in days, not since he came to check on me the other night.

"How are you feeling?" Theo asked, dramatically. A huge grin appeared on his face, hinting at our inside joke. My *first* inside joke.

"I'm obviously feeling much better, you idiot," I whispered across the table. Ezra's eyes flashed to mine in shock and little horror, but Theo and I just laughed until the moment was forgotten.

Theo had been texting me throughout the week to check in. Not too much, like he knew I needed the rest, but just enough for me to know he cared. He even sent me pictures; one of Latke balancing on Theo's head, and one of my brother asleep on the couch with his mouth hanging open. The rest were all penguin videos. I especially liked the one of them marching down a flight of stairs. And of course, the occasional "how are you f...Nope, not gonna give in."

"What's the plan for tonight, AG? Think you have what it takes yet to crush me on the Xbox?"

"Dude, we're going to Stowe, remember?" Ezra announced.

If he'd picked up on my new nickname, he ignored it. *AG. Adventure girl.* Something else that was just ours. I fought hard to suppress a grin.

Ezra had warned me about this trip last week. Apparently, a girl he knew had a cabin on the mountain thirty minutes from us and invited them to stay for the weekend. Ezra was suddenly obsessed with snowboarding in the winter, and he had not shut up about this trip since he was home.

"You know I can't board, Ez. It's too risky. Coach would murder me if I got injured during hockey season."

"Whatever. Just come hang out then. Katie's friends are hot. And they have a jacuzzi." I didn't know why Theo looked at me then, like I was somehow part of the equation in this. The conversation had nothing to do with me.

"Nah. I'd rather chill here. You should go."

"Seriously?"

"Yeah. Mrs. Klein?" Theo turned toward my mom, still at the stove making another batch of bacon. "Would you mind if I stayed here while Ez is at Stowe? I don't want to intrude, but someone should keep Ellie company, right?" He winked at me. *Oh my god.*

"You're always welcome here, whether the other kids are home or not. You know that.

"Thanks, Mrs. K."

EZRA PACKED up his snowboarding gear and left for Stowe right after breakfast. There was some serious tension between him and Theo, but I didn't dare mention anything. Theo was acting like everything was normal. He told me if I was feeling up to it, he would take me skating, but I let him know that wasn't in the cards this year.

So we played video games instead.

The four of us spent most of the day in the basement. Me, Theo, Noodle Kugel and Latke. My cat was glued to Theo's lap, purring like her life depended on it. I wished I knew what she liked about him so much, because she never showed that kind of affection to anyone else in our family.

Noodle stayed by me on the couch, cuddling in close. He always knew when I wasn't feeling my best, pushing a little harder against me like he was there to draw out all my pain. He even let me use him as an arm rest when my limbs succumbed to exhaustion.

Before dinner, I took a nap. Well, I was told to take a nap, so naturally, I lay in bed for an hour, staring at the ceiling and waiting out my mom. And that's when I heard it, my dad talking to Theo. I'd opened the door to let Latke out a few minutes earlier and never bothered to close it.

"It's very nice of you to spend time with her, but I want you to know you are under no obligation to."

"Umm, I don't feel obligated."

Then my mom joined the chat. "You're so good with her. We really appreciate it." God, they made me sound like an injured horse.

"Sure. No problem."

"Just let us know if you need some space. We can be the ones to tell her if it's getting to be too much for you."

I could hear Theo walking away, heading down the stairs to the basement. I hated my parents for talking about me like that. Hated them and hoped they were wrong. Hated them and wanted to kick and scream and run away as far as I could go.

My phone vibrated on the bed next to me, pulling me out of my pity-party.

THEO

Feeling any better?

A shaky breath whooshed out of my lungs. If there was one thing I could be sure of, Theo left that conversation to go text me. I forced myself not to squeal.

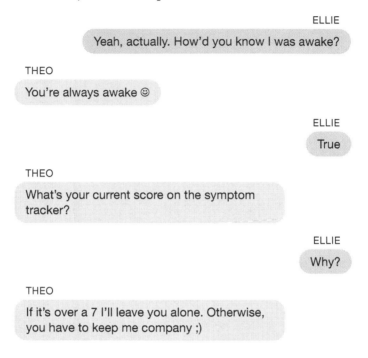

ELLIE

Yeah, actually. How'd you know I was awake?

THEO

You're always awake ☺

ELLIE

True

THEO

What's your current score on the symptom tracker?

ELLIE

Why?

THEO

If it's over a 7 I'll leave you alone. Otherwise, you have to keep me company ;)

Theo and I had texted a lot over the last year, ever since I got my first phone for birthday number fourteen. In fact, he was the first contact I added. Sometimes he would ask about my health, if I would ever be allowed to visit them at Avon, but mostly we just chatted. I sent him pictures of Latke and Noodle and he would tell me about hockey practice or what teacher was giving him a hard time. And of course, penguin videos.

In another world, I might have been cool and texted him back something flirty, but I couldn't get that conversation with my parents out of my head.

ELLIE

Did you stay here because you feel sorry for me?

THEO

I guess you heard me talking to your parents just now?

ELLIE

Yup

THEO

I don't feel sorry for you

You're my friend, and I wanted to hang out with you. I'm not sure why they don't get that

ELLIE

Thanks

Just making sure I didn't ruin your NYE

THEO

I wasn't gonna say anything in front of your mom, but your brother's friends drink a ton. I don't, so it's weird to hang out with them. I knew it would be a shitshow all weekend

I discovered last summer that Theo didn't drink. Ever. He was sixteen, so it wasn't exactly a wild revelation, but compared to Ezra, it was. I hadn't known that Mr. and Mrs. Fox were killed by a drunk driver. But when I found out, it all clicked.

THEO

I promise, I would much rather spend the weekend with you

Plus, you make the best grilled cheeses

ELLIE

You're using me for late night snacks?

THEO

Among other things

Other things? What other things? *Breathe, Ellie.*

THEO

Like your cat that's in my lap right now ☺ I'm thinking about making it official

ELLIE

I don't think she's the relationship type. She loves her freedom

THEO

I guess I'll have to keep searching for my true love then

So...you coming down here or what?

Theo and I both faked small appetites at dinner. It wasn't easy with how delicious my mom's lemon chicken was, but we had already made plans for secret grilled cheeses and brownies at midnight.

Resting in bed through the afternoon had me feeling energized, like my body somehow knew to store it away.

We stayed in the basement, enjoying the pillow fort we had yet to take down and waited for the signs and sounds of my parents going to sleep. They were early risers and never stayed up until midnight on New Year's.

I'd half expected Mom to shoo me off to bed when they called it a night, but she either forgot where I was or had no problem with me and Theo being alone together down here.

"I think the coast is clear," Theo whispered. I checked the

time on my phone—only three after eleven—and we made our way up to the kitchen.

I started on the brownies since they would take the longest. I had already crushed up a bunch of leftover candy canes from Christmas. I knew they would help cover up the taste of the coconut sugar, and they would help give the almond flour a chewier texture. My lupus diet was becoming more manageable as I learned to cook with different ingredients. It was all about balance. When I added the crushed candy to the batter, Theo started to drool. He really did love to eat.

We finished our feast right at midnight and said the proverbial "Happy New Year." There was an awkward moment when I thought he went in for a hug, but we just sort of bumped heads. And since Theo never, ever got full, he grabbed the rest of the brownies to bring down to the basement.

"Movie?"

"Sounds good." There was no way Mom and Dad would be okay with me staying up this late, but I wasn't about to ask for permission.

"Thanks again for the grilled cheese. I think my dad would be happy we kept the tradition going. You know, in case he's watching." He looked at me, his mouth tilted up on one side. The sad-but-not-too-sad Theo smile. I loved that smile.

"But what if your mom's watching too? Do you think they're up there having it out about years of lies and secret grilled cheeses?"

I was rewarded with a full belly laugh. Loud enough that he apologized in fear of waking my parents.

"I kind of hope they are. They loved to bicker. Like, it sounds weird, and no one wants to watch their parents fight, but whenever mine did, they were smiling. Sometimes my mom couldn't even hold in her laugh and whatever they were arguing about would be forgotten in seconds."

"I love that." Another smile only I could see. I was getting greedy for them. I'd had so much of Theo to myself this year, and I already knew this holiday break would be hard to top. All of our little traditions, they were everything to me.

"What do you miss the most now?" My question settled over his features as he chewed the inside of his cheek.

"Honestly, I can't think of anything." He swallowed thickly and his expression soured.

"Sorry, should I not have asked? What's wrong?"

"No, El. I love that you asked, that you always ask. No one ever asks about them anymore." He blew out a long breath. "Does that make me a horrible son? That I can't think of anything right now? I shouldn't be happy, not without them here. But I am."

I always struggled with these conversations, yet somehow always started them anyway. I didn't know how to deal with grief, and I wasn't sure I ever would. But I always wanted to try with him.

"They wouldn't want you to be sad. And just because you can't think of anything specific right now doesn't mean you don't miss them. I think if they are watching, they would be really happy for you. They probably love watching you play hockey. And I'm sure your dad is jealous of my superior grilled cheese, but he would want to you enjoy them anyway." Theo wrapped his arm around my shoulder and pulled me toward him for a hug. Latke was buried between us on the couch, trapped in his tight grip. "And I'm sorry for bringing it up. I promise I won't ask again."

Theo's hands found my shoulders and he pushed us apart, his eyes bouncing between mine. "Don't do that, El. Please don't stop. I love when you ask, I swear."

"Okay." My voice was softer than usual, but the force of his gaze on me at that moment made me feel breathless. This whole week, every look from Theo held some new weight to it.

"Can I ask you something?" His voice was lower now too, shaky. It sounded hesitant and hopeful and a little reckless.

I barely mustered out my "mm-hmm," my eyes trained on his face, searching for clues. Why was it so hot in this basement all of a sudden?

"Would it be weird if I kissed you?"

Oh my god. Time stood still. In my chest, my heart beat like a million hummingbirds, their wings wild and out of control. Something on my face must have given me away because his hands swiftly dropped from my shoulders and back onto Latke.

Theo wanted to kiss me? *Me?* I would be lying if I said I hadn't thought about it before, about what it would be like to have more than his quick hugs and side squeezes. In my quiet moments when I'd felt my loneliest, I imagined what his hair would feel like between my fingers. I'd close my eyes and picture it, shining like rays of sunlight during golden hour. I thought about feeling the muscles I noticed grew a little more every year, having his mouth on mine the way I had only read about in books.

"No one's ever kissed me before." I wasn't sure why I admitted that; I could have so easily lied. But I never wanted to be anything but honest with Theo.

"Oh. Okay."

No! I completely ruined the moment. Theo wanted to kiss me, and my fearful little heart screwed everything up. I had to fix this.

"Maybe you could teach me?"

Well, that caught his attention. Theo's startled gaze caught mine before it turned into a grin. "Yeah?"

"I mean, you taught me how to skate. And play video games. And make the best snow angels." His smile stretched wide across his devastatingly beautiful face. "Maybe you could teach me this too."

His eyes sailed across my lips, to each plane of my face and back. Something mimicking restraint coated each feature.

"All right. Maybe I will."

Chapter Fifteen

Theo

Now

"I'm not making snow angels with you. That's silly." She pouts and crosses back over to the fire, gathering the pillows and blankets she'd set up earlier. I didn't want her to put anything away, though. I wanted her to leave every mark she could on this cabin.

"So? What's wrong with being silly?" And since when does Ellie shy away from having fun, especially with me? Where the hell was my adventure girl? "Please? For me?"

I give her my best sad face, puppy dog eyes and all.

"Ugh. I am not in the mood to see a grown man cry today, but we can't. Look outside, Theo."

She's right. Snow is still falling in thick sheets, swirling wildly in the wind. It's gotten worse since I shoveled earlier. Not the kind of weather to play in, but perfect for a cozy day inside.

"All right. Change of plans. How about a movie?" I close

the laptop and set it aside, knowing she'll be grabbing for it soon enough.

"How are we gonna watch a movie? You just said the internet's out."

"It may be hard to believe," I say, walking over to the TV and opening up the cabinet below. "But I have a special artifact, something our generation has mostly forgotten. You may have read about it in your history books."

"*A DVD player?* Wow." She crouches down next to me and takes in the equipment with a sparkle in her eye. "You're right. I thought they were extinct."

"I've got a bunch of DVDs in this cabinet. Why don't you pick something while I go grab snacks."

In the kitchen, I search for anything and everything I can remember Ellie likes to eat. I'm trying to hide the stupid grin on my face, but I'm beaming like a giddy teenager. Watching a movie with El, in the middle of a snowstorm, it feels like those stars I'm always wishing on finally came through.

"Theo, do you have anything other than Christmas movies?" she yells from across the room.

"Most of these are from when I was a kid. You know how much I love Christmas movies." I head back to the living room, chuckling at my collection already splayed out across the floor. "I thought you did too."

"Of course, I do." She takes the offered spoon and peanut bar jar from my hands. "Thanks. You have the crunchy kind? Fuck, yes." A huge spoonful finds its way between her lips, and I watch her savor the treat as if in slow motion. Her eyes don't stray from the jar or the spoon until she's licked it clean. "That was heavenly. And I was just surprised that everything was Christmas-y, that's all." She shoves the jar back into my hands. "Please take this away before I devour the whole thing."

I take it back into the kitchen and start on the popcorn. "There's more than just Christmas movies. Keep looking."

"Hmm, *Pirates of the Caribbean*? That's a solid maybe." I turn and lean against the counter, watching as she picks up each box carefully, turns them over in her hands, and inspects as if they might hold secrets. "Hard no to *King Kong*. Love that you have *Narnia* but maybe a little too on the nose with this storm. *The Dukes of Hazard*? Really?" I laugh, enjoying her commentary. It already feels like old times.

"Oh my god!" she screeches. "Is this the full set of *Planet Earth*?" I freeze. "I haven't seen these in forever. Can we watch?" Her interest shouldn't surprise me. Ellie and I have watched hundreds of animal documentaries together. But for some reason I'm getting choked up. I'm remembering all the ways we fit together and all the ways that no other woman has ever felt right to me. Even for something so silly as not wanting to watch my favorite series.

"O-*kay*," she continues, exaggerating the word. "Since you've gone mute, I'll take that as a yes. *Ice Worlds*, here we go."

I collect myself and bring the popcorn with me to the couch. She's already started the episode and is completely engrossed by the screen. When we were young, my favorite thing to do with Ellie was watch shows about animals. I loved teaching her all the facts my mom bestowed upon me, finding out which ones were her favorite, having her challenge me with all the things she knew that I didn't.

But my second favorite thing was sneaking glances at her face while we watched. Her expression was always so full of wonder, it was hard to look away. Today, I'm trying my best not to stare, to not let her see how badly I still want her. How badly I still want everything we used to have.

"*Ice Worlds*," I eventually respond, taking a seat a few inches away from her. "Let's do this."

"I'm kind of hungry again. Got any more pizza?"

"A freezer full of it." We haven't left the couch since we hit play, but we've now also watched *Caves* and *Ocean Deep*. She never liked going in order, and something about watching the same way we did in high school feels inexplicably right.

I head to the kitchen and pull open the freezer to check what I have. "Cheese, pepperoni or supreme?"

"Supreme, obviously. You know I don't turn down extra toppings." I catch her expression shift, unsure.

"Right. Should've known." I should know. But I don't. Because it's been seven years, and I'm not sure if I even know her anymore. We've fallen into old patterns watching animals on TV, but I'm swiftly reminded that she has an entire life in California that has never included me. It might as well be a whole different dimension.

"Actually, do you mind if I grab a quick shower?" It's clear she's using this as an excuse to pull away from the awkward path we've stumbled upon. The idea of calling her out sings to me, but I don't. It's not worth risking the headway we've made today by forcing her to talk about the past.

"Sure. Pizza will take twenty minutes anyway. Everything you need's in the bathroom upstairs."

"Thanks."

By the time Ellie comes back downstairs, hair still wet from the shower, I'm halfway down a thought spiral. The things I don't know about her are piling up one on top of the other and I'm verging on meltdown status. But for whatever reason, knowing her current pizza order feels like the most important thing in the world.

For years I knew where she slept, what seat she favored at the kitchen table, how much syrup she put on her pancakes and the fact that she preferred whipped cream on waffles. I knew that she wore her hair down to cover the small rashes on her neck during a flare, that she loved animals more than people, that I was the only exception to that rule.

Now I'm looking at her, and she still has the same beautiful face, wide eyes and long hair I dream about getting tangled in. She still has the same laugh I hear every time I close my eyes at night. But all the years we've been apart, all the pieces of her I haven't discovered, they're eating away at me.

"What's wrong?" I'm a mess right now, and I'm sure I look it. I'm not exactly trying to hide it. "What happened?"

"I need to know." Pent-up ache leaks into my voice, and again, I don't try to hide it. I'm desperate, pining for all her details.

"Need to know what?"

"Everything." I watch the movement of her throat as she swallows, my eyes glued to the spot below her ear. The spot I used to run my tongue along that made her entire body shiver. "Tell me everything I missed. Please?"

"Oh. Okay." Her expression softens. "Pizza first?" A small smile breaks free from her lips lighting up her entire face, brown eyes glistening.

"Sure. Let's eat."

"It sounds like California suits you."

"Yeah, I guess so." She seems less sure than I am for some reason, but it sounds like everything worked out for her. She always wanted to explore the world, gain some independence. I was surprised with the way she cut everyone off, especially me, but it kind of makes sense now. She wanted freedom and she got it, with nothing in her way.

Part of me feels guilt over how angry I was when she left. Shouldn't you only want the best for someone you love? Even if it means having to be selfless? But that train of thought suddenly halts when she says, "I miss the snow."

Fuck if that doesn't sound like she's saying she misses me. It might be irrational, but I can't think of snow without Ellie, and I pray it's the same for her.

It has to be.

"Why'd you retire?" As soon as she says it, we both go rigid. This is the first hint she's given me that she's kept up with my life at all over the years. How lucky for her, that she had the opportunity. I want to revel in the fact that she followed my career, and yet I'm just angry I couldn't follow hers.

"Well, I tore my MCL twice. And once they recruited that new center from Sweden...I figured I'd rather go out on my terms than wait for the team to cut me. I never meant for it to be my career long term anyway." When I was younger, it was the only plan I had. But after I lost my parents, all I really wanted was a family again. I knew they were gone, but getting the village back felt like finding a piece of them. It felt like the first step.

"Sugar Valley was always the plan," she whispers, barely loud enough for me to catch it. But I do. And I wonder if she's thinking about prom now too.

Her demeanor shifts. It's a slow change as she curls into herself a little more with each passing second, sinking deeper into the couch. These memories that keep getting stirred up between us, are they not happy ones? Maybe I missed something, somewhere along the way. All my memories with Ellie are blissful. Until the ones at the very end.

"Do you travel a lot though, for the job? I'm sure you get to see snow then."

Her head jerks at my sudden change in topic, and the corners of her mouth pull up in a tight smile. I don't want to spook her, so if it means managing her emotions when all I want to do is shake them out of her, that's what I'll do.

"Not really. Most of the places we scout are in warm or temperate climates, more desirable for vacationers. But I did go up to Banff once. You would love it up there."

I don't tell her I've been. That I thought of her the entire time.

"We did two weeks in Argentina scouting out a few spots in Mendoza—wine country—and the forecast actually called for snow one day. I was thrilled, but nothing actually stuck."

"You're so worldly."

"Well, I had to live up to the 'adventure girl' moniker somehow, right?"

"You were always adventurous in spirit. I'm just glad you got everything you wanted."

"Everything?" She tilts her head to the side, eyeing me, like she's trying to decode that one word.

"Yeah, AG." The nickname sits between us. It feels good to use it again. "When we were younger you'd ask me if I thought every ocean looked the same, or if they'd be different on each coast. Do you remember?"

"Yeah." She laughs. "I was very concerned that the color of the water would be different, and I just *needed* to know. The only beach I ever went to was in Maine. I figured the whole world couldn't look like *Maine*."

"Well, how many beaches have you been to now?"

She grins. A genuine smile that I've been waiting to see for seven fucking years. "A few. Maybe more than a few."

"And what's the verdict? Do you have a favorite?" I'm

tripped up by the eagerness in my own voice. I need these answers from her like I need oxygen.

"New England is pretty wonderful. I think maybe I appreciate it more now, since I've been to so many other places." She pauses, worries her bottom lip. "But nowhere I've been has stolen my breath like Big Sur. The ocean, the cliffs, the vastness of it all. Nothing compares."

Big Sur. Let's go there together, I want to say. Instead, I land on, "And was the water different there?"

"Not different, but just, *so* blue. You would love it there, Theo. Camping in the trees, nature everywhere. I mean, the *birds*." She throws her whole body into the word, giddy. "The hiking is beautiful. Hard too; I could only do a few trails, but—"

"Why didn't you call me?" I interrupt. Because it sounds like she thought about me. It sounds like she didn't just forget I existed for the last seven years, and I need more answers than I'm getting.

"What?"

"Why didn't you call me? Why didn't you tell me about Berkeley? I wouldn't have tried to stop you from going."

"Oh, I know." Her words are laced with something bitter.

"What the fuck does that mean?"

She pins me with a stare, and I realize immediately that I said the wrong thing. She's not looking for a fight right now, but maybe I am.

"I get why you left. I do. And I think I'm glad, because it sounds like you found everything you were looking for." Her brows pinch together in confusion, but I keep going. "All I wanted was for you to be happy, but...I wish you would've called me. I wish I could have been a part of your life still. I hate learning everything this way. I thought I meant more to you than that." My throat is thick with tears that I refuse to let spill, making every word more painful than the last. "Why did you cut me off? Why didn't you call me? Text me? Anything? Why?"

"I..." She takes a long shaky breath. "It just hurt too much. After—"

Sparks shoot out of the walls and we both jump off the sofa. The crackling echoes through the living room, and then silence settles, thick and heavy. We stare at each other, mouths hanging open. What the hell?

The lights flicker a few times for good measure, provoking some squeals from Ellie that are honestly adorable. But then the power shuts off altogether. Shit.

"I probably need to go fill the generator. I promise I won't let you freeze." I grab a jacket and a flashlight—a real one this time—and trudge out to the detached garage.

I move as quickly as I can, remembering how cold the house got last night. But when I reach the generator, it's still full. The blinking red light tells me it's turned off somehow, so I check the back of it and the ground around, looking for what could have tripped the power. My fingers are now fully frozen, so I go through the motions to restart the machine.

How is it still so full? Generators burn fuel like cars. If it's working properly, it should be close to empty by now. I only had enough fuel for a day, maybe a day and a half. If the actual power doesn't come back tomorrow, we'll have to dig our way out of this snow.

After I get the generator up and running, I see the lights flicker on and know we'll have heat for the night. No matter how perplexed I am, I'm still nervous about how much fuel is in there. I saw multiple power lines knocked down by this storm. And considering the snow is still coming down, I don't expect anything to get fixed in the next twenty-four hours.

Is it possible I'll only have one more day with Ellie? I need more time. This thought carries me back inside the cabin where

Ellie looks as relaxed as can be, curled under my favorite blanket.

"Hey, you okay in here?" She glances up at me with a tentative smile. I'm eager to finish our conversation but right now, the bigger concern is making sure we have power tomorrow. "I need to go check on a few of the other buildings. Gonna take the snowmobile out. Mind if I leave you alone for a bit?"

"Don't worry about me. I have peanut butter and electric heat."

"That's my girl." Her eyes bulge at the comment and I think about apologizing. Fuck that. She's always been mine. I just need to remind her.

I grab some gear and load up my snowmobile to head to the other side of the village. None of the businesses have opened yet but they've all been getting ready, so I figure it won't hurt to see if they have any fuel I can borrow. No one else seems to be waiting out the storm in the valley.

When my search comes up empty, I head back to the cabin, not letting myself enter full panic mode. Worst-case scenario, we use this trusty ski machine as a plow to get out of the valley and find some cell service. The main town is less than fifteen minutes from here and has a small hotel. It'll be tough if the storm doesn't quit, but I'm sure we can make it there if we run out of options.

But that's not really the worst scenario, because the worst possible outcome is that Ellie has no more reason to stay here.

That I lose her.

Again.

Chapter Sixteen

Ellie

December 23, 2013

MAYBE I WILL.

Three words had been running on a loop in my head for the last three hundred and fifty-four days.

Maybe.

I.

Will.

The night itself had been mostly uneventful, but that didn't stop it from living rent-free in my head all year. After I ruined the perfect almost-first kiss, we proceeded to binge-watch *Heroes* until we both fell asleep. I'd woken up on the couch, cuddling Noodle, and Theo was already back in his bed. The following day, before we could have any more alone time together, Ezra came home early from Stowe. Apparently, he felt bad ditching Theo—who'd given me a secret wink when they did their bro-hug—and they both went back to Avon to run drills together.

It wasn't like I hadn't talked to Theo since. We texted

often. But he hadn't been back to our house at all. He usually came home for some holiday or another, but hockey took over his life this year. Mom and Dad brought it up at dinner sometimes, talked about how serious he was taking it, doing everything he could to get a college scholarship. He'd stayed in Connecticut over the summer to teach a junior league camp and was always training or working on the weekends when Ezra came home.

But texting wasn't enough, and Ez was getting more and more annoyed any time I mentioned Theo's name.

One day. One more day—and a creative way to get him alone—and I could finally find out if he still wanted to kiss me.

I knew how sad this was. I was about to be sixteen and still waiting for my first kiss. And it wasn't because I couldn't get anyone to kiss me. Everyone at my school was kissing. It was practically an extracurricular activity. I understood why Mom didn't like the idea of a co-ed boarding school. From what Kat told me, they were sneaking into the boys' dorms every other night. Two of my friends were already having sex, and they were both younger than me.

Kevin Daniels tried to kiss me once. Well, first he asked me to the fall dance. But of course, I wasn't allowed to date. He took my refusal as an "I wish I could go, but I'm not allowed, so please stick your tongue down my throat instead." That was not how I meant it.

I ditched Kevin's tongue the second it came for me, and even though he was cute, and popular, I had no regrets. My first kiss was going to Theo Fox. No matter what I had to do to make it happen.

"Ellie, come here," Mom called from the kitchen, her voice a little unsteady. "Ez just called. He's bringing home his girlfriend for the break." Her face was hovering somewhere between distress, delight and flat-out confusion. It felt like she was asking me for help.

"Girlfriend? Did you know he had one?"

"Nope." The smile-scowl twitch made another appearance. "He said she's from Vancouver, and also Jewish, and that she didn't want to fly all the way home. He felt bad letting her stay at school by herself."

Dad walked past me to grab a banana from the fruit bowl and patted my shoulder. "I think it'll be nice to have a full house. Another girl for Ellie to play with, right sweet pea?"

Yeah, dad. Because all I want for my sixteenth birthday is *a girl to play with*. Sometimes I wondered if he even realized I'd hit puberty. He was back in his study before I could respond.

I glanced back at Mom, but she still looked dazed, her mouth pinched tightly. She was not happy about this turn of events.

And neither was I. "Does this mean Theo isn't coming?" I knew she could hear the dread in my voice, but I didn't care. He *had* to come this year.

"I don't see why he wouldn't. Oh, but who knows. He probably has a girlfriend too. Maybe he'll call to let us know he's spending Christmas with her. Seems like everyone is springing surprises on me this year." Mom walked away nonchalantly like she didn't just shred my heart to pieces with that apocalyptic scenario.

No, no, no, *no*. I prayed she was wrong. He had to come. He would have said something to me if he wasn't coming, right? I grabbed my phone to text him, but he beat me to it.

THEO

> See you in a few hours! I'm driving Ezra's car so I can come a day early. Amber has another day of exams, so Ez's waiting to go with her

ELLIE

Great. Can't wait to see you!

I hoped that wasn't too eager. Was it possible he could tell I was internally freaking the fuck out?

ELLIE

What's Amber like? That was a surprise.

THEO

Yeah, he waited till the last minute so your mom couldn't say no. And you'll see. She's cool. Very enthusiastic

ELLIE

Enthusiastic? You gotta give me more than that

THEO

Nope. We have more important things to discuss

I wondered what that meant. Important things? We? As in something important between *me* and *Theo*? I had a million questions to ask but Theo's next text whisked them all from my mind.

THEO

Any first kisses I should know about since last year?

Oh my god. *Oh my god.* This was actual flirting. No mixed signals or hidden messages or—shit. I needed to respond.

ELLIE

Nope

Nope? That was so pathetic. I could do better than *that*.

ELLIE

Haven't found a worthy accomplice

That was banter-y. Right?

THEO

Good

I wanna be your first

"You're really not gonna tell me where we're going?"

"Nope. It's a surprise that I know you'll love."

"Fine." I crossed my arms against my chest and turned to look out the window, mostly to hide the ridiculous grin I was sporting.

Minutes after Theo arrived from school, he told my parents he was taking me skating. Mom handed over my skates without question, always trusting Theo with me. Her favorite babysitter after Ezra. But once we got in the car, he told me we were going somewhere special. And he gave me nothing else. For over thirty minutes.

So far, it was all hockey, school, and my attempts to pry info from him about the elusive Amber. Nothing about the kiss. Not the could've-been-kiss, or the could-be-kiss, or the fact that I still hadn't had a first kiss. No mention of kissing *at all*, even though it was the only word my brain seemed capable of conjuring at the moment.

I really needed a distraction.

"How's Raj?" I had met Theo's new roommate a couple of times over FaceTime. He was the other star player on their hockey team. "Does he still call you Foxy?"

"Yeah, the whole team does now. Do you think it's because of my awesome flow?" He ran a hand through his bronzed hair, flipping his head a bit for drama. He'd grown it out to his chin now, and I *really* liked it.

"No," I replied with a hint of nonchalance. "I think he just wanted to come up with a nickname as bad as the one you gave him."

"The Mirage? No way. That is the *best* nickname. He's so fast on the ice, the other team can't tell if he was ever really there. A mirage. *Mi-Raj*. It's nickname gold, Ellie." He gave me a deadpan look and I had to stifle my grin even more.

Laughter was still pouring out of me when I felt the car slow. When I peeked out the window and saw the sign, I think I stopped breathing.

My heart leaped and I swiveled to face Theo. "Sugar Valley?" My voice cracked.

Why were we here?

"Yep. I talked to one of my mom's old friends who lives nearby. Remember Fox in the Snow?"

"Obviously." Of course I remembered. Who could ever forget a café with an actual hot chocolate bar and flavored whipped cream? I still dreamt about those snowflake marshmallows every birthday. And maybe sometimes I thought of Theo as *my* Fox in the snow. Especially after making snow angels last year.

"Well, the owner—Cindy—we've kept in touch since..." He trailed off. I remembered now, his dad telling us that the owner of the café was Carol's best friend. So close in fact that she named the café after Theo. It was nice knowing Theo still had this small part of his mom. "She let me know the place is sort of abandoned but she said the rink was still here. I'll make sure it's safe first but...Will you skate with me?"

I tried and failed to hold back tears as we parked and

hopped over the gate that marked the village as closed. It was clear he was crying too even if he hid it better than I did. I had four years of memories washing over me.

He had fourteen.

His palm squeezed my hand a little tighter the closer we got to the rink, and once it was time to get on the ice, he let out a long, unsteady breath.

"What do you miss the most?" I asked. It felt like the right time.

He made a small sound, something deep in his throat. Not a sob, but still guttural. It broke my heart. His head tilted up as he slowly spun, taking in the entirety of the village that was such a huge part of him, of his family, of his legacy. And he finally responded, "This."

The tension around us fell as soon as a smile broke from his lips. He was looking at me in that way only Theo could. And just like that, neither of us were sad anymore.

There was a thin layer of snow on the ice, but Theo walked across the rink to test for any weak spots before we laced up our skates. I loved how he always protected me but never made me feel weak.

That first step on the ice, I felt it. The chill in the air fizzed with memories, twirling around us in a light breeze. The energy that made me fall in love with skating. It was here. It was alive.

"Show me your moves, AG."

Noticing the wind, I pulled my hair into a braid, and then I took his hand to do a few laps together. Once I had my bearings, I let go and flowed into a one-foot glide—*still got it*—raising my other leg into the air behind me. That was always my favorite trick; it felt like I was flying.

My arms transformed into wings and my long braid caught the breeze of my own creation. Feathers coasting through the sky. I bent forward until I could reach down to the ice with my fingertips.

"You're so beautiful when you skate."

I righted myself and found Theo idling small circles on the ice, watching me.

"Come here." His words held a compulsion to obey, and I skated his way until he grasped my hand and spun me in a circle around him. Laughter filled the air around us as he spun me faster and faster. And then suddenly he was pulling me closer, until we were only a few inches away from each other.

The breeze between us stilled as we both caught our breath, but our gazes never faded from one another.

"I really want to kiss you, El"

"I think you should."

Amusement shone from his face for about three seconds before his lips met mine.

The world stopped spinning. The wind paused in a spell of meditation. My heart sped past the sound barrier. The moment was so perfect that it couldn't be contained by science. Magic shimmered all around us.

Theo's mouth was soft and warm. Gentle. Exactly how I had imagined it would be. A piece of hair fell from my braid, and he tucked it behind my ear, staying connected to me as he pulled away, resting his forehead against mine.

The taste of his lips lingered on my mouth like caramel, sweet with a flicker of salt that had me craving more, more, *more*.

I leaned into him, drawing our lips together again, and let my face be cradled in his hand. I was so happy I could cry, every emotion incandescent.

He angled his face to the side and deepened the kiss, urging me to part my lips and sink further into the heat of him. I was surrounded by ice and snow, but I was melting like an ice cream cone on hot pavement.

He held me tightly, strong arms wrapped around my body, sheltering me from the wind and the world around us. My legs betrayed me and started to wobble—weak knees due to his kisses or my balancing act on skates, I didn't know.

Eventually he drew back and ran his teeth across his bottom lip, hazel eyes fixed on my mouth.

"I don't think I need to teach you at all."

I scoffed, smiling at him. I was pretty sure Theo just called me a good kisser. How could this day possibly get any better?

He took my hand and pulled me into another loop around the rink. We skated until our noses were bright red from the chill and our muscles were shaky with exhaustion. And finally, we drove back home.

We arrived just in time for dinner with my parents.

Theo and I could not stop stealing glances at each other. There were even a few times his socked feet brushed mine under the table. I was glad Ezra wasn't back yet because he definitely would have noticed.

Dad was acting weird and jittery, rambling about nonsense. Theo, ever the polite guest, did his best to look engaged. Meanwhile, Mom was clearly lost in thought, no doubt about the girlfriend who would be arriving tomorrow.

"Oh, screw it. I can't wait another day." My dad exclaimed, dragging all of our attention to him at the end of the table.

"Honey," Mom scolded. "Ezra will be here *tomorrow*."

"Then we'll celebrate again." She shook her head, but didn't seem all that mad. I had no idea what they were talking about.

"Theo," my dad announced. "I've got some news. Some very exciting news."

Theo's eyes grew wide like he had a sense of what was happening, but I was still completely in the dark.

"I know it's a little unorthodox for me to tell you this way, but—" Dad was getting choked up. What the hell? "We're offering you the scholarship. Full ride. Do you want to be an Ice Bear, son? Our hockey team sure could use you next year."

I had seen Theo cry before, small tears when he talked about his parents, even earlier today. It was never like this. He was a flurry of emotions, laughing, smiling, tears welling his eyes. He threw me a look before standing up and giving my dad a bear hug. Now my emotions were running away from me too.

"Do you know how proud of you I am? I didn't even have to sway anyone. And you know I would have." They pulled apart, weeping giving way to laughter, as my dad kept his hands clasped tightly on Theo's shoulders. They were the same height now.

"Thank you," Theo choked out. "It wouldn't have happened without you, sir. I could never repay you for everything you've done for me." Their sniffles were contagious, and my mom and I embraced out of sheer need. "You don't know how much this means to me."

Dad squeezed his shoulder a few more times and the closeness between them caught me off guard. I'd never put much thought into it before but my parents loved Theo. They loved him like another son. Ezra was accepted to Harvard *and* Dartmouth last month and while both my parents had been thrilled, this reaction was in a different stratosphere.

"There's something I've been wanting to share with you, about your father." Theo's expression shifted into something skittish as they took their seats at the table again.

"My dad?"

"I think it was the second year we went down to the village, when we had more time together. We grabbed a beer while you kids were all skating or tubing or who knows. When I told him I was the dean at VU, he went on and on about sending you to college one day. How he never got to go but that you were so much smarter than him. How you were destined for greatness. And then he offered me a bribe to get you in." Dad started to chuckle, more to himself than the table, like he was lost in a memory.

Theo gaped. "A bribe?"

"Christmas trees for life. He obviously didn't know we were Jewish." Laughter rang through the room at that.

"Oh, he was just screwing around. At least I think he was. But he said it was his dream for you to go there, how every penny he saved was to send you to college. I think he just wanted to see if I had any pull." Dad swallowed thickly. "You were such a good kid. Ezra adored you, and you were so good with Ellie, getting her those little birthday presents. I figured right then and there I would do whatever I could to help you, even though I doubted you would need it. And after that horrible accident—" Dad blew out a long breath, then took a few more. "I just want you to know that your dad would be so proud of you, just like I am."

"Thank you," Theo said, barely audible. "I'm really glad you told me. And—" He paused, closed his eyes for a moment. "I'll do everything I can to bring you a championship."

"I like the sound of that. My Ice Bears haven't won the frozen five in almost a decade now." VU's actual mascot was the Maple Tapper, but that wasn't tough enough for the hockey team, so they sort of had their own. A hockey jersey with a roaring polar bear and Theo's name on it was going to be my new weekend uniform.

Everyone got up to share hugs, and it felt good to let mine

with Theo linger a little longer than would normally be appropriate. Before we broke apart, I said, "Did you know a group of polar bears is called a celebration?"

Theo tossed his head back in a genuine howl of laughter and dropped a tender kiss to the top of my head, no one being the wiser.

WE CELEBRATED the good news with ice cream until Mom saw one yawn and sent me to bed. She'd tutted something about skating being too intense for me. My smugness over the true intensity I'd felt on that ice won out over annoyance at being treated like a kid in front of Theo.

And anyway, between the kissing, being back at Sugar Valley, and the news that Theo was going to college *twenty* minutes from my home, I was feeling drained. But exhilaration hovered close by.

THEO
8:30 bedtime is brutal

ELLIE
More brutal than having a bedtime at all?

THEO
Touché

Think you can sneak down here?

ELLIE
Doubtful. Mom's been checking in on me every 15 minutes. She's really losing it this time

THEO
I know you're just upstairs, but I miss you

ELLIE

Yeah? What do you miss the most?

THEO

Hmmm

The way your face gets all scrunched up in jealousy when Latke lets me pet her

ELLIE

She's with you now, isn't she?

THEO

Purring in my lap

ELLIE

Traitor

THEO

I can't help it if the ladies love me

ELLIE

I guess I'm not so special huh?

THEO

Nah. You're my penguin, El

❄

Theo and I took Noodle for a long walk the next morning. My parents were used to us hanging out together, but for some reason anything else felt suddenly explicit. Even when he asked me to come play video games in the basement, I had this nagging sound in my head—definitely Mom's voice—that said it wasn't allowed. And after that text, well, Theo was very present in my dreams last night.

The walk turned out to be even better. With the winter

chill, no one was outside who didn't have to be. And with zero prying eyes, Theo and I were completely alone.

As soon as we turned the corner from my street, he pulled off one of my mittens and interlaced our fingers. He held my hand inside of his pocket during the entire walk, even when he used his other hand to play fetch with Noodle.

Theo kept me warm and smiling. He also told me that yesterday was the happiest day of his life. I was pretty sure getting a scholarship to his dream school was the main reason, but I refused to believe our kiss on the ice wasn't a contributing factor.

Ezra's car pulled up right as we made it back to the house and I got a rush of anxiety about meeting Amber. Theo refused to tell me more about her, and my mind was coming up with all sorts of wild scenarios.

I had never met a girl Ezra dated before. I had never met any girls he even talked to. I only knew from Theo that Ezra was constantly dating. Apparently, he had a different girlfriend every week.

"Hey, sis. This is Amber." A stunning blonde with serious boobs held on to my brother as they walked into the house with us. My first impression was *good for Ezra*. Deep down I knew my brother was good-looking, but Amber was in another league.

Until she started talking.

Because she never, *ever* stopped.

"Because Laura liked him first but it was just so obvious, you know? I mean, Ezzy and I look so good together. Don't we, baby? Ugh, of course you know we do. Everyone at school calls us Ezber, like we're a real celebrity couple! I mean, we kind of are and, like, I do love my school but oh my *god* being with all girls can just get exhausting, you know? They're always so competitive and it's just so nice to be able to get away sometimes. But it's such a good school and the teachers are wonderful, and I would have never met Ezzy if I hadn't left home."

The original question via my father was "where are you from?"

"The food is so good Mrs. Klein, I'm just not eating carbs right now, or anything with a face. Poor Ezzy has to deal with my hunger swings—that's what I call my mood swings when I'm really hungry—he's such a saint. Aren't you baby?"

The lunch continued as Amber bogarted the entire conversation. Mom flinched every time she heard her say "Ezzy" and I tried not to laugh too audibly. Theo was grinning ear to ear, in between throwing me knowing glances across the table.

My parents clearly wanted distance from Amber after, so they ordered us pizzas for dinner and banished us to the basement.

We had set up the pillow fort to watch Christmas movies but Theo and I both stayed on the couch, as my brother was tangled up with his girlfriend.

They weren't full-on making out or anything, but Ezra could not take his hands off of her and it was making me a little nauseous. Theo tried distracting me by showing me the tricks he'd taught Latke last night, but since she was a cat, and couldn't actually do any tricks, it wasn't helping.

"Do you know what they call a group of slugs?" Theo whispered to me.

"Ew. No, what are they?"

This time he spoke so close to my ear I could feel his breath. "An Ezber."

I snorted.

I covered my mouth quickly, but *Ezber* was so wrapped up in each other, they never heard a thing.

Mom mentioned at lunch that Amber would stay with me in my room, but at this point I didn't see her complying with the house rules. No problem for me, but what was Theo going to do? This was his bedroom. I gave him a pleading look that let him know I was desperate to get rid of them.

"Ez, can we chat for a sec?" My brother picked his head up from Amber's neck and pinned him with an annoyed look. Begrudgingly, he walked over to the bathroom with him, and they shut the door to have a private conversation.

"Have I made a horrible impression?" Amber's voice came suddenly from beside me as she sat down in Theo's spot on the couch.

"What?"

"I just, I can't tell if you like me. And I was so nervous about meeting you, and now I think I fucked it all up. Please don't hate me."

"Of course I don't hate you. But why would you be nervous about meeting me?" Why would anyone care what *I* thought of them, especially a popular-looking girl like Amber? I bet she'd texted more friends over this break than I had in my whole life.

"Promise?" She rested her hands on my shoulders, forcing us to face each other. "I just know how important you are to Ezzy, and I really like him. Do you think we could be friends?" She continued with her questioning, but I didn't hear it. My brain was solely focused on one curious revelation.

"You think I'm important to Ez?"

"Umm, yeah! Whenever he talks about you it's obvious how close you are."

"He talks about me? To you?" Nothing about this conversation made sense to me. In my head, Ezra never even thought about me when he was away from home.

"Are you kidding? Like, *all* the time. Apparently, you're a genius. He always says you're the smart one in the family. And he told me about that website you're building, the one that tells you what your animal soulmate is. Which, by the way? *So cool.*

And he said you're this really amazing ice skater too. Honestly, if you weren't related, I would be insanely jealous. He loves you so much."

Ezra and I had our good and bad times. I would always remember how he came through for me, standing up to Mom and Dad about letting me switch schools. And after his apology that had followed, I thought things might change between us. But the second winter break ended, it was back to normal. So why would he talk to Amber about me like that?

The guys came out of the bathroom then and interrupted the maelstrom of uncertainty in my head. I had always liked the word befuddled, but didn't get many opportunities to use it. Well, I was currently very befuddled. It felt like my whole world had been turned upside down.

When my gaze caught Theo's, he gave me one of those head tilts that said *come with me*. He already had Latke perched across his shoulders and Noodle not far behind as he disappeared up the stairs. I got up to follow him, eager to chase that warm smile of his. But then I realized I'd never even responded to Amber.

Stopping short, I turned around to find her and my brother cozying back up to each other. Eye roll. Based in his body language, I didn't think Amber had any reason to be nervous. He didn't care what anyone else thought of her.

"Hey, Amber?" I called.

"Yeah?"

"Mom and I always make waffles on Christmas morning. Do you wanna help us tomorrow?"

Her flawless smile gleamed. "I would love that. Thanks, Ellie."

. . .

When I reached the kitchen, Theo didn't say a word as he brought his finger up to his lips. Mom and Dad were already in bed, but we stayed silent as we walked up the next set of stairs to my room.

"I'm gonna stay up here," he said, shutting the door behind us.

"Here?" My room?

"Oh god no, El. I didn't mean it like that." He set Latke on the bed and rested a hand on my shoulder. "Ez asked if they could stay in the basement, and for me to sleep in his room. He knows there isn't really any privacy up here so..." Theo was correct. My brother and I had adjoining rooms with zero noise-cancelling walls. It was extremely annoying, and I was grateful he actually considered it before making me listen to them all night. My brother was full of surprises today and all of them made my face hurt from too much smiling.

"Okay. That was really nice of him, actually."

Theo nodded in agreement. "Are you tired?"

"What do you think?" I murmured.

"Movie? We could watch on your iPad."

We settled on my bed with the iPad between us, but I couldn't help feeling anxious about Theo lying next to me. I was shaking.

"Are you okay?"

"Umm, just a little cold." He ripped off his hockey sweatshirt and handed it to me. I slipped it on, and his scent surrounded me. It was delicious, but it did nothing for my nerves.

"If I'm making you uncomfortable, I can go back to Ezra's room. I really don't—"

"I'm not uncomfortable. I'm extremely comfortable actually." I moved a little closer to snuggle into him. I couldn't help myself. "I was just nervous Mom might come in or something."

Theo never made me feel anything but good. But the thought of her throwing Theo *out* made my heartrate soar.

"Oh. She'd probably freak out, huh?"

"Honestly, I don't think she's ever even considered me having a boy in my bed. I'm not sure what she would do. If she found us in here together, I bet her first assumption would be that I'd stopped breathing or fainted or something and you were helping me. She'd never think you were in my room just because you wanted to be."

Theo scoffed, and there was an edge to it, like he understood everything I was saying and wasn't happy about it. "Do you think I should go?"

"No. This is too cozy. Let's risk it." He wrapped an arm around me and pulled me closer so my head could rest on his chest.

"We'll keep the movie really quiet. And the second we hear someone coming, I'll sneak over through the bathroom. I promise."

"Okay." I pressed into him further. And then it hit me: Theo and I were *cuddling*. Definitely more than just-friends cuddling, or even just-friends-who-sometimes-kiss cuddling. It felt intimate and terrifying and so inexplicably *right*. Like the nook between his arm and ribcage was created just for me.

I knew he was muscular. Him and my brother were both twice the size of most high school guys I knew. But feeling the ridges of his chest, the swell of his bicep, knowing that I had access to touch him like this, it was making me feel a little wild.

My hand began to wander aimlessly, reveling in everything I felt. It wasn't like I had any clue what I was doing, but it seemed like I had kissing somewhat mastered. Why couldn't I grope him a little? He was *hot*.

"El?" His knuckles grazed my chin and I tilted to look at up him.

"Yeah?"

"Can I kiss you again?"

I nodded my approval and he bent to reach my lips.

Kissing Theo on the ice was magic.

Kissing Theo in my bed was a roaring fire on a winter day. I melted against him slowly, butter in a pan, falling into his embrace like it was a damn rabbit hole and I was starved for an adventure. His fingers wove their way through my hair until tingles forged a path from my scalp down to the base of my spine.

I felt electric. I felt a bone-deep warmth that I didn't know existed. I felt and felt and felt, until all I could focus on were his soft lips pressed against me.

Theo kissed a path down my jaw, and I heard a faint groan come from the back of his throat. The sound vibrated against my skin, scattering goosebumps everywhere. iPad forgotten, I slipped my leg over his without intention, wanting to get closer somehow, wanting to get completely lost in him.

But then he pulled away. I wasn't sure what sound I intended to make, feeling the loss of his mouth, but the whine that escaped me was not it.

"I just don't wanna move too fast."

"Oh. Okay. Sorry," I muttered.

"El." He brushed his lips against my cheek. "Do not be sorry. You're perfect." Another velvety kiss. "There's no rush. I want to do this right."

I wasn't completely sure what he meant, but I trusted Theo more than anyone else in the world, so I didn't question him. He pulled us back into the perfect spooning position and I felt my eyes grow heavy. He promised he would stay until I fell asleep and that he wouldn't let anyone find him in here if they came looking.

The last forty-eight hours had felt completely unreal, flawless even. It was like I had opened a book to my own dull story and rewritten the words, creating events that only existed in dreams.

Was this how my life was now? Was Theo *mine?* The idea was almost preposterous. But not completely.

I figured I should make the most of the time I had, just in case. I turned over, still tucked in Theo's arms so I could stare into his perfect face. The face that wanted to kiss me, that did kiss me, that liked kissing me enough to do it again.

"You're my favorite person," I revealed, letting the words slip out and dissolve in the heat of his body.

"Me too, El."

"No, I mean it. You're the only one I like more than dogs." His grin spread wide making his eyes crinkle at the edges. And then he kissed me again.

MY BROTHER WAS AN IDIOT.

He knew, as well as our whole family did, that Theo was an early riser. Whenever he stayed with us, he was the first one up and would usually take Noodle for a walk before anyone else got out of bed. Which he did this morning.

Unfortunately for my idiot brother, that meant Mom assumed the basement was empty when she went down to collect our pizza boxes for the recycling.

Mom had never been strict with Ezra like she was with me, but finding him sleeping naked on the floor with his girlfriend tipped the balance.

Dad stood at the kitchen counter, his face fire-engine red, as Mom huffed and clarified—enunciating every single word—the rooms they'd assigned. You would think that my idiot brother would be embarrassed, but the second my parents were out of earshot, Ezra pulled me and Theo aside to work out a new—stealthier—sleeping arrangement for the rest of the week.

He was incorrigible, my idiot brother, but his plan really worked in my favor.

My parents' room was on the first floor of our house, so only Ezra and I slept upstairs. It was pretty easy to hear someone come up the stairs, but the issue was switching rooms once you heard them coming up.

Ezra's plan was fairly simple: since Amber was supposed to be staying in my room on the air mattress, that's where he would be. If Mom came up to check on him, he could run through the adjoining bathroom and be in his bed before she got there, as long as he was listening.

Since I would rather have swallowed a grenade than share my room with *Ezber*, he said I should sleep in the basement—with Theo. Yeah, Theo and I both had a reaction to that but held it together enough for no one to notice. Ezra made a good point that if Mom did find out I wasn't in my room, I could just say I fell asleep on the couch watching TV. It happened all the time.

My birthday was spent full of plotting our sleeping arrangements and eating Christmas waffles while huddled in the blanket fort. The same blanket fort that, if the stars aligned, I was going to share with Theo once everyone went to bed.

And somehow, against all odds, my idiot brother's plan worked. Mom only checked that he was in his room twice, and he'd escaped in time on both occasions.

I'd driven myself to exhaustion when they left, using incense and essential oils to perform a cleansing ritual on my room, but I also got to cuddle with Theo for six glorious nights.

I really loved my idiot brother.

Chapter Seventeen

Theo

Now

"Let's not be sad anymore, okay?" Ellie greets me at the door. "I decided, while you were gone. I'd rather just enjoy being snowed in, so...pillow fort Christmas movie marathon?"

Even though I've spent the last twenty minutes in the cold, dissecting how we'd pick up our conversation where we left off, El's revelation beings heat back to my toes in less than one.

She looks cheerful, giddy even, and my breath catches when I see what she's done to my cabin.

"Did you move the mattress downstairs?" I ask, dumbfounded. How the hell did she carry that thing? Her eyes track my own, wandering around the room.

"I did. Now no one gets the bed."

"Savage." I grin, taking in the space she's set up for us.

She's pushed the couch back to make room for the mattress, which is covered in every sheet and blanket I own, some I'm not even sure where they came from. Cushions from the back of the sofa create a barrier on three sides and extra pillowcases are tied together creating a Rapunzel-esque canopy from the back of the couch to the bottom of the mattress. She left a few cushions on the sofa so it still looks usable but all the pillows in this house are either laid out in the middle or stacked around the perimeter. She crushed it.

"This is a pretty exceptional pillow fort."

We both cast our eyes down at the same time to the mattress-cushion concoction she's created. I wonder if it looks as much like a time machine to her as it does to me. When I hear her suck in a breath and look over to see her eyes squeeze tightly shut, I know it does.

She may have built this as a distraction, not wanting to talk about the past, but all she's done is remind me of the perfectly fucking perfect week ten years ago when we spent every night alone in her parents' basement.

"Well, I hope you're okay with it. Death came for me twice getting that mattress down the stairs," she mutters. "I'm not moving it again." There's my Ellie, always going for the pivot these days.

"Wanna light the menorah?" I offer. Her shoulders drop away from her ears and she smiles, following me into the kitchen. We work together to set up the nuts-and-bolts menorah. It's a work in progress.

"Remember New Year's that year?" I say, grabbing the matches. I refuse to pretend like she won't know what year I'm referring to. She nods. "That was the most awkward shit I've ever experienced. If you hadn't been there with me, I don't know. I don't think I would have survived it."

Her laugh turns wheezy as we recall the horrifying moment that Ezra decided to break up with his girlfriend, at their home, on New Year's Eve. And how he hid in the basement with me all night to avoid Amber, leaving Ellie to console her new friend.

Our week leading up to that night was blissful. The four of us spent our days going tubing, bowling, basically enjoying all the best winter activities Ellie's mom would allow. And while it wasn't new for me to spend my break with her and Ezra, it was nice seeing Ellie have a girlfriend too. She and Amber had bonded over Christmas Day waffles and their mutual love of winding Ezra up.

Each day, Ellie and I got more creative, finding pockets of privacy for our lips to meet. After our first kiss on the ice, I was addicted to the feel of her, to the warmth that unfurled every time we touched.

And the nights, they were just for me and Ellie. Curling up in the pillow fort with Latke and Noodle, watching nature documentaries and sharing random animal facts until our eyes grew heavy. Kissing until her lips were swollen and she'd made a complete mess of my hair.

OUR FIRST NIGHT *in the fort, as soon as we were alone, Ellie looked at me so seriously I was afraid I'd done something to piss her off. Relief flooded me when she finally spoke.*

"Should we burn these sheets or wash them discreetly? I'm not sleeping on them." Relief flooded me and I laughed under my breath, keeping my voice down.

"Are you afraid of Ezber cooties?"

"Yes." She deadpanned. "Deathly afraid."

"All right. Help me get rid of them." I started stripping the sheets and blankets we just put on yesterday while Ellie sprinted up the stairs without a word. When she returned moments later, she was wearing rubber gloves.

"I'm not taking any chances."

We dumped the contaminated bedding into the corner and replaced it with the sheets and duvet from my bed.

Once the fort was back to her standard of coziness, we fell into it and each other. I couldn't believe it had only been two days since our first kiss. There was no hesitation as we tangled ourselves together.

"I really like kissing you," she said, still close enough that her lips brushed mine when she spoke. I wished we could always be this close. "Does it always feel like this? Does it always feel this good?"

"No." How could I explain how different I felt with Ellie? In that moment I almost wanted to tell her to kiss another guy from her school. Just so she'd know the difference. "It's better because we like each other. I like you so much, El. It's ridiculous how much I like you, actually."

Our noses brushed and I felt Ellie's smile before I could see it. She whispered, "Ridiculous." Then she kissed me again.

THAT NIGHT FELT so momentous I never let her out of my arms. The same ones that held her last night, that still itch to hold her now, that never want to let her go.

She quickly recites the prayer for the second night of Hanukkah, and we make our way back to the fort.

"My brother was such an idiot. Is he still that bad? With women, I mean."

Her question catches me off guard and I raise a brow. "You don't know? I thought you guys were so close now."

"Not really. We talk sometimes, like a few times a year? And we text a little." She speaks so nonchalantly that it has to be true, but a part of me wonders *how* it could be true. My expression must match my confusion because she narrows her eyes and says, "What?"

"He just...he talks about you a lot. How happy you are in San Francisco, how you have all these amazing friends. Whenever we're with your parents he goes on and on about how great you're doing on your own. He kind of rubs it in their face how happy you are, since you left home."

Not that he ever talks about anything important, like where she works. Nothing that could have helped me keep track of her. It's become a sort of unspoken rule between us that I don't ask about Ellie. Instead, I wait for any morsel he'll give me on his own.

But he's never let any of us forget that Ellie is happier in California. Every year when we're together at Christmas, every time he tells us, I feel a special sort of kinship with Judy, Ellie's mom. She might not know about the bond we have, but I do. Neither of us can stand the idea of Ellie being better off without us.

"That's weird," she comments. "I never complain to Ezra when I'm not in a good place, but I never gloat about my great life either. I don't talk about myself much at all. Most of our conversations revolve around him. It was all med school all the time for four years, and now it's just stories from his residency."

When she's in a bad place? I wonder if she's talking about her lupus flares or something else. Is it possible Ezra doesn't know what he's talking about? That maybe she isn't really better off these days?

"Is he wrong?" I ask.

"About what?"

"El, come on."

"What? If there's something you want to know, just ask me."

"Are you happy?" I pin her with a stare, urging a truthful and straightforward answer. I need it more than she realizes.

"Yeah, sometimes." I can't stop myself from grinning. "What are you so smug about? You don't want me to be happy?"

"Of course I do. I'd just rather you be happy with me."

A flicker of a smile grazes her lips, but it evaporates as quickly as it came. Now she looks pissed.

"Don't say stuff like that to me."

"You don't want me to be honest?"

"Honest? You want to talk about honesty? Seriously?" Her chest heaves and her skin starts to redden across her neck, but I have no idea what has her so upset.

"El, what are you talking about. Are you okay?"

She reaches a hand in her pocket, and I track the movement of her thumb over a stone. She still has it. I guess if I can't comfort her the way I used to, I'm glad something else can.

"Forget it." She huffs out a breath. "Can we just...talk about something else? Pretty please?"

I give her a pleading look, because whatever is going on, I want to fix it. But she's stoic and I'd rather enjoy the night than fight about something I don't even understand.

"Come here," I say, reaching out for her hand and coaxing her down to the floor. Her body softens into the pillows, and she lets out a contented sigh, draping the blanket over both our legs. And then I turn on *Elf*.

Chapter Eighteen

Theo

August 21, 2014

WHEN MY PARENTS were still alive, there was one thing my mom continuously said to me: Marry your best friend.

It always felt strange for my mom to show such an interest in my future love life when I was still a kid, but after I lost her, I treasured those life lessons like they were scripture.

She and my dad were high school sweethearts. Well, sort of. They grew up together and were best friends, but they both dated other people until they were twenty-five. Mom loved to tell me why none of the other men worked out for her, how none of them made her laugh like Dad did. She'd say that you could only ever have one favorite, one person you wanted to spend every moment with, one person that could make any bad day better; and if that wasn't the person you married, you'd always regret it.

I don't think I understood what she meant until I had my first girlfriend. Laura and I met when I was sixteen, while I was coaching hockey camp and she was coaching tennis. I liked her and was attracted to her, but I realized after a couple of months that I would always choose Ellie if I had the chance. I knew she was the person I would always want to spend Christmas with, the one who I could talk to about my parents, the one I texted every time I found a new penguin video because I knew she'd enjoy it as much as I did. She was my favorite person, long before I had the guts to kiss her.

The summer before I went to college was one of the best times of my life. Marriage wasn't exactly top of mind just yet, but I knew my happiness drew from one thing: I was falling in love with my favorite person. That first Christmas Eve when we skated together at Sugar Valley, I fell into Ellie's orbit without even realizing the shift had occurred. And I had only sunk deeper every year after.

My love for her had become the constant with which I measured truth. Not a day went by without thinking of her.

Grief followed me like a shadow. Every time I felt it withering away, it came back as sure as the rising sun. I didn't think it would ever disappear, but Ellie helped me turn it into something malleable. I could choose how to focus it; into my favorite memories, into making my parents proud of who I had become in their absence, into loving her the way they had hoped I would love my best friend one day.

Mr. and Mrs. Klein offered to let me stay with them for my last month before starting college. It was my and Ezra's last chance to spend real time together before we went our separate ways to school. He was the closest thing I had to family, a brother in every way that mattered. Spending the better part of high school as roommates, not to mention all our holidays together...Life was going to look very different with him in Boston and me in Vermont.

But even thinking about that made my guilt rise, because the person I was most excited to spend time with was Ellie.

For three weeks I navigated hanging out with Ezra and trying to find any excuse to include his sister, which he hated. Luckily for him, Mrs. Klein was also working against me.

It was summer. We spent most days going hiking or hanging out at the lake. All things I had never realized Ellie wasn't allowed to do. The truth of it was that I'd never understood everything Ellie missed out on until that year.

But after weeks of frustration over seeing so little of each other—we mainly texted and snuck into each other's rooms at night—some good luck finally came my way.

"Theo, I hate to ask this of you. I know it's your last weekend before classes start and you might've wanted to get settled in the dorms, but it would really be such a help if you could stay with Ellie. We'll only be gone three nights."

"*Mom!* I don't need a fucking babysitter," Ellie screamed as she ran down the stairs and into the kitchen. She wasn't nearly as happy as I was at the surprise turn of events. Then, after she caught her breath, "I'm almost seventeen."

Mrs. Klein ignored her and started walking me through the lists of doctors and a shit ton of medications. She showed me the symptom tracker I was already familiar with, telling me things to "look out for," like Ellie would hide it from me. And then the thermometer. She wanted me to log Ellie's temperature every day.

Was this super fucking weird? Sure. But honestly, all I could hear was that we would be alone for three days while Mr. and Mrs. Klein got Ezra settled at school.

I was *thrilled*.

"Are you ready to go on an adventure?"

Ellie grinned at me. We'd been making out for the last

twenty minutes, ever since her parents and Ezra drove away and I told her I planned a special day for us. I finally came up for air and checked the time on my phone. We needed to get going.

"I'm ready for anything, as long as it's with you." She winced at herself, and sure, it was kind of cheesy, but I also knew she really meant it.

Another twenty minutes later, we were on the road heading to one of my favorite summer spots in Burlington. Emerald Cove Park was a gorgeous hiking area with crystal clear water for swimming on a hot day. And it was almost completely flat.

I knew Ellie could handle it, no matter what her mom might think. This would require less exertion than she used to kiss me. And just in case, I made sure everything we needed fit in one backpack so I could give her a piggyback ride if she ever got tired.

We stopped at Ellie's favorite deli to grab sandwiches, snacks, and the largest bottles of water they had. We both applied sunscreen before we left the house and again after we parked the car. We would be following the most shaded trail the whole way, only getting full sun once we hit the lake.

I really had thought of everything. I liked to think that if I could actually tell Ellie's mom what we were doing, she'd be pleased with my preparedness.

"This is so weird." Ellie said, after stopping for a quick drink. "You're a winter person. I'm still adjusting to seeing you in shorts." She giggled, definitely *not* checking out my legs.

"Well, prepare yourself, AG." I whipped off my T-shirt, knowing we were getting close to the water. It was eighty-five degrees and humid. And Ellie was right, I was a winter person. I belonged on the ice, in the snow, curled up with my adventure girl in a pillow fort. Summer was lasting way too long.

"Can we really swim in that?" Ellie eyed the lake as we rounded the corner.

"Of course. Why do you think I told you to wear a swimsuit?"

"I don't know. I just—I've never been swimming outside before." I chuckled as I saw her watching the other hikers wade into the water. I always thought Ellie was mature for her age, even when I'd met her at nine years old. But she was also sheltered. There was so much she hadn't seen, hadn't been able to experience yet. I wanted to give it all to her.

I set our stuff down under a bench and took her hand, leading us to the small beach. "Come on. I need to cool off. We can just dip our feet in if you want." But once we touched the water, she immediately let go of me.

"Screw that. I'm swimming!" She ran into the ice-cold water and winced the farther out she went. But as soon as she was waist-deep, she dove under just as gracefully as she floated across the ice.

I stood there frozen, watching her as she came up for air. She spun in circles, making waves with her arms stretched out. She laughed as she kicked up and transitioned to floating on her back. I couldn't take my eyes off her.

She met my gaze. "What are you doing over there, weirdo? Come swim with me!"

I wasn't sure why I couldn't move. It felt like quicksand was holding my feet down. All I knew was that I loved seeing Ellie this way, beaming and carefree. *My adventure girl.* It made me so happy that it made me angry for all the times I had seen her in a different light. All the times she had to stay home and miss out on something fun, all the times she was isolated in her room because Ezra didn't even want to keep her company, all the times we lived too far away from each other for me help her have this kind of freedom.

It was overwhelming, everything winding through my head. I wanted to take Ellie and run away, show her the world. It was wrong that *swimming in a lake* was bringing her this much joy. I decided in that instant I would do everything in my power to give Ellie a real adventure one day.

And then I ran through the water and joined her.

ORIGINALLY, I had planned to take Ellie out to dinner. I wanted to make this day together—our first real date—as special as I could. With her parents being so strict, I wasn't sure when we'd get the chance again.

But after we got home and showered, El said she was feeling tired and wanted to stay in. I trusted her to let me know if she was actually unwell, so I didn't push. She had enough of that from her mom. And we did have a long day in the heat. Anyone would be tired after that if they weren't used to it.

I offered to go pick up Chinese for dinner. I knew it was her favorite even though it wasn't on her mom's approved list. Maybe *especially* because it wasn't on the list. She stuck to vegetable stir-fries, sauce on the side. I offered to share some orange chicken, but she let me know that she'd been sleeping a lot better when she cut down on sugar. Then she told me to get some eggrolls too.

She knew how to take care of herself, how to follow her doctor's guidance as well as what her own body was telling her. Why couldn't her family see this side of her? The fact that her mom thought I needed to *watch* her this weekend still baffled me.

I got home with the food and set everything out on the kitchen table. I heard no sound from El so I figured she must have been napping. Thinking I would give her some space I went down to the basement. I could always heat up the food later.

As I reached the bottom step and eyed my bed, every bit of air left my lungs.

Candles studded the floor, bathing the entire room and a half-naked Ellie in soft twinkling light.

"What's going on?" I stuttered, lost for words. Ellie, *my* Ellie was laid out on my bed and balancing on an elbow, ankles crossed in a tantalizing way.

"You don't like it?" She sat up on her heels, her expression shifting, clouded in uncertainty.

I sped over to her, not wanting her to feel dejected in any way. I took both of her hands in mine as I said, "I love it. Whatever this is. I'm obsessed with it. Especially this outfit." I let my fingers roam over the tiny tank top she was wearing, and the even tinier shorts that matched.

Reflexively, I grabbed on to her ass and pulled her into my lap. Her lips found mine, drawing my breath out of me as she tangled her fingers in my hair. She straddled me, then pulled me down with her as she lay flat on my bed.

"I just wanted to do something special. For our first time." She kissed me again as I drank in her words. Our first time?

I knew Ellie was a virgin. Hell, I was her first and (hopefully) only kiss. I didn't consider myself to be all that experienced, but I had had sex before and she knew that, knew everything about the girl I'd dated. There were no secrets between us, and it was before our friendship became *more*. I understood why she thought I needed this, but it felt way too soon. We had barely done anything besides make out.

"Ellie, hold up." I sat up and pulled her with me. "What are you talking about? Who said we needed to have sex tonight?"

"I just thought...since my parents were gone..." Her gaze

fell and my heart tumbled after it. She looked so vulnerable I could have cried.

"Hey, look at me. Please, El?" Her big brown eyes turned upward, watery with apprehension. "You are extremely tempting right now. Do you have any idea how sexy you are?" That got me a small smile, but I knew her confidence was still wavering.

I scooped her up to sit on my lap again, pressing kisses to her neck and shoulder until she squirmed a little. "Do you see what you do to me? I can't keep my hands off of you."

"But you don't want to have sex?"

"Of course I do. I just don't think it should happen the first time I'm alone with you in your parents' house. Let's just go slow, okay?" I was already bursting with frustration over how little time we spent together this month, and I knew once school started it wouldn't be any different. I wasn't prepared to call her my girlfriend—that would require her family knowing about us, and I definitely wasn't ready to tell Ezra. I had no idea how to make this work and keep his friendship; he'd been clear he was against it before it ever started, getting pissed over nothing but late-night grilled cheese sandwiches. And if I couldn't give Ellie a real relationship, there was no way I was going to go this far with her. Not until I could give her the type of commitment she deserved.

"Okay."

"Please don't read into this baby. You know I want you. It has nothing to do with that."

"Did you just call me *baby*?" It wasn't my intention, but a change in topic was more than welcome.

"Is that okay?"

"Absolutely not. Nope. Don't ever call me that again."

She was serious.

"Okay. You don't like pet names?"

"I mean, in theory, they're kind of sweet. But Mom and Dad still call me baby and sweetie and sweet pea all the time. Sometimes it feels like you're the only person who doesn't still see me as a little girl..." I felt her thoughts rolling back to the sex-rejection in the way she averted her eyes, tugged her shirt down over her hips.

"Ellie." I ran my hands along each side of her face, forcing her to make eye-contact with me. "Eliana. In my eyes, you are definitely not a little girl." I pulled her hair over her shoulder and dragged my hand across her collarbone before sliding down one of her straps. I tugged it just a little so I could kiss the top of her breast. It was the most intimate we had been together, but knowing her eagerness to go all the way, I figured it was time to up the ante a little.

"Mmmm," was her only response.

"Is there anything else you'd like me to call you?" I softly dragged my lips against her skin and she arched closer to me. "Honey? Sugar? Cupcake?"

"I liked it when you said Eliana. No one ever calls me that." Her words stretched as I scraped my nails up her side.

"Done." Her lips found mine again as she swung a leg over to straddle me fully. I kissed her mouth, her jaw, her throat. I pressed my lips against her until she panted out every single breath. I was desperate to show her how much I wanted her, even if it wasn't the right time for us to have sex.

But the more she pressed herself against me, writhing and rolling her hips, the more difficult it was to keep our relationship PG-13.

Her fingers dove into my hair, pulling it taut while she kissed me. A small moan spilled from her lips as she ground herself down on me harder, trailing her lips down my neck and digging her fingers into my skin.

"Eliana," I murmured against her temple. "Do you want me to touch you?"

I kissed my way down the side of her neck, nibbling her ear as I went. She whimpered, and it vibrated through me. I felt her nod and then heard, "Yeah. Yes. I think so."

I had to reign in my laughter. Even when I knew she was completely out of her comfort zone, I loved how honest she was with me.

She watched intently as I dragged a hand down between us. As soon as my fingertips reached her waistband, she sucked in a sharp breath. I didn't get the chance to ask the question before she was nodding again. "I'm sure."

I slid my hand down farther, until I could feel the heat radiating off of her.

"Do you know what you like?" I asked.

Her wide-eyed expression told me enough, so I kissed her again.

"Let's find out together."

WAKING up after one of the best nights of my life, my mind raced.

Little flashes of yesterday with Ellie swam through my vision; her smile as she ran into the lake, the mix of confidence and vulnerability she showed me last night, the feel of her. I woke up with a grin the size of Texas and an urgent need to kiss her.

But when I rolled over, there was no Ellie. Her pillow was cold.

It wasn't a secret that she often had trouble sleeping, that she tended to wander the house at night when she got restless, so I wasn't too concerned.

That changed when I went upstairs to find her lying flat on her stomach in the sunroom.

"El? Are you okay?" I crouched down on the tile.

She turned her head toward me and groaned. "Cool floor. Feels good."

I rested my palm on her face and was met with skin so hot it could sizzle.

"Are you sunburnt?" Fuck. I took her hiking, pushed her to swim. I'd spent the day thinking how unreasonably strict her mom was, but what if she was right? What if I hurt Ellie?

"Not burnt, just a fever." She rolled onto her back and smiled up at me, the tiniest hitch of her lips. "Good morning."

Good morning? "Ellie, what can I do? Do you need medicine? Should we go to the doctor? How do I help?"

"Calm down." She sat up. "It's just a flare. I already took some Tylenol for the fever and left a message with my doctor to get a prescription filled for steroids. I'll be fine." She rested a hand on my shoulder, like I was the one who needed comforting. "Would you mind getting me some more water?"

She lay back down as I made my way to the kitchen. The scent of peppermint permeated the air from a half-empty teacup in the sink. I could see a few pill bottles out on the counter as well as her symptom tracker filled out with today's date. She had already logged her temperature three times, every hour on the hour. It was only ninety-nine, but I could still feel the heat of her face simmering on my skin.

It felt like an invasion, but I couldn't help myself from looking closer at the tracker, at what she was feeling. She gave a score of *moderate* to thumping headaches, joint pain, chest pain and body aches. Fuck.

How often did she have to go through this? She didn't seem concerned at all, like laying half-dressed on the tile floor at six in the morning was completely normal. Maybe this *was* her normal, and I just never realized what it was actually like for her. I felt like a fucking idiot.

"Are you in a lot of pain still?" I brought her the water and sat on the floor next to her, feeling about as useless as a disconnected light switch.

She adjusted a bit, letting out a small sigh when she placed her cheek on new section of tile. "Yeah. I'm used to it though. Just wanna kick the fever because it makes everything else worse."

"You really need steroids? What about more Tylenol or Ibuprofen?"

A joyless laugh tumbled from her lips. "Treating this kind of pain with Ibuprofen is like trying to cut down a tree with a butter knife. Prednisone may have a bunch of shitty side effects, but it's honestly a miracle for my joints."

Fuck.

"I'll be right back. Yell if you need anything, okay?"

I ran downstairs and grabbed my iPad. I wasn't even sure what I was doing but suddenly I had ten tabs open of Reddit threads and Google searches.

How do you fix lupus?

Best ways to kill a fever.

What lupus symptoms are serious?

When to go to the hospital for lupus?

What is a thumping headache?

How to cure a migraine.

Is chest pain dangerous?

How to do an at-home breathing test.

How long should a fever last?

How long before a fever is dangerous?

"Hey. What are you doing?" I startled and nearly dropped the iPad. Ellie was at the bottom of the stairs, and the seven-thirty-eight on the screen told me I'd been hunched over it for more than twenty minutes. I tossed the iPad back on my bed and turned to face her, gently grabbing her wrists to check her pulse.

"I'm so sorry, I lost track of time. I was trying to figure out how to help you."

"I'm fine. Promise. I'm used to it, ya know?"

"I don't know, though. Like I had no idea it got this bad, El. How often does this happen?" My voice was desperate, but desperation was all I felt.

I needed answers. Needed to know every detail about this illness, about how I could protect her. No wonder Ellie's mom's rules were always so rigid. Why wouldn't she want to protect her daughter from suffering like this? *I think I finally understand.*

"Umm, probably once every few months? Sometimes more. I promise it's not that bad. I'm usually just exhausted and the pain isn't always this severe. Sometimes it's even over after a week."

"A week? Fuck, Ellie. That's horrible." I rushed over to hug her, but she immediately pushed me away.

"Aches. Sorry. It kind of hurts if you touch me." Her gaze bounced around the basement as she chewed her cheek. Shit. I didn't want her to feel embarrassed about any of this.

"That's okay. I just need to learn. Tell me what helps. What makes you feel better?"

Ellie proceeded to grab the pillows off my bed and lie on the floor. She propped her head on her palm and walked me through all her details. How the aches were mostly joint pain from inflammation, how sometimes it felt better for her to stretch her limbs on the ground where she could spread out and switch positions, and how her skin was extra sensitive to touch —not in a good way. She told me about the pills she only took during a flare, how bitter they were, and the peppermint tea she drank to help rid the taste of them.

She explained that the best coping mechanism was rest and relaxation, that her stress hormones were always the biggest concern to her doctors, so anything to help her stay calm and relaxed was the best medicine. She even took out the stone I had gifted her from her pocket and told me she always kept it on her, that it really helped.

"I usually spend most of my time watching TV or listening to music, but it has to be stuff I've seen or heard before, nothing that needs my full attention. So it's usually—"

"*Gilmore Girls* and Taylor Swift?"

She smiled in response, and we were both quiet for a moment. I loved proving how well I knew her, and I guessed she liked it too. But then she shifted again, and I caught the subtle wince she was trying to hide. She was still in pain.

"Was this my fault? Did it happen because you were in the sun yesterday?" I knew I shouldn't make this about me, but I needed to know. The pangs of guilt were relentless. Like I wanted to steal Ellie's pain and force it upon myself. Anything to help her.

"No. I mean, I don't think so. You made me put on so much sunscreen. And we walked in the shade most of the time. Really, it's not your fault." She paused to take a long drink of water and change positions on the floor. I was impressed with how well she treated herself. It was like she didn't need me at all. "They're honestly so random. Like, okay. The doctors tell me to avoid stressful situations because they can lead to flares. But having Mom gone and spending the night with you, I've truly never been less stressed."

My mind traveled back to everything we did last night. We didn't exactly discuss it, but I was pretty sure that was Ellie's first orgasm. Or at least the first one from a guy. Was that stressful on her body somehow? Or maybe she was breathing too hard, or—

"I can see your brain spiraling. Please do not read into this. Nothing we did last night caused this; I swear."

"But—"

"Theo, I'm tired. And my hips and shoulders are killing me. And I really hate that you're seeing me like this. Can you please not overthink it?"

Silence fell between us; I had no idea how to respond to that.

"Listen to me. Yesterday was one of the best days I have ever had. I never get to be outside like that and I loved every thing we did together. I feel pain all the time, but you made me feel *good*. If it caused this, I have zero regrets."

"But I hurt you."

"Stop. Please stop. Don't turn into my mother. My lupus has always been mild, okay? I know you're about to spend the rest of the weekend googling this shit, but I'm begging you not to. I'm tired, maybe a little weak, but I can handle this. My health is under control, as much as it can be. I'm so tired of missing out on everything just to be safe all the time. There's more to life than playing it safe." That same desperation I was feeling floated into her voice. "Please don't let this change anything between us."

I wouldn't able to stop blaming myself, I knew that. But I could pretend for the rest of the weekend. I could do it for her.

"Okay. Can you just do me one favor though?" She nodded her head. "I just want to know what you're feeling. Like, any time you have pain, or you're extra tired, anything. Please just let me know. I promise I won't ever tell you what to do or what not to do, but I have to know what's going on with you or I'll go insane."

Her lips twitched before she pursed them, sucking in one of her cheeks. "I agree to your terms."

I moved the sectional to make a bigger space on the floor in front of the TV. I propped up pillows and cushions wherever I could to offer a range of seating options. I tried my best not to ask more questions, which I was only mildly successful at, and I turned on *Gilmore Girls* because I knew it was her favorite show.

Begrudgingly, I left my iPad alone for the rest of the weekend. If she didn't want me looking for more information, I could grant her that wish. For now, my singular goal in life was to help Ellie relax.

Chapter Nineteen

Ellie

Now

I SUCCESSFULLY IGNORED ALL seven of Theo's attempts at flirting last night.

Sort of. Success is relative, right?

But I did brush his comments aside enough that we could eventually just talk. The way we used to, when we would stay up all night talking about nothing at all.

When I started to yawn, he pulled me in to a cuddle and I didn't argue. He was right. It *feels* right. There's no point in denying it. The storm will be over soon, and I'll leave Vermont and never have to deal with all these messy emotions ever again.

Only, the storm isn't passing. Through the cabin's window, I can see at least another foot of snow has fallen since last night, and Theo waist-deep in it on the front steps.

I get up and open the door to groggily ask, "What are you doing?" while simultaneously rubbing sleep from my eyes.

He jumps, one gloved hand coming to his chest as the other grips hard on the shovel. "Shoveling." *Okay, Mr. obvious.*

"Why?" I don't even wait for an answer as I turn on my heel and lie back down under the blankets.

He throws the shovel down and crosses the threshold, kicking off his boots and snow pants and shutting the door with a click. "So we can go somewhere." Cryptic. Because where the hell are we going when the cars are still buried in snow?

"Also, good morning." He comes to sit down next to me. "You still look so pretty when you sleep."

I blush. He's getting more and more brazen with the flirting and it's getting equally more difficult to ignore it. Especially when he leans down to brush a soft kiss on my temple.

"Theo. What are you doing?"

"First, making you breakfast." He pops up to stand. "Then I'm going to finish shoveling. And then I'm taking you on a date."

"A date?"

"A date." His face is pure mischief. I want so badly to hate it. "I know there's seven years of space between us, but you're here now, and I know you're planning to make a run for it the second you can. So while you're stuck here, just go on one date with me. Please?"

There is a lot to unpack there, but he's right. About all of it. "Where are you planning on taking me? We're snowed in, remember?"

His smile gleams. "I stole something from your house a few years ago. To be honest I had no idea why I did it, it just felt compulsive, like I had no choice. Now I think I must have been psychic or something, like I knew this day would come."

He runs upstairs before I can decipher his words. I'm still stuck on the part about him stealing from me.

Within minutes, Theo is bounding down the steps like a

kid on Christmas morning. Except instead of eagerly rushing to open presents, he's handing one to me.

My old skates.

The last pair Mom bought me before she made me cancel my lessons. When she said it was becoming too stressful on my body even though it was my favorite thing in the world. The skates I wore when I did my first and last jump on the ice.

The skates that I balanced on with weak knees the first time Theo kissed me.

These skates were one of my most prized possessions, yet I never took them with me to California. I can't remember why I left them behind, probably because I didn't bring anything that reminded me of Theo.

He stole these from my house. Why? What could he possibly have wanted with them?

I look up from the boots and meet his gaze. He's been watching me. Watching me recount all the memories held between the leather and laces in my hands. His lips lift up on one side, the unsure smile that says he's still waiting on my reaction, but he hopes it's a good one.

"We're going skating?"

The smile grows. "Where else would I take you for our second first date?"

THEO SPENDS the rest of the morning shoveling snow. The man is built like a lumberjack, and I would be lying if I said I wasn't enjoying the view. The yoga butt has nothing on a hockey player.

He creates a walkable path to get us to his snowmobile—which is thankfully a two-seater—and once we reach the perimeter of the ice, I can see all the other work he'd been doing when I wasn't watching.

Reindeer Rink shines like a beacon.

My favorite place in the world.

"Have you skated at all since you've been gone?" Theo comments as I take a few steps on wobbly legs.

"I have, but only a little. It normally takes me a second to get my bearings." Not long though. In a blink, I'm gliding flawlessly, loving the feel of my old skates and my favorite rink.

My first year at Berkeley—my first birthday there—I was so incredibly homesick. It was too warm, too bright, too vacant of my best friend. I had asked Maya if she knew of any outdoor skate facilities in the area, and she took me into the city to Union Square. It felt bizarre to go skating in a T-shirt and jeans but getting on the ice softened the blunt edges of my sadness.

After that, we went every year. Our own little tradition.

"You still look good. Show me some tricks, AG."

AG. Adventure girl. Those two letters, the name only Theo has ever called me, they burrow into my chest, chipping away at the heart of stone I've been cultivating all these years. I wear them like a badge of honor as I quickly braid my hair and cross the rink.

Theo is a god on ice, more elegant than any man his size should be. He smoothly glides forward and back, side to side. His hair is cut short now, but I can still see it swaying in the breeze like it used to.

I take his hand and lead us in a lap around the rink, twisting on my skates until he's satisfied with my moves.

Time ripples around us, blurring every line of now and then, until I'm fifteen again, praying that Theo Fox will kiss me. But he doesn't kiss me this time. He holds my hand. He spins and dips and lifts me. He never lets me fall.

The past seven years were supposed to be my adventure, but none of it was as exhilarating as playing with Theo on the ice right now.

Is there anything that ever will be?

I'm dying to ask him about the skates. Why did he take them? When?

I know it shouldn't matter, but somehow these answers I'm searching for feel like puzzle pieces to all the chasms in my heart.

Theo missed me. I hoped he did. I would never pretend I didn't know that was a possibility. It was just never enough to erase the betrayal. But now I'm feeling the need to remember that betrayal, to stamp it into my mind, because my emotions are messing with my head.

I pull away from Theo to skate on my own, spinning on one foot and then two, circling again and again until I start to feel dizzy. Until my breathing meets the pace of my skates. My vision gets a little more blurry with each spin, but I can't get myself to stop.

Time has been steadily warped by this rink, and I can't seem to keep track of *when* I am. Is it my last day before turning sixteen, experiencing the sweetness of my first kiss? Or the day I met Theo almost twenty years ago? Is it prom? Is it now?

I am lost to these feelings. Drowning in their depth. Trapped in some sixth dimension of memories with no escape route. And little desire to leave.

"El! Stop!" I've been spinning. And spinning and spinning and spinning. Theo's hands grab my shoulders to stop my movement and hold me in place. "Are you okay? What was that?"

I blow out a shaky breath, not sure if I'm on the verge of tears or a panic attack. Is mercury in retrograde? Would that be a viable excuse right now? My legs shake so heavily I can barely stand.

"Breathe, El." Theo pulls me along the ice until we're on solid ground. He kneels in front of me to help remove my skates, stopping short of the laces. His hands rub up and down my calves, with enough pressure that I can feel his heat through the fabric of my fleece leggings.

I follow his instructions, taking exaggerated breaths in and out at the pace he demands. He continues massaging my legs and I let my eyelids flutter shut.

In, out. In, out.

Up, down, Up, down.

"That's it, just keep breathing." My eyes are open again, clear. His voice soothes me to the bone. I can't stop myself from watching his face as his hands work my sore muscles. His cheeks are pink from the cold, his stubble glittering in the bright sun. He's gotten even more beautiful over the years, and I'm hit with a knife to the gut knowing he isn't mine anymore.

That he never really was.

God I miss him. Even when he's right in front of me, both hands splayed against my body, I miss him. It's a deep ache, violent waves in the middle of the ocean churning through my chest.

I keep breathing.

In, out. In, out.

Eventually the pain will go away.

It always does.

Chapter Twenty

Ellie

December 24, 2014

"LOBSTERS?"

"Happy birthday." Theo grimaced. "Please say you like it. I was trying to get creative."

I stared down at the snow globe filled with two lobsters wearing Santa hats.

"It might by my new favorite. Where did you find this?"

Theo eyed me sheepishly. "Maine. Had to sneak out after our away game."

"What? Why would you do that?" I was scolding him, but I couldn't stop grinning. Theo could get me whatever snow globe they carried at Target, and I would be perfectly happy, but knowing the effort he put in to make these gifts special had me falling completely in love with him.

And I was in love with him. There was no denying it. I wouldn't be telling him that any time soon, but it was a fact of life that felt as sure as gravity. Sometimes it felt like he had been gifted to me by the stars.

"Remember last time you came by the dorms?" he asked.

Of course I did, and it wasn't because my trips were infrequent. I was there almost weekly.

Dr. Patel, my endocrinologist, suggested I start Kundalini yoga a few months ago. My blood tests had been mostly normal for the past few years, but the one thing that had always been concerning to her were my cortisol levels. She believed that my other symptoms and even the cadence of my flares could be moderated if I could find ways to regulate my stress. If Mom hadn't been with me, I would have gladly shared my own ideas.

A Kundalini class I found online was offered three nights a week and was only a few blocks from the VU campus, somewhere I could easily drive myself now that I had my license. I actually really enjoyed it. I liked moving my body, breaking a sweat, feeling my muscles burn, even if it was mostly due to deep stretches. I liked the meditation too. Clearing my mind was liberating.

I also only went once or twice a week, and used the other times to visit Theo. I was typically flushed when I got home from either place. Mom never knew the difference.

The last time I hung out with him at his dorm was a couple of weeks ago, before hockey and cramming for finals made it impossible. We had been...Hmm. What had we been doing? It would've either been watching TV with his roommate Raj —*Mirage*, as the entire VU team called him, thanks to his Avon legacy—or hooking up with Theo while Raj was out partying.

"Shit. You don't remember, do you?" He scoffed.

"Just give me a sec!" I whisper-yelled. We were in my room. He came up right before midnight to give me my gift. I doubted Ez was asleep yet, so we were being extra quiet.

And then it hit me. We *had* been watching TV, cable actually, after they had somehow broken their Roku. We were watching old reruns of *Friends* and they said something like... lobsters mate for life?

My expression turned knowing and he beamed at me.

"You're my lobster, El."

"I thought I was your penguin."

"You're my everything."

I pounced. Arms hooked over his shoulders. Legs clamped around his hips like a barnacle. Lips coming together so swiftly I wasn't sure who initiated the kiss.

He held me against him while he walked to each side of my room, first locking the main door and then doing the same with the bathroom.

We fell onto my bed, still connected, always connected. I never grew tired of kissing Theo. I only ever wanted more.

"Wait. I forgot to tell you," he whispered. "Do you know what a group of lobsters is called?"

"Theo, come on." I kissed him again, lightly shoving his chest with both hands.

"No, you're really gonna like this one. I swear." His eyes twinkled as he grinned up at me. Who was I to end one of our traditions?

"All right. Tell me."

He pulled me down and flipped us, so we were laying on our sides. Our heads shared my pillow, barely a breath between us. His hand squeezed my hip as he leaned closer to whisper in my ear. "A risk."

WINTER BREAK that year was nothing short of magical. All week, our trio was inseparable; me, Ezra and Theo. Ez didn't even try to ditch me for New Year's.

Things were very different when Theo and I could be alone, and we did find time for that after everyone else fell asleep at night. But he was always my friend first. Even when I had to stop myself from kissing him so Ezra wouldn't see, I was in heaven.

"There's a new camp at Stowe. They added a lodge and outdoor rink on the south side of the mountain. Should we go? I think they're doing fireworks tomorrow too," Ezra offered. We were sitting at the kitchen table, even though we finished breakfast a while ago.

"Is that the reggae skate?" Theo asked. "One of the guys from my team was talking about it."

"Yeah, I heard that too. I'll make sure to bring the pen."

I never understood the reasoning behind it, but Vermonters *loved* reggae. Maybe being so far from anywhere tropical had us seeking out the sunshiny vibes through music.

"El?" Theo looked at me, awaiting confirmation. "Wanna go?"

"Hell yes."

"ELLIE, I think we need to have an intervention," Ezra said from the front seat of the car. He and Theo had been talking hockey non-stop on our drive to Stowe, so I was surprised by the sudden interest in me.

"Excuse me?"

"*Gilmore Girls*. It needs to stop. I can hear you watching it through our wall at night, and I can't get that damn song out of my head. I'm afraid I'm gonna start singing 'where you lead, I will follow' at the gym."

Theo laughed and added, "Dude, she's never gonna stop. She's obsessed with that show." I had to hide my massive grin. Yes, I watched it regularly. But this week, I kept it playing at night to cover up any sounds I was making with Theo.

"But why? Why are you so obsessed with it? You must have

seen every episode ten times at this point. What is so good about two women who never stop talking?" Ezra inquired, a little bit rudely in my opinion.

I stayed silent, enjoying the banter from my brother even if he was making fun of me. Theo continued to laugh, throwing me sly, knowing glances over his shoulder and through the rearview mirror. This topic may have come up with us a few times before. I couldn't help it. It was my favorite show.

And it wasn't exactly a mystery as to why.

"First of all, Stars Hollow is the perfect small town and I want to live there." Fact. "But mostly, I just like watching the dynamic between Rory and Lorelai. They're best friends and they tell each other everything. They have all these fun traditions like movie nights and eating ridiculous amounts of food. It's like the most amazing mother-daughter relationship that could ever exist and—"

"I get it," Ezra replied, gently cutting me off. "I get it now."

Theo parked the car and we all jumped out, excited to see this brand-new skating rink. Ezra threw an arm around me and whispered conspiratorially, "Screw Mom. Let's have some fun."

He handed me the weed pen after taking a quick hit. I had smoked once or twice before but never with Ezra. Raj always offered it to me when I visited the dorms, and everyone I knew at Champlain Academy smoked.

"Really?" I snatched it from him before he could change his mind.

"You tell Mom or Dad I gave this to you, and we'll never speak again." He looked at me pointedly. "And not because I'll be pissed—and I will—but because they will never, *ever* let me be alone with you for the rest of our lives. You know that right?"

He wasn't wrong.

"They'll never hear a peep from me. I sister-swear." He looked down at my pinky finger hanging in the balance between us and laughed. I shrugged and took a small hit, the zing traveling down my throat and into my chest, then offered it to Theo.

"Nah, I'm driving. I'm sure there'll be enough of that shit in the air to get buzzed anyway."

Ezra ran up ahead, saying he saw someone he knew from school, and Theo took advantage of the opportunity immediately, lacing our fingers together for a stolen moment.

"If you feel funny or tired or anything you let me know, okay?"

I saw the sincerity in his eyes. He wasn't telling me what to do, even if he still worried about me. I was never a burden with Theo, I only felt looked after. Cherished."I will." I squeezed his hand before letting go, knowing my brother could turn around at any moment.

"Good." He threw me a quick wink. "Let's do this."

We ran ahead, chasing the sound of the music until we made it onto the ice.

February 21, 2015

RAJ MAHAL

Operation Bang Theo is a go

He thinks I'm taking him to see the Bruins, so you better bring it or he'll be disappointed

ELLIE

Did you change your name in my phone?

And he won't be disappointed

RAJ MAHAL

Yeah. Raj Theo Roommate was lame

ELLIE

Also, we agreed on Operation SURPRISE Theo, and all you had to do was clear his schedule!

RAJ MAHAL

Be honest Ells Bells, you wanna bang. And it's his birthday! I had to come up with something he'd buy

You're welcome

COORDINATING a birthday surprise for Theo with his roommate was...interesting, to say the least. I loved Raj. He was hilarious and so entertaining. But he also never turned it off. If he wasn't flirting or messing with his friends or coming up with nicknames, he was probably asleep.

But I needed him.

My parents let me know last week that they'd be going to Boston for parents' weekend at Harvard. They were going to be gone for two whole nights, and it was the first time they had ever been willing to leave me home alone.

And parents' weekend just so happened to fall on Theo's birthday. The stars were aligning for me.

Preparations began as soon as Mom and Dad left the house. Theo had made my last nine birthdays magical. I was finally going to return the favor. Thankfully, Raj gave me a list of all of Theo's favorite foods. As well as I knew him, I had mostly seen him eat pizza and grilled cheese.

I had started cooking even more this year and was loving it. Cooking my own meals made it easy to follow the anti-inflammatory diet recommended by my doctors, and I could actually eat stuff I liked. Pinterest was a godsend and always had tons of stir-fry's and Mexican recipes to satisfy what my mom dubbed my "eccentric tastebuds."

Cooking a whole weekend of meals for Theo felt like a very grown-up thing to do. And I had to admit, I was hoping that if I could show Theo how mature I was, our relationship might finally shape itself into something real.

He had made it clear that everything between us needed to be kept secret, and I understood. I did. It wasn't like I was dying to tell my family either. But my biggest fear wasn't that they'd disapprove of Theo. They loved him like a son, which should have bolstered my confidence. Instead, it made me worry they would want to find him a better match, a potential surrogate daughter-in-law.

Theo and I were closer than I ever could've dreamt, but I was still frustrated over not having a title. After this special weekend though, there was no way he wouldn't see me as girlfriend material.

ELLIE

Happy birthday eve! What are you up to?

THEO

Playing Xbox with Raj. We're going down to Boston tomorrow though. Wish I could see you instead

ELLIE

Me too *Kissy face emoji*

I got you a present though

THEO

I don't want anything but you AG

ELLIE

I'm pretty sure you'll like this

I left it outside your door

"What? When was El here?" I could hear Theo's voice through his door, as well as Raj laughing at him.

"She's sneaky, dude."

Seconds later, the door to Theo's dorm opened and a very bewildered Theo looked back at me.

"Surprise!"

"Are you kidding me?!" He scooped me up in his arms, planting kisses all over my face, and carried me into his room. "This is the best gift ever." He lowered me down next to his bed. "It feels like Christmas."

"Happy birthday." I wrapped my arms around his neck but kept our lips from touching. I was very aware of Raj's presence still in the room, and it wouldn't be unlike him to sit back and watch our every move. The harmless creep that he was.

"How are you here? I thought you went to Cambridge with your parents?"

"I lied." I smirked at him. "They went without me. Wanna have a sleepover?"

He looked over to Raj in a desperate way that made my heart want to explode. He wasn't even entertaining the idea of saying no.

"Foxy, you really think I bought you Bruins tickets for your birthday? I like you, but...nah." Theo's confusion doubled, marring his expression with doubt before a smile crept in.

His attention was back on me. "You planned all this?"

"Well, I had to make sure your whole weekend was free. We've got a packed agenda. Grab your stuff because I'm taking you with me."

He ran around his room scooping random clothes into a backpack and met me at the door in lightning speed.

"You kids have fun," Raj yelled after us. "And use protection!"

THE NEXT MORNING, I woke up in my own bed with Theo for the first time.

It felt decadent, stretching and rolling into his heat with my eyelids still sealed.

"Morning. You look really pretty when you sleep." He placed a gentle, familiar kiss on my forehead. "You kind of smile. It's so cute."

I cracked one eye open and found a sleep-mussed Theo gazing at me. "I probably only do that when you're here."

We lay there cuddling for who knew how long, cocooned in the sheets. Eventually, Theo asked if I wanted to walk Noodle with him.

"How about you walk Noodle while I make us breakfast?"

"Again? That dinner was incredible. I'm not sure if I'm even hungry." I wouldn't be surprised if he never ate again after finishing off the entire tray of enchiladas last night. It was very impressive. He finished most of the guacamole too.

"I was just gonna make smoothies for the road. We've got a long drive ahead of us today."

"What?" he replied. "What are we doing?"

"It's a surprise!" His look of excitement and gratitude blended with something soft and caring made my heart all gooey. I wished we could be like this every day. "Don't forget your passport. Raj snuck it in your bag."

I LASTED about thirty seconds into our drive before telling Theo where we were headed. My buzz was bordering on oppressive.

The Montreal Biodôme was described online as an "immersive ecosystem experience." It was part-aquarium, part-aviary, part-zoo, part-science center, all recently renovated. I must have watched at least ten videos about the place since I discovered it two weeks ago.

The reason we were going: they had *three* types of penguins. And this was the one thing I managed to successfully keep to myself on the drive.

"It sounds awesome. How did you find out about it?"

Hmm, couldn't exactly say that I googled "closest penguins to Vermont." But even if they didn't have his favorite birds, I knew this was the perfect place to go for his birthday. February was dreary. I didn't even want to go skating outdoors. And while staying in and watching *National Geographic* together would have made for a fantastic weekend—mostly because of the cuddling—this was going to be even better.

"I just thought, we both really love animals. And it sucks there's nowhere to go in Vermont. My parents took me and Ez to the New England aquarium in Boston once and I loved it. This is a lot closer though."

"I've been to the Boston one too. This actually sounds way cooler. What are you most excited to see?"

Was this boy trying to force the word "penguin" out of my mouth? Jesus.

"The otters." Not a complete lie. If I saw a pair of them holding hands I was going to absolutely lose my shit. "Also, I got us tickets to one of the planetarium shows. I saw it was called *Frozen Worlds* and clicked to buy without reading the description. I'm kind of excited to go in blind."

Theo turned and offered the sweetest smile before swiftly facing the road again, mumbling something about "precious cargo." I grinned and plugged my phone in, starting the road trip playlist I spent hours on last week. I'd just reclined my seat and closed my eyes when I heard him murmur, "Best birthday ever."

THERE WERE OTTERS HOLDING HANDS. I didn't *not* cry.

There was also Theo holding my hand, the entire time we explored the Biodôme. Something so simple shouldn't have been this monumental, but after a whole year of sneaking around my family and hiding out in his dorm, it felt epic.

We started the day at the planetarium, had lunch while we geeked out over everything we'd just watched, and spent most of the afternoon googling the collective nouns for every new animal we stumbled across.

My favorite was definitely a "wisdom of wombats."

Our magical day ended at the penguin exhibit, Theo's grin stretching wide and his arms hugging me as tight as a boa constrictor. We watched them play and swim and flap their flippers at us. Theo asked me to name them all. I tried my best. More than one got dubbed Oreo.

Eventually we found ourselves sitting on the floor and leaning against the wall. Watching other onlookers walk by was just as entertaining as watching our favorite flightless birds.

"I wish she could have come here with us."

There was no need to ask. I knew he was talking about his mom. Theo aways said he got his love for animals from her, from all the times he helped her out at the sanctuary and all the animal factoids she would pepper him with as a kid.

I selfishly wished one of my parents were a vet. How might life have been different with someone like Carol Fox as a mother? I thought of her often, how she'd reacted to my mom's rigid rules, even when all I'd wanted was a pony ride.

"What do you miss the most now?" It had been a while since I asked him. This year's holiday break had been filled with long days hanging out with my brother, and blissful nights sneaking around my house. There hadn't been time for nostalgia. I wasn't sure if that was a good thing or not.

"It's not really something I miss. But I was thinking about how much I wish she could have met you. I think about that all the time, actually."

Angst coated his features, like this non-truth was painful for him to think about.

"Theo, I met her. You really didn't know that?"

His eyes flickered toward me, his focus as heavy as tungsten. "Really?"

"Yeah. I think the first time I was eleven. She let me pet the mini horses." *She told me you talked about me. She told me we were friends.* "And then, Mom let me go back once in the spring for a full tour. Carol was so nice to me. She even got Mom to let me ride one of the donkeys—you know, for like one minute." We shared a gentle laugh as our gazes connected. "They sort of fought about it and...I really loved her. I'm sorry I never told you."

Theo's eyes turned glassy as I offered up every detail I could remember, and then he pulled me into a hug as fierce as the tigers we saw earlier. I wished I had told him this before, seeing now how much it moved him. It was hard to understand how Theo dealt with his grief, but I knew that memories were everything to him. In my periphery, I could see the sunny, melancholic grin on his face, but still, I felt selfish. Like I had been keeping this one for myself, not allowing him to store it with all the others.

Theo didn't know that I had my own arsenal of preserved moments. That they were everything to me. That every one of them was connected to him.

I had no idea how long we sat there on the floor, holding each other in front of the penguins, enjoying the moment of being together in public without consequence. I would have stayed there with him forever.

Dinner was planned again for our second night together, but Theo's lips collided with mine the second we got home, and food was easily forgotten.

It was a heady feeling, truly having the house to ourselves, no one else knowing he was here.

We kissed against the front door, Latke slinking around our ankles. We kissed in the kitchen, Theo propping me up onto the island until we were the same height. We kissed in almost every room of my house, ending up on the couch in the basement.

I was perched on his lap with my hands in his hair, pulling and scraping, his mouth pressed to the hollow of my throat, when he said, "God, I love you."

"What?" I breathed, still panting from Theo's kisses.

"Shit. That wasn't—" Theo brushed a hand through his hair, gaze downturned and a grimace covering his mouth. "That's not how I wanted to say that."

Did that imply he didn't mean it? I was afraid to speak. Afraid I could ruin the perfect moment, or somehow propel the bad one.

"El? Are you okay?"

"Mm-hmm." I nodded, still forcing neutrality.

"Did I scare you?" he asked. I shook my head and narrowed my brows, willing him not to take it back. "I do. Love you, you know? I'm sorry this wasn't romantic, but it was getting hard to hold it in." Why didn't he *start* with that?

"I love you too," I all but hummed.

"Yeah?"

"Yeah."

And then we were kissing again.

Theo did this thing when he kissed me. He would rest his knuckles against my jaw while his thumb stroked the column of my throat. Up and down, slow and purposeful, like he was tracing a path he had memorized. The first time he did it, it tickled a little. No one had ever touched me with that kind of reverence before. But every time after, his touch grew more familiar, until I craved it as much as his lips.

Now, as his thumb moved in time with his mouth, it felt like warm honey cascading down my neck. Electricity buzzed between us. A new surge with every movement, every time a different part of my body connected with his.

Theo's mouth traveled down to my collarbone, nipping and sucking on the delicate skin, eliciting sounds I was sure I had never made before. Everything he did felt incredible. I loved him so much I felt like my chest might crack open.

"Do you want to?" The words slipped away from me, a mind of their own.

The first time I propositioned Theo for sex, I was terrified. The relief I'd felt when he said we should wait made his rejection a little less painful. But now, I wasn't scared or apprehensive. I was needy for him. I wanted to erase every molecule of air between us.

Our foreheads met as Theo peeled his mouth off me, his hungry hazel eyes boring into mine. "Yeah. I really do. But I don't think it's the right time yet."

"Why not?" I sighed.

I watched his brain work, furrowed brows giving away his thought process. But then his expression morphed from solemn to sultry. Whatever his initial reasoning had been, it became something playful and teasing.

"Eliana," he exhaled, shivers skating up every inch of my skin. "There's still a lot we haven't done yet."

I trembled against him as he reached for the hem of my sweater. He lowered his head and started laying hot kisses across my stomach. Wow.

"Can I go down on you?"

"Umm..." I'd asked for sex. I should have been okay with this, right? But somehow it felt more intimate, more vulnerable.

"I think you'll like it," he said, his voice shaky and optimistic.

A quick "okay" tumbled from my lips. He started sliding my leggings off as he glided his own body farther down the couch.

"Just tell me if you want me to stop. You're in control here."

I liked the sound of that. Almost as much as I liked the feel of him as he pressed his mouth between my legs.

"Tell me when it feels good, okay?"

"It, umm, feels good," I whimpered.

His light chuckle vibrated against me, making my hips roll toward him. He lifted his head and kissed the crease of my thigh before he admitted, "I've never actually done this before. Tell me when it feels *really* good." Our eyes met as his confession washed over me. I was thinking I liked sharing a first with Theo. It made me less nervous. "You with me, AG?"

He resumed his teasing as I nodded and *mm-hmm*'d my response. Within seconds I was offering the feedback he requested, and then again, and again, and again, because it just kept getting better. Until I lost the ability to speak entirely.

Theo held on to my hips tightly as I fell apart underneath him, and I was unable to stop the laughter breaking free from my lips.

"That was funny?" He crawled up the length of me, confusion marring his face.

"No. That was awesome," I said through a few shaky exhales. "Can we do it again?"

Theo laughed with me in between pressing kisses to my collarbone.

"Sorry if I was talking too much," I mumbled.

"Are you kidding? That was hot."

"Yeah?" He nodded enthusiastically. "Okay, my turn," I said, pushing off the couch and swapping positions.

"Huh?" he asked.

I straddled his legs and found the button on his jeans. "Tell me when it feels really good, okay?"

Chapter Twenty-One

Ellie

Now

"You scared me, El," Theo says, undoing the laces and sliding off my skates. "I thought you were in pain or having a flare or something. Your face went white as a sheet."

He helps me into my boots and onto the snowmobile for the short ride back to his cabin. I'm not sure why I haven't said anything yet, but my focus is still on my breathing.

When we're back inside, he gives me a warm flannel pajama set to snuggle into—the pants are huge—and tucks me into the blanket fort.

I'm burrowing myself deeper into the cushions when he returns again with a bowl of popcorn and a steaming mug of hot chocolate.

"Are you feeling better?" he asks after I blow some steam off and take a tentative sip.

I let the cocoa warm my throat and take another deep breath. "Yeah. Sorry about that. I think I was just overwhelmed."

"I get it. I really do. I've been living here for over a year now, but sometimes I just get hit with the most random memories. Like I'll be walking on the north side and see the Pizza Emporium sign, and suddenly it's like Dad's right there. I swear I can hear him ordering, making me promise I won't tell mom he asked for extra cheese."

"I miss The Pizza Emporium. I know it was just food coloring, but I swear their crust tasted better."

He chuckles. "It did. It was doughier somehow."

I laugh, but I know my smile doesn't meet my eyes. So many happy memories, but so many sad ones too.

"Tell me," he urges. "What were you thinking about?"

How do I explain what I was seeing? It wasn't just a memory; it was a whole life. The life I had with *him*. I stare down at my mug, watching the powdery bubbles float to the surface, not knowing how to respond. But he won't relent. "Tell me."

My voice is barely a whisper, but I murmur, "Us."

He takes away my mug and sets it on the coffee table. Then his fingers are sliding through my own, locking our hands together.

"Ask me," he says. "Ask me the question you always ask. The one I've been thinking about every Christmas for the last seven years." His hazel eyes capture my gaze, locking me in a trance, making me forget every reason I ever cut ties with this perfect man. "Ask me."

"What do you miss the most?"

"You."

The word falls from his lips like a star falling from the sky. It happens in slow motion, eons passing by, yet somehow so quickly I almost miss it, a comet flying across the horizon. It's barely a breath, the same breath he exhales against my mouth as his lips crash into mine.

A heady mix of chocolate and nostalgia greets my taste-buds. In seconds I am gone. The part of my brain warning me not to get wrapped up in Theo is officially on sabbatical, vacationing in a remote part of The Maldives with no service.

The softness of Theo's lips, the taste of him I always associate with Christmas, the scent of snow and spruce that never leaves his hair even in the heat of summer—they're the only thoughts left in existence.

And then there's a touch of salt, a tear that hits my lips. Is it his or mine?

Theo pulls away and wipes the wet drops from his cheek. "Fuck, I've missed you. So much."

His lips are on mine again, needy and sucking, drawing us closer together. "I missed your pillow forts, and your grilled cheeses." His mouth carves a trail across my jaw, searing my skin, setting me aflame. "I missed holding you. I missed you asking what I miss." He moves lower, his tongue finding all the sweet spots on my neck.

"I missed the look you gave me every year when you were waiting for your snow globe, for that smile that belonged to me." Hot breath along my collarbone that makes me quiver. "I missed the way your entire body shakes when I touch you." He pulls the delicate skin into this mouth, teeth grazing my flesh exactly how he used to.

Theo knew my body better than I thought anyone ever would, and it looks like his memory is firmly intact.

Each kiss draws out more memories, and I start to make my own list of everything I missed. Secret cuddles in my room at night, the steady sound of his heartbeat against my cheek, holding hands while we walked Noodle; the way he kissed me, the way he touched me, the way I felt more myself around him than with anyone else. The list is endless.

"Sometimes I missed you so much," he starts, the words coming out on an exhale, "it was like I forgot how to breathe."

Our lips connect again in a magnetic pull, and it feels like this moment was inevitable. How could I ever stay away from this man?

"Did you miss me, El? Did you miss me like I missed you?" His eyes shine, gold flecks sparkling through the green. God, I adore those eyes. All I can see in them is love.

"Every day." I try to catch my breath, but Theo's lips steal it from me. He presses his hand against my lower back and slides it to my hip, tugging until my body is flush to his. Until I can feel every inch of him pressed up against me.

"I want you so bad, El. I've wanted you since you drove your car into that frozen pond." He sucks my bottom lip into his mouth and moans. "No, fuck that—I've wanted you since the last time I said we should wait."

Dangerous.

This is dangerous territory. Kissing, letting our hands wander, opening up old wounds. We're being reckless.

"Why did you always make us wait?" I manage to get out, afraid yet eager for his answer.

His eyes lock on to mine, filled with a mixture of lust and regret. "I thought we had forever. I wasn't in a rush."

Words become gratuitous after that. There are too many things I do not want to say, do not want to ask, do not want to know. And there are so many better uses for our lips.

Theo must agree, because his mouth is *everywhere*.

Clothing slips from my body through sheer force of Theo's will. My shirt, my bra, and every bit of flannel he wrapped me in all vanish until there's nothing between us but magic in the air.

His head moves down my chest at a blistering pace before

settling above my hips. He is Magellan, exploring so thoroughly that he may as well be drawing a map with his tongue.

God, how I missed this. Theo and I may have never gone all the way, but not-quite-sex with him was still a million times better than any of the men that came after. Theo was *thorough*, he worshipped me. He ruined me for all other men when I was seventeen.

His tongue makes lazy circles, moving up and down from my breasts to my navel and back again. He hooks his thumbs over my thong and pulls it down with him as he sinks lower, my last line of defense.

"Do you think about me?" he rasps. "When you touch yourself." His lips mark my inner thigh with a scorching kiss, erasing every bit of cold I felt today on the ice.

"Yes." The word stretches like taffy from my lips as I arch my back, responding to his touch. Lips on my thigh, fingertips sliding up my hip, hair tickling my most delicate skin. It's overwhelming.

"Do you think about me when other men touch you?" His words are a growl, vibrating against me as I squirm beneath him. His strong hands clamp down my thighs, forcing my body still.

"Yes," I whimper. My head falls back as he touches me exactly where I want him.

"Do you think about my hands or my mouth?" He's teasing me. With his words and the languid strokes of his tongue.

"Both," I admit without giving it a moment's consideration. He's all I ever think about.

"Good."

And just like that, the dam breaks loose.

He buries his head between my legs, kissing and licking and sucking until I'm writhing against him, helplessly moaning his name as I climb over the edge. He holds our connection, and my limbs go soft beneath his touch. The link anchoring us fizzes with heat. Then he's crawling up my body with a satisfied smirk painting his expression.

"Eliana?" I know the question he's asking. I don't even have to think about it.

"Fuck me, Theo. Now."

Part Three:
Karma

"You kept me like a secret, but I kept you like an oath."

Taylor Swift

Chapter Twenty-Two

Ellie

December 27, 2015

MY EIGHTEENTH BIRTHDAY didn't feel right from the start. It was supposed to have been this momentous occasion, crossing that invisible path into adulthood. It was supposed to create a whole new world, full of independence and responsibility and finding yourself.

Not for me.

The first strike against me was only being a junior in high school. When I was younger, missing so much of elementary school and getting held back a year didn't seem like a huge deal, but every year that I got closer to the big one-eight, the age gap between me and the rest of my class felt wider.

But the real issue was my parents, my mom mostly.

Sometimes it was hard to blame her. I could never understand what it might feel like to have a child diagnosed with a potentially fatal illness. I knew how devastating it was for her. It was in her nature to try and protect me, prevent the worst from happening, keep me safe. She really was trying to be a good mother.

But the older I got, the more I realized how stifling she was. I started comprehending my doctors' visits more and more, particularly when they reiterated how mild my symptoms had been from the start. How the stability of my labs and testing over so many years meant that—as long as I kept up with my medicine and lifestyle changes—I was mostly in the clear.

And it became almost impossible not to resent her.

How much of life had I missed out on because she was cautious to the extreme? Because she spent so much time and energy trying to "fix" me? I felt more like a project than a daughter, and this was what really did me in. Of all the things I missed out on, having the kind of mother-daughter relationship I had only seen on screens or heard about from friends at school, that was what I wanted more than anything.

"Which one's that?" Theo said, resting his hands on my shoulders and peering at the screen. He'd been doing some reading for his second semester classes while I researched colleges with him in the basement.

"Dartmouth." One and a half hours. Not far enough. I clicked to my other tab. "And Brown. It's a long shot with mom but they have a pretty good computer science program." Four hours. Too far for my mother to agree and still not enough somehow.

At first, she'd said I would be living at our house and commuting, no questions asked. When I threatened to hitch-hike to Canada and survive as a stripper rather than attend college while living at home, she (Dad) agreed I could live on campus. Within a reasonable distance of course.

Vermont University was the obvious choice. Theo was there, making it attractive to me, and Mom and Dad worked on campus. But I was itching for more distance. Middlebury was on the approved list, and it was almost a full hour's drive. I would see Theo less, but it would also be more difficult for Mom to show up unannounced.

Yet somehow it *still* felt way too close. I didn't want an hour between us. I wanted *years*. I wanted all the years back that she robbed from me. All the years that I could have been a real adventure girl.

"You should apply to Berkeley." Theo's comforting rumble in my ear brought me back to the now. Then Noodle flipped onto his back next to me and his stretched-out paw hit so many buttons I had to close the computer.

"In *California?*" The idea was ludicrous. Mom and Dad didn't fly. I had never even been on a plane before. Any family vacations were by car or train.

"Yeah. Don't they have the best program in the country for computer stuff?"

"How do you know about *computer stuff?*" I quipped.

"You are into computer stuff. Therefore, I am into computer stuff," he said matter-of-factly. "I may have looked it up recently. Just wanted to see what schools were best for you."

I never needed a reminder of how much of my heart I'd given over to Theo, but moments like these did it anyway. His thoughtfulness shone like a starlit sky.

"I've always wanted to go to California. But I think I'd miss the snow," I mused.

"Damn straight you'd miss the snow. I don't know how anyone lives without it. You should apply though. Even if you don't go, wouldn't it be cool to know you got in? It'd be a good opportunity to brag about all those online courses you've taken. You could even show them the website you built."

These were all things I had been planning to include in every application, but I didn't argue with Theo. Everything he was saying latched onto my heart. I knew I couldn't have the experience I wanted, but maybe just knowing it existed, in some alternate universe, would be equally as satisfying.

"All right. I'll apply. Just for fun." I opened up the laptop again—moving Noodle's paw off my thigh—and started my research.

WE WENT to Reggae Night again for New Year's Eve this year, but it felt different. Ez seemed annoyed at me, and after he had a few beers, he wasn't exactly pleasant to be around.

Whether he meant for me to or not, I heard him call me a third wheel and ask Theo why I never had any of my own friends to hang out with, among other hurtful comments. When Theo turned him down to follow some random girls back to their cabin, he got just as annoyed with him.

It was clear he didn't like how close Theo and I had become, even though I was sure he never considered there was anything romantic between us. I couldn't really figure out why he was so against our friendship. Especially when he'd spent so many years helping to cultivate it.

ELLIE

What's his deal?

I texted Theo as soon as we got home and went to our respective rooms. Ezra had followed Theo to the basement, so I didn't even consider sneaking down there. I was also starting to feel some pain in my knees.

THEO

Not sure. Maybe I'll ask him after he stops throwing up

ELLIE

Ew. I've never seen him drink that much

THEO

Yeah, he's usually not so bad. He was
definitely in a mood though

Sorry we had such a shitty New Year's. I'll try
and make it up to you next year

Next year. Despite how upsetting having my relationship
with Theo be a secret, I always held on to the certainty that it
wasn't ending. There was always next year.

ELLIE

It's ok. I still love you

THEO

Love you more

If I wake you up in the morning, will you walk
Noodle with me? I feel like I've barely had a
moment alone with you this week.

ELLIE

We'll see. I can feel a flare coming on so I'm
not sure how I'll be tomorrow

THEO

What hurts?

ELLIE

My legs mostly. Might just be from skating. I
took some drugs so hoping I feel ok in the
morning

Prob won't sleep though ☹

Within thirty minutes, Theo was slipping through my
door.

"Shouldn't you be helping Ezra?"

"He finally passed out. Kind of stole my bed, so I figured I could take his." He sat down on the bed next to me and started sliding his fingers through my hair. "How's my Ellie?"

"Meh."

He slipped under the covers, curling himself around me without actually touching. Theo was fluent in my body language, always knowing what I needed. He didn't try to massage anything, just gently pressed one soft kiss to my shoulder.

"Tell me if you want some space, okay?"

"Actually..."

"Tea?" I nodded against him. "Lemon?" Another nod. "I'll be right back."

Sometimes it felt like Theo was too good. He had already spent half the night taking care of my brother, and now me. Who took care of *him*?

This question plagued my thoughts the rest of the night. Even after he came back with my tea and agreed to watch *Elf* in bed until I got sleepy.

Because no matter how well Theo seemed to keep it together, through his grief and his pressure with school and hockey, everyone needed someone to take care of them. Everyone needed a crutch sometimes. I wondered if Theo had one, if maybe it was me, if a time might ever come when he would need me as much as I needed him.

By MORNING I was feeling much better, and not just because Theo had fallen asleep in my bed.

He woke up nervous about getting caught and fled downstairs quickly to change. It was kind of adorable. He was halfway down the first flight when he ran back up to ask me about all of my symptoms and get an update on my pain level (a two—yay!) and see if I was up for a walk (absolutely!). And after he got dressed, he appeared again with a fresh cup of peppermint tea and my favorite beanie.

"Sure you're feeling better?"

"I am. Just my hips this time. Not a real flare. I'm seeing Dr. Canter next week though, so I'll see what she says."

"You told me it's usually stress-related, right?" We crossed the street, and he looped Noodle's leash around his wrist so he could hold my hand.

"Yeah. That's what they tell me at least." My doctors were constantly talking about stress levels, stress hormones, stress relievers. That word grated on my ears, hearing it so much. Of course I was stressed. What eighteen-year-old wasn't *stressed*? Add in a chronic illness, an overbearing mom, and a secret boyfriend—sure, I was *totally* zen. No amount of yoga was going to clear my head completely. "I'm not sure if I buy into it though. I always have some anxiety. So why do I only get flares every few months? Nothing's different."

"Ez was different last night. That could've been a stressor, right?"

"Umm..." Maybe? I would never blame my brother for a lupus flare, no matter how rude he was. "Anything's possible, but I think it's more about internal stress than something like my brother being a dick. They always warn me to go easy on myself with school, not overdoing it with extra coursework, stuff like that. If there's anything I'm that stressed about, it's where I'll be able to go for college, or just generally dealing with Mom, or..." Our non-relationship. Couldn't say that.

There was an expression on Theo's face I couldn't read. Like he was holding back, chewing on words he wasn't sure how to say. I knew he struggled with my lupus, knew how desperate he was to understand it, to fix something that was unfixable. So I didn't question him.

We got back to the house with Noodle in tow, just as Ezra reached the top stair.

"Mom, can you make pancakes? I feel like shit," he grumbled, dragging his feet to the table and slumping down.

Mom gasped. "Are you sick?" She sprinted toward me and pulled me further away from the kitchen. "You need to put on a mask, Ez. And stay away from Ellie. You should be in your room!"

He didn't budge. "Jesus Christ, Mom. I'm hungover, not contagious. You can stop worrying about your precious Ellie."

The way he said my name then, *precious Ellie*, it was biting. The words clawed at my skin.

"Well, in that case," she replied. "You can make your own pancakes." She turned to me and did the obligatory temperature check. I was beyond grateful that I hadn't had a fever the night before. "What do you want to eat, sweetie?"

Ezra started laughing at the table, the maniacal sound pouring off him in waves, twisting with the smell of alcohol. He reeked.

"Actually, I wanted to make pancakes. For everyone." I opened the fridge and grabbed ingredients. "Blueberry okay, Ez?"

"Whatever," he muttered, before laying his head down on the table.

"I'll help," Theo offered as my mom huffed and disappeared from the kitchen. My family was not looking great today.

Theo came up behind me as I added batter to the griddle and snuck a feathery kiss to the back of my neck. It was impulsive and irresponsible while everyone else was in the house. Maybe that was why it felt so good.

"Don't worry about Ez," he whispered in my ear. "He's just

stressed with school. He loves you." One more soft kiss below my ear. "Just like I do."

I turned and raised a brow at him.

"Okay, not exactly like I do. No one will ever love you like I do." He pressed another kiss into my hair before jumping back when we heard footsteps.

"Morning, Dad."

"Morning, Mr. K." Theo and I spoke simultaneously.

Dad grumbled quick hellos to us before smacking a snoring Ezra on the head.

"Ow! What the fuck?" His head whipped up, leaving a pool of drool in its wake.

"Do we need to have a conversation about your drinking?" Dad announced loudly enough to make Ezra wince.

"It was New Year's Eve. Can you lay off?"

Dad started screaming at Ezra, so I scooped the finished pancakes onto a platter and brought them down to the basement for me and Theo. I had no desire to listen in on that conversation. Neither did Theo.

But the walls weren't thick enough, and we both heard when Ezra yelled, "Now you give a shit about me? When I'm almost twenty-one and had a few beers over the holiday? Nice parenting, Dad. Good to know you actually do realize you have two kids. I'm over this shit."

And then we heard the front door slam and the roll of an engine as Ezra's car spun away.

April 17, 2016

THEO

You'll never believe the call I just got from your mom.

ELLIE

My mom?

WHY WOULD she be calling Theo? This couldn't be good.

THEO

Yep. Get this. She wants me to take you to...

I waited a full minute.

ELLIE

THEO

THEO

Prom! *fireworks emoji*

What? My mother seriously asked him to take me to prom? As what? A fucking favor? Just when I thought she could not get any worse, she pulls something like this to humiliate me further.

Did she think I couldn't get a date? Because I was asked to go. *Twice*. Since I'd never been allowed to attend a dance before, I assumed that hadn't changed. And I didn't want to spend a night with any other guy than Theo anyway.

Getting out of going had been easy. All I had to tell my suitors was that I already had plans that night. I still couldn't utter the word boyfriend without feeling like a complete fraud, but the guys didn't push; they'd been cool with it.

But what was I supposed to tell Mom?

This was why I wished we didn't have to be a secret anymore. Maybe if Mom and Dad realized that Theo saw me as an adult, they would too. It might have been the only way for them to get my permanent invalid status out of their heads.

> **THEO**
> Hello?

> **ELLIE**
> Sorry, just letting it all soak in. I can't believe she did that. Like I'm some charity case

I could picture the conversation between them too. Mom acting all sweet, telling him she would have asked Ezra to do it, but he was just too far away, and Theo was always so *good* with me, so would he mind taking one for the team. Just so I could play normal teenager for the night.

> **THEO**
> Yeah. Not gonna lie, it was weird. But hey, at least I get to see you all dressed up and spend a night together without having to lie to anyone

> **ELLIE**
> But I can't go to prom

> **THEO**
> Why not?

> **ELLIE**
> Because I told the two guys who asked me that I couldn't go

> **THEO**
> My Ellie's a heartbreaker huh?

My Ellie. Never my girlfriend. Would he even be jealous if I went to prom with someone else?

ELLIE

Oh you know it

THEO

Better keep you all to myself then

SHOPPING FOR DRESSES with my mom was one of the most unpleasant experiences of my life. First, because I was eighteen and she still found it appropriate to share a dressing room. I had to wear a sports bra to cover up two hickeys. Second, because she only wanted me to shop in the junior's section. And third— and I knew this was my fault—because I decided it was a good time to ask about going to Brown.

"But it's in Rhode Island, sweetie."

"Yeah, I've looked at a map. I know where it is."

"Ellie." Her gaze pinned me down as she dropped her head to the side. She was looking at me like I was dumb. "We talked about this. Ninety minutes or less. Otherwise I'll never be able to see you."

"You know the point of college isn't to have my mom come visit me, right? Some kids go all the way across the country. Like—" Nope. Not the time to mention California or my Berkeley application. Had to stay on task. "I think it would be a good opportunity for me to gain some independence."

"You're already independent, baby. You're perfect the way you are."

Why did it always feel like she was talking to a toddler? I was half waiting for her to pinch my cheeks.

"Will you please just think about it? Brown has a much bigger computer science program than Middlebury or VU, and the campus looks amazing. I'd really like to apply there."

"But—"

"Mom, I know you mean well, I do. I know you want to keep me safe and healthy, but you need give me the chance to fuck up!"

"Ellie," she placated as usual.

"I need space to breathe, Mom. To live. To screw up and discover my actual limitations. I know school will be hard for me. I know working a full-time job will be hard, maybe even impossible. But how will I even know what I'm capable of if I never try?"

"You're telling me you want to go away to school so you can push yourself to the limit? That is exactly why you shouldn't be on your own. That is reckless and irresponsible and—"

"Maybe it is!" I knew other shoppers could probably hear us, but I was beyond caring. I took a steadying breath and continued. "But I want the choice. I would hope that you have enough faith in me to know I'll make smart decisions. I just want to be able to choose for myself. For once in my life."

So what if choice breeds uncertainty and regret, isn't that what freedom is? Having the ability to regret things? Being able to make a decision and knowing you'll deal with the consequences, good or bad? I wanted that power. I wanted it desperately.

Nothing I said was enough. We ended the day with no spoils and no resolution to the college conversation. When we got home, I begged her to let me go shopping on my own another day, to do one thing for myself. I hated how reliant I was on her, but without a job, I was completely tethered to my parents financially. I knew I was lucky we could afford college, especially thinking about how hard Theo worked for a scholarship, but what was the point when I was completely lacking in autonomy?

Mom didn't like the idea of me shopping without her, but

she caved once I used the argument that she picked my date so I should get to pick my dress.

The next week, I scoured boutiques all over campus until I finally found the right one, the one I knew Theo would love. It was a simple silk slip that somehow gave me curves, but it was the color that really called to me. Sure, white was a little bridal-esque, but I wasn't actually going to the dance anyway. No one would be able to judge me. And I knew exactly what Theo would think when he saw me in it.

"You look like snow," Theo said, his voice catching. He ran his hands down the length of his thighs like he needed something to occupy them. Then he kissed me.

He waited until we were in the car of course, but I saw the look on his face before we left the house. The moment he opened the door he was tongue-tied, and I knew I had been right about the dress.

"I like you in a suit," I murmured. "I know you said you have to wear them for hockey all the time, but I don't think I've ever seen you in one."

He smiled, loosening his tie before taking it off altogether and tossing it in the backseat.

"This thing is so uncomfortable. But luckily I don't need it where we're going."

"You mean to your dorm?" I asked.

"Nope." His eyes danced with mirth.

"I thought we were gonna watch that new series about whales?"

"I decided we should do something else, something special. We don't always have this much time together. And you don't always look like that."

"Theo! Spill!" I grinned and shoved at his chest before I noticed where he was exiting the highway. We were heading to Sugar Valley.

I had only ever visited once when there wasn't snow on the ground, the time Carol gave me and Mom a tour of Moon River, the animal sanctuary. I didn't even remember what the rest of the village looked like in the spring.

Theo drove us toward the tree farm that was scattered with balsam firs and white spruce of every height. It was clear the farm hadn't been tended to in years, but it was still beautiful. And the aroma sent my system into overdrive. It was the same smell I associated with birthdays and happy memories and more than anything, Theo.

"Okay, you have to stay in the car for a few minutes so I can set everything up." Normally I would argue, but I was brimming with nervous energy. The good kind.

My eyes tracked him disappearing behind the copse of trees, and with him went my earlier trepidation over the prom-or-no-prom decision. Sitting at my vanity and curling my hair today, I'd let my uncertainty get the better of me. *Should I take Theo to prom? Should I just go through the motions, with the rest of my class? Should I have said yes to Brad or Chad?* Now, though...anticipation flickered across my skin.

I had never done things the conventional way, whether by choice or not. And being here with Theo, not even knowing what was about to happen, I was certain there was nowhere else I'd rather be.

The sky was painted a murky shade of lavender as the sun hid behind the mountains to the west. It was just dark enough that my vision sparked when I saw the lights turn on. Hundreds of them, twinkling among the trees like constellations falling from the sky.

I rushed out of the car and found Theo in the middle of the glittering scene laying a large blanket on the ground.

He looked up and caught my gaze, a smile stretching from his lips. "Dance floor." He nodded to the blanket. Then he made his way to a speaker propped up on a tree stump and started swiping on his phone. Taylor Swift's "Christmas Tree Farm" rang around us, and his eyes found mine again. I laughed. This wasn't exactly the kind of song couples danced to at prom—in May.

But then he changed the song. It was something slower, tropical. I remembered it from the first time we went to Reggae Night at Stowe. He told me that night it was one of his favorites, how he wished we could have skated alone while it played.

"Dance with me?" he asked.

I fell into Theo's arms and swayed to the music, still unconventional, and so perfectly *us*.

We slipped off our shoes, and Theo removed his jacket, getting more comfortable as the night wore on. His hands wandered over my silky dress as we danced, driving me wild with his heated touch. When the sky turned black and darkness crept over us, the lights shone even brighter, bathing us in a shimmering luster. No one could ever tell me this wasn't better than going to prom.

There was only one thing holding this night back from sheer perfection.

"Theo?" The song was slow, Ed Sheeran maybe? Theo held me tightly against him while my cheek rested on his chest.

"Yeah?"

"Why aren't we boyfriend and girlfriend? I mean, I feel like we are most of the time. But I really hate keeping this all a secret." It was easier to ask when he couldn't see my face, his chin balancing on the top of my head. I felt him try and pull back so we could look at each other, but I held us in place, wanting the metaphorical distance.

"I'm sorry, El. It's not fair to you." He tugged a little. "Please look at me?"

I pulled away as our dance came to a halt, his arms still circling my waist. He dipped his head to kiss me, and it was a soft, barely-there caress of his lips.

"Can you put up with me for a little longer?" he pleaded. "I just don't wanna fuck this up with your family. I know it's still lying, but I'd rather let them think this started after you went to college. If they knew I've loved you since you were fifteen, they would probably ban me from ever seeing you again."

Was he wrong? I had no idea what Mom and Dad would say. I wasn't allowed to date. Did that mean I wasn't allowed to love Theo?

In my heart, I was still more worried that they would think Theo was too good for me. Mom constantly reminded me that I wasn't a *normal* kid, or a *normal* girl. I wasn't supposed to think about boys at all, because why would one be interested in a sick girl like me?

Maybe Theo was right. Waiting until I was out from under Mom's thumb made sense. Even if they didn't like the idea of us together, once I was gone from that house, it wouldn't matter. They wouldn't be able to control me anymore. Not completely.

I rolled Theo's words over in my head a few times before I picked up on the most significant part. "You've loved me since I was fifteen?"

He grinned. "Longer. But if I say that out loud, I feel like a creep."

"I think I've loved you since I was nine. Since you gave me my first snow globe."

Theo pulled me in closer for a kiss, his fingers tangling

through my hair. "Give me another year and I promise everything will work out. Can you wait for me?"

Of course I agreed. I would do anything to be with Theo. In that moment, I wondered why I was pushing Mom so much on college. Shouldn't I want to stay in Vermont? To be as close to Theo as possible? I couldn't imagine willingly putting more distance between us than we already had. Even thinking about being on opposite sides of the country made my chest ache.

Theo grabbed the snacks he packed from the car, and we sat down on the blanket.

"I love being here, even without the snow," I admitted, my voice blending with the soft notes from the music. We were munching on spoonsful of crunchy peanut butter—my obsession—while we star-gazed. "It still feels magical."

"I'm getting it back," Theo all but declared.

"What do you mean?" I turned my body to face him fully, noting the determination in his eyes.

"I signed with the Bruins. After I graduate next year, I'll be playing professionally. And the second I have enough money, I'm buying this back. I just need to talk to the owners. Convince them to sell." My ears rang and my pulse quickened. *Holy shit.*

"*Theo.* How did you not tell me any of this before? That's amazing!" I leaned over to steal a quick kiss. "You're seriously going to be a Bruin? I'm gonna buy everything I can find with your name on it! And you'll have to sign it all, obviously."

"Don't get too carried away. I'll be starting on the development team." He nudged my shoulder so he could wrap his arm around me. "Hopefully not for too long though. Providence sounds boring." He sucked in a shallow breath. "And too far from you."

"We could always blackmail Mom into letting me go to Brown. Got any dirt on her?"

"I wish. Has she said anything else about it since your last talk?"

"Nope. I tried talking to Dad, but he just said he'd have to talk to her about it. Dead end."

There was a long beat of silence, and I wondered what he was thinking about. For me, it was calculating how often I would get to see him after next year, trying to map in my head which approved colleges were closest to Providence or Boston. But when he finally spoke, I realized he was thinking the same thing.

"You know none of it matters, right? Wherever you go to school, wherever I end up playing, it won't change anything between us. Even now, I know we don't get to see each other as much as we want to, but it will all be worth it. Because one day in the not-so-distant future, we'll see each other every day. You'll be sick of me."

"Never!" I leaned in for another kiss and his strong hand gripped the back of my neck, squeezing as he kissed me back. His kiss was filled with so much promise, a future I could taste on his lips.

He pulled back from me, barely an inch between us, but enough space to find my eyes. "It's ridiculous how much I love you."

"Ridiculous," I repeated on a whisper. I squeezed my eyes shut, urging the tears to stay lodged in each socket. I'd spent so much of my time in my head, going back and forth about what our relationship meant, why we had to keep it private, how my parents were doing everything in their power to impede it without even knowing.

I lived in my anxiety, unable to escape the constant internal questions. But then Theo said things like that, and it made my head quiet. Even if it only lasted a moment, it was a moment of peace that he gifted me.

"Would you ever want to live here?" he asked.

I started at the abrupt change in subject. "*Here*, here? Like with the trees?"

He laughed. "I mean here, at the village. I don't know. I always have this vision of you and me living in a cabin in the woods, going skating whenever we want, helping out at the animal sanctuary if I get it up and running again." I heard him sniff. "It probably sounds stupid, but—"

"It sounds amazing. But won't you be living where your team plays?"

"Yeah, I will. But not forever. The goal is to get back here, eventually."

We cuddled under the starry sky a while longer. Until his alarm went off letting him know he had to get me home. I spent the whole time imagining what it would be like to live with Theo.

In a little cabin in the woods.

Chapter Twenty-Three

Theo

Now

FUCK ME, Theo. Now.

Ellie's voice rings through my head. *God* if those words don't do something to me. I scoop her off the couch and decide there's no time like the present to live out the number-one fantasy I had throughout high school and college. Walking us into the kitchen, I lay her out on the island.

Her skin is still flushed from coming on my tongue, and I take a moment to admire her body displayed in front of me. Ellie was always beautiful. Even when she was a teenager, she had these big brown eyes that made you want to write a love song. As she got older, her smile could bring me to my knees, no matter what was going on around us.

All those things are still true, but she's different now. Her body has curves, a suppleness that didn't exist when we were younger. It's all been hidden under her winter clothes this week and I can't seem to get my fill, no matter how long I look.

"Theo?"

"Sorry. I'm just gonna be honest. I sort of zoned out staring at your tits."

"Yeah, I noticed." She blows a piece of hair out her face as she leans forward, balancing on an elbow. "You wanna do something about this?" She grabs onto my erection and smirks. "Or should we try making snow angels instead? Hmm?"

I don't remember ever hearing that kind of snark come out of her mouth. It surprises me, but I don't hate it either.

"You've changed so much." She scrunches her face and I know I've offended her. "No, come here," I say, pulling her up to me, letting my fingers trail down her bare skin. "You're different. And I like it. There's *nothing* I don't like about you, El."

"I'm not a kid anymore," she whispers against my mouth, reaching for my shirt and tearing it off. Then she finds her voice again, the new one that's so intriguing. "And I'm done taking no for an answer. Don't make me wait any longer."

"I won't." I kiss her, deeply, proving the truth of my words. There is nothing I don't like about Ellie. "And not everything has changed. You still make the same sound right before you come." I trail my lips down her throat and whisper, "Three quick breaths. I missed that too." She gasps and I steal another kiss.

I say a quick prayer to the kitchen gods that I still have a pack of condoms in my junk drawer—it's been a while—and after a quick and successful search, I lose the rest of my clothes and slide one on faster than I ever have.

"Finally," Ellie crows, just before I press into her.

"Have you ever...?" It's a question I don't want to ask, but an answer I need to know. It slides through my lips as we draw together, erasing all the space between us.

"Yes." The answer comes out under her breath, followed by an even quieter, "And every time, I wished it were you."

Fuck. It should have been me. It should have *always* been me.

She wraps her arms around my neck, lifting her hips and digging her heels into my back. There's a split second when I wonder if this is right, if this is good enough for our first time together after all the waiting. But it feels effortless, *natural*, and we find the perfect rhythm in seconds.

"Ellie," I rasp. "Fuck, you feel good." She whimpers in response, letting her head fall back as I chase the perfect angle. I hold her to me, not wanting any space between our bodies ever again, like I can erase the years we spent apart as well.

Our skin feels magnetic. Our bones, our blood, seeking out their other half. My lips refuse to leave her neck. Her hands mold themselves to my shoulders until we're one being, one breath, one heartbeat drumming together.

"Is this what you imagined?" I breathe out, both palms pressed to her back, lifting her a little higher off the island.

She moans against me, before she reaches for my hand and slides it down between our bodies. I always loved when Ellie took charge, but this time there is zero hesitation. It's like all her insecurities have melted away, and I can't help but wonder if it's me or time that has had that effect.

I follow her lead, letting my fingers find all the spots that draw out more sounds, that make her hips move closer.

"It's better," she cries out in between breaths. Her panting slows as she presses her mouth to my shoulder and gently bites the skin below my neck. "How are you so good at this?"

My movements pause and I grab her chin, seeking eye contact with the woman I love. We're both gasping for air, breathless with need for each other. Sweat slides down my chest as I pull her face to me, our noses grazing. "It's good because it's us."

Her heels dig into the backs of my thighs in response, and I lose myself in her again; in the sounds she's making, in the marks she's creating on my back, in the heat of her.

I wrap my arms around her back, my fingertips branding the nape of her neck and the skin along her ribs and walk us toward the steps until I have her up against the wall. Her legs squeeze my waist as I have her pinned to me.

"Is this okay?" I ask, my nose buried in the crook of her neck again. I can't fucking get enough of her.

"Are you kidding? You don't have to be gentle with me. I won't break. You've got Stanley Cup hockey muscles." She squeezes her legs around me tighter still. "Use them."

Her hands trail from my shoulders to my wrists, to my abs, scratching and squeezing each swell and groove of my body. I lift one of her legs and throw it over my arm, reeling in the little squeal she gives me that is drenched in approval.

Minutes pass as I we rock against each other, falling deeper into this spell of our bodies, trying to feel every inch of skin, trying to fuse what's broken.

"Theo," she murmurs under my ear, her voice shaking, needy and expectant.

"I got you."

I walk us back to the pillow fort and lay her down as gently as I can. My body follows hers down, pulling her to me, already missing the way she tastes.

"Tell me what you w—"

She presses her hands into my chest and pushes me hard enough to roll us over on the mattress. Her hands stay clasped to my skin as she moves her legs to straddle me. "No more talking," she chirps into my ear.

Her lips capture mine and she rolls her hips forward, seating herself fully.

I easily obey the command, lying back to enjoy the view. The view of her taking exactly what she wants from me. The view of the most beautiful girl I've ever seen, naked and riding me.

The view I thought only existed in my dreams.

THE FIRST YEAR I spent without Ellie, while she was on the other side of the country, I dreamt of her almost every night. Sex appeared sporadically, but usually, I just woke up thinking she was still wrapped in my arms.

Now, I've had her every way I've imagined, and I just want to keep holding her. It doesn't hurt that she's naked. Naked cuddling is something we rarely had the opportunity for, so I'm making up for lost time.

The problem is I can't stop thinking about lost time. All the time we didn't have together over the last seven years. I'm not sure how to focus on the future without understanding the past. I want to pretend that I'm over it, that I don't need the answers I have been searching for throughout her absence.

That I'm not terrified it's about to happen again.

But I don't know if I can.

Dusk hovers outside the window, alerting me that my time with Ellie is ticking away. But then I'm distracted by a red bushy tail.

"Ellie, look." I'm not sure why I'm whispering. It isn't like they can hear us through the door, but I point to the window, wanting her to see the small family of foxes playing outside.

"Oh my gosh!" she exclaims, sitting up and covering herself with the quilt. "They're adorable."

We watch as three foxes roll around in the snow, jumping and diving headfirst into the fresh powder. I've seen a few of them around the village but never like this. Without the regular cars and people, they must feel safer than usual, like this terrain belongs to them.

"They're beautiful. Do you know what they're called? A group of them?" she asks me, her features wide with anticipation.

"I'm a Fox, Ellie. Of course, I know." I press a kiss to her neck, right under her ear. The breathy sound I'm rewarded with feels like some kind of drug. "Sometimes they're called a leash or a skulk, but my favorite is an earth. An earth of foxes. Like they have their own little world."

"I love that." Her lips tug into a smile. It starts small and widens until it reaches all the way to her eyes. The kind of slow smile that turns my heart to mush. "I finally got to see a fox in the snow."

She turns in my arms until her back is flush to me and we watch the foxes play until they disappear into the woods. We keep watching even after they're gone. I love this view. There's a reason I built the cabin here. You can see the southern mountains in the distance, a sliver of the tree farm to the east, my favorite rink if you look straight ahead.

Tranquility via a simple windowpane.

"Did you see that?" Ellie points to where a fluffy rabbit has just run across the yard. "He was huge!"

"Yeah, we get a little of everything out here in the valley. I even saw a black-and-white spotted one the other day. Like a little cow-rabbit."

"You sure it wasn't just a skunk?"

"I'm sure. I also happen to know the collective noun for rabbits. But I'm not sure you could handle it."

"Theo, come on. I think I'll be okay."

"I don't know. It's almost *too* cute."

"Tell me!" She twists and wiggles in my arms before pinching my side.

"Okay, okay. You win. They're called a fluffle." She turns to me and her brown eyes go wide like they used to whenever I'd surprise her at my dorm with eggrolls.

"Really? You're not making that up?"

"I wouldn't dare. Collective animal nouns are sacred, El."

"I want to be in a fluffle," she muses.

"I'll be in a fluffle with you."

I lay her onto the mattress and kiss my way down her neck, her chest, all while contemplating what someone would call us, if there's even a word in the English language that could simplify what it's like when we're together.

Nothing big enough exists.

Ellie is asleep in minutes after we fall back onto the pillows, her neck still flushed and her hair a tousled mess. I'm amazed at how easily she sleeps these days. I can't stop staring at her. Can't stop thinking about the past. Can't stop worrying about the future.

There is a desperation seeping into my bones, desperation to keep us in this perfect bubble as long as I can.

I slide off the mattress and grab some clothes, taking careful steps to avoid the creaks in the floorboards. I need to clear my head, and more importantly, I need to check on the generator. Our power seems to be working just fine, but I wouldn't be surprised if it's running on fumes.

It's only a matter of time before I have to let Ellie know what's going on.

"WHAT THE ACTUAL FUCK?"

The generator is almost completely full. It looks the same as it did last night when I filled it with the last of our fuel. It should be empty. Which tells me it's clearly broken. So how the hell do we have power?

"Hey." I turn and find Ellie in the garage, wrapped in two quilts and wearing a pair of my boots that must be twice the size of her feet. She looks ridiculous, but I'm glad she came outside prepared. Even if the garage is fully heated, the ten steps to get here are not. "I thought I heard a drunken sailor."

"Sorry if I woke you." I realize for the first time how quiet it is out here. The storm seems to have passed for now. It's cold enough that none of the snow has melted, making driving impossible, but the air is eerily silent. No wonder she could hear me. "I, umm, need to show you something."

I show Ellie the generator and soon find she has no idea how it works, so I walk her through that as well.

"So, it's just...working? Without using any fuel?" She finally understands my bewilderment.

"Basically. I don't have another explanation. But however it's working, I don't know how much longer it'll last." I catch her gaze, needing to see her reaction to our predicament. "We may want to leave now, just in case. All the heat is electric. You know how fast the cabin freezes up once the power goes out."

She watches me with an open mouth, like her lips can't decide which words to let slip. "Leave?" she asks.

I can taste her reluctance. It energizes me. It gives me all the hope I need.

"Or we can chance it, live on the edge while we wait to see what happens. Worst-case scenario, I can get us out of here on the snowmobile and get to a place with cell service. It'll be tough, but doable." I watch her nibble the inside of her cheek, weighing the options. *She's fighting back a smile.*

This is my Ellie—*my adventure girl*—grinning back at me. The girl I fell in love with making snow angels at midnight. The one I've been waiting not so patiently to return to me.

"Fuck it." She smirks, dropping the quilts. I almost choke on the vision in front of me: a stark-naked Ellie in nothing but my snow boots. She walks over to the snowmobile and perches her ass on the edge of the front seat. "Let's be lobsters. I feel like taking a risk."

Chapter Twenty-Four

Ellie

December 22, 2016

Two DAYS.

Two days and Theo would be here for Christmas. Two days and I could finally tell someone about the email that was burning a hole in my inbox.

Two days and I could have the conversation I had been dying to have, with someone who would take me seriously, who would be able to celebrate this alternate universe with me before it disappeared back into the ether.

Two days passed, but then my brother called.

ELLIE

Ez just said he won't be back till Christmas Eve because you two are going to Stowe together. What's going on?

THEO

Yeah

He was kind of pissed last year that we didn't get to do much, just us

I'm a hot commodity with the Klein family ;)

ELLIE

I feel like I haven't seen you in forever between hockey and school. I was so excited for today.

THEO

It's just an extra two days apart. Please don't give up on me

I'll be thinking about you the whole time

Gotta jump in the shower before he gets here. I'll see you soon, El

ELLIE

As long as you'll be thinking about me in the shower...

TWO MORE DAYS.

Not just two days waiting to see Theo, but two days with no response to my last text.

Yeah. I was losing my mind.

I had woken up on Christmas Eve *knowing* he'd messaged me, grabbing my phone with a ferocity that I never had first thing in the morning. But seeing the void where all his messages were meant to be, it filled me with a strange pit of dread. Something was wrong. I didn't know what it was, but I knew it existed.

Theo had never once not responded to me. Never not called when he said he would. He was always reliable, always respectful, always perfect. And while I wanted to be the coolest version of myself, the girl who wasn't needy or clingy, I couldn't stop myself from making a call.

Three calls. Three times I tried calling over two days and each one went straight to voicemail. Something had to be wrong.

And when Ezra showed up, very noticeably *sans* Theo, I knew I was right. Something was very, very wrong.

"Where's Theo? I thought you were driving over together from Stowe?" Mom asked, leaving me grateful not to be the one to do it.

"Oh, he didn't tell you? He's spending the holiday with his girlfriend's family up in Montreal."

"His *what?*" The words spewed out of my mouth along with some weird croaking sound as I tried to keep my lungs from malfunctioning.

Theo did not have a girlfriend. He had me. *His Ellie.* There was no way he could have kept this from me. But then I heard it, distantly through the screaming in my head, Ezra was telling my parents about her. Chloe. She was a cross-country skier, half French, and gorgeous because of course. She was *real?*

How was this possible? How could he have lied to me? We were...we were...fuck. I didn't know how to finish the thought. What were we, actually? To me, Theo was everything with a capital E. He was the only person who *got* me, who saw me, who made me feel like I was worth something.

But what was I to him? My home life was so sweltering he wanted to keep us a secret, because who would ever want to date a girl with parents like mine? Theo could have any girl he wanted. I doubt Chloe had a nine o'clock curfew at nineteen or had to fake going to yoga class just to see him. I bet she had experience with boys, had tons of friends, had a whole life for herself.

A cross-country skier? Really? She was probably healthy and perfect, just like Theo. And why wouldn't he be with a perfect girl? Why *shouldn't* he?

I felt dizzy. Everything in my vision that was once clear started to blur. I could feel the gazes of my family land on me, seeing this visceral reaction to something they didn't understand, and I ran up the stairs.

Tears cascaded down my face as I sprinted to the bathroom and emptied the contents of my stomach. I gagged and heaved until there was nothing left in my gut but sadness and despair.

I had never trusted another human being the way I did Theo. How could he do this to me?

And then I thought, could he actually do this? I slumped onto my bed and grabbed my phone.

ELLIE

Is it true? You're not coming?

I felt stupid for texting him, considering he hadn't responded to any of my calls, but then the typing bubble appeared, and I held my breath.

THEO

I'm so sorry Ellie

He was sorry. Fucking *sorry*?

For what? For lying to me this whole time? For making me believe that he loved me? For ignoring me for two days so he could let my brother break the news to me? For making Christmas plans with someone else on *our* holiday, on my birthday?

THEO

Let's talk when I get back in town, okay?

Happy birthday

I *roared*.

My anguish wasn't comparable to anything I had experienced in life. The pain surged in my blood, my bones. My lungs were on fire, too brittle to let me cry another tear. I felt like I was dying.

"Ellie?" Mom entered the room without so much as a knock. Just another reminder of how pathetic my life was. Almost nineteen and with zero privacy. Couldn't she give me a moment to grieve in peace?

"What do you want?" I didn't have the energy to pretend away how I was feeling.

"Look, sweetie. I know you're upset about Theo. We all are. We've spent your birthday and Christmas together for so long I can't remember what we even did before. Well, we didn't celebrate Christmas, that's for sure." I silently thanked her for the reminder, not trusting the expletives that were begging to leave my mouth and attack. "Don't be so upset, baby. He has his own life too."

"I'm not upset!" I couldn't stop myself from lashing out. I was so tired of her never taking me seriously.

"Ellie. Come on. I don't know what's gotten into you, but you need to snap out of it, okay? Getting worked up like this isn't good for someone like you." She paused for a quick temperature check because why *wouldn't she* be more concerned about me working myself up into a flare than my actual feelings. "Maybe it's my fault for letting you go to prom with him. I just wanted you to be able to be a normal kid for a change."

"*I am normal!* You're the only one who doesn't see me that way. And Theo didn't take me to prom because he felt bad for me. He likes me."

"Of course he likes you," she said, her voice sugary sweet. "But that doesn't mean he can't have a girlfriend. You're like a little sister to him, baby."

I couldn't listen to any more of this. How was I supposed to prove her wrong? Tell her about Theo going down on me in the shower last time they left me home alone? God, part of me wanted to. And part of me knew that, even then, she would just think I was delusional.

She only ever saw what she wanted to see. She barely knew who I was. Aside from my illness, did she think there was anything else worth knowing?

"I want to be alone."

Mom looked like she wanted to argue but eventually left my room—door open, of course.

I stayed upstairs through dinner, headphones in the whole time so I wouldn't overhear them talking about me.

"Hey, Ellie, can I come in?" A couple of hours had passed when Ezra knocked loudly enough for me to hear over the emo music in my ears.

I didn't want to see him. I knew he was laughing at me, just like Mom and Dad. My anger toward Theo for keeping us a secret grew exponentially at the realization. *My whole family thinks I'm pathetic.*

"What do you want?"

He came inside and shut the door. He actually looked concerned. "I wanted to talk to you, about Theo."

"I could care less about Theo, okay?" I wasn't sure why I took this route, but I refused to let Ezra see how torn up I was about my not-boyfriend. I didn't want him to have anything to go back to Theo with that would further my embarrassment.

"It's okay, Ellie. Just tell me what's going on."

"It has nothing to do with Theo. I mean sure. I don't like that he bailed at the last minute. We have a tradition." Because

I could at least call him out on that. He was bailing on Ezra and my parents too. "I'm just fed up with Mom and Dad about college."

"Oh. This isn't all about Theo?" He motioned to the room around me. "Mom was pretty sure you're in love with him or something."

Was she for real? Could she have *found* a better way to kick me while I was down? This ended *now*.

"In love with him? Give me a break, Ez. I'm not nearly as pathetic as you all think I am. I'm just dying to get out of this fucking house, but Mom is determined to keep me as a prisoner forever." I huffed out a breath and realized that while I was definitely lying about Theo, I was also being honest.

I had *the* college acceptance letter sitting in my inbox. The one I was planning to show Theo when he got here. The college no one else even knew I applied to because it was only ever a dream. The one that was three thousand miles farther away than anywhere on the approved list.

The one I couldn't stop thinking about. Because Theo told me it didn't matter, that wherever I went to school, and wherever he played hockey, nothing would change with us. Apparently, he was right. Nothing would change, because we were never what I thought we were to begin with.

Fuck him for making me dream like that.

"I'm angry because they won't let me go where I want for school, okay? That's it. It just happened to coincide with Theo bailing."

A whole range of emotions skated over Ezra's features. Uncertainty, guilt, and resignation all visible, albeit confusing. "Sorry, Ellie. I can try talking to them for you? I want to help. Maybe Dad will listen to me."

"Don't bother." I offered the biggest smile I could muster— it was tiny—because he was actually being really nice to me.

"Will you do me a favor and tell Mom I'm not feeling well? I'm gonna go to sleep and I really don't want her up here bugging me."

"For sure. Feel better, sis."

THEO

> Happy New Year! Hope you and Latke aren't having too much fun without me ☺

> Just got back from Montreal. Can we talk? I've tried calling you a few times but it just goes to voicemail

> Did Ezra say something to you?

> Please call me back? I really don't want to do this over text

<<You have successfully blocked this number>>

HE DIDN'T WANT to do this over text? What was *this*? Tell me about his girlfriend? Break up with me? Explain how he could keep seeing us both?

No thanks.

I might not have been experienced with boys, or ever actually dated anyone else. I might have lived a sheltered life and come across shy or reserved to some people. But I had a fucking backbone. It didn't matter how much I thought I loved Theo, no one was allowed to treat me that way.

I did some major soul-searching after my birthday. Well, I made the decision to be over Theo. My heart wasn't exactly cooperating, but my brain was on board. No more energy was going toward caring about Theo.

The best part was that I quickly realized he was the only tether I had to Vermont. The only reason I ever felt okay about being stuck here.

Sure, I had friends at school. But no one that I was super close to. They all had these huge lives outside of their time with me. The same went for my brother. Our relationship ebbed and flowed these days, but even through the good times he was away at Harvard.

I wanted to matter, to make my mark. And the only person I truly believed I had accomplished that with was Theo. I thought I was stamped as a permanent fixture in his life. I was wrong. So there was nothing left for me here, which made me especially reckless.

I knew what I wanted, and I wasn't going to give up without a fight. The fight of my fucking life.

I marched into the kitchen, filled with the determination of an Olympian.

"Mom." I waited for her to acknowledge me. "I got accepted to UC-Berkeley. That's where I want to go to school."

She was dumbfounded, stuttering words I could barely make out. But I couldn't tell if she was confused on her behalf or mine. "UC, as in California?" She finally got out.

"Yes. It's the top computer science program in the country. Feel free to say congratulations. Or not. I don't really care as long as you let me go."

"Okay, enough with the attitude, sweetie. Since when did you apply to schools in California?" She braced her hands on the island, arms locking in place. "We never even discussed this."

"Of course we didn't. Because you would have said no. You didn't even want me to apply to Brown and that's in Rhode

Island! I got in there too by the way." And I would have been begging to go there right now if it weren't for Theo. Turned out colleges liked my story. I wasn't exactly trying to use lupus to my advantage, but it was part of me. Part of the reason I was so desperate to go away to school. Between that, my stellar test scores, and all the online coding classes I had already taken in secret, colleges found me pretty desirable.

At least someone did.

"Ellie..." Mom looked flummoxed, her usually rosy cheeks going pale. It was like she didn't recognize me, wasn't sure what language I was speaking. But I was not backing down this time. I didn't care if she cried. I didn't care what reasoning she had saved in her arsenal titled "Why Ellie Can't." Because people-pleasing Ellie was gone. I was finally going after what *I* wanted. And this was the only thing I wanted.

It was all I had left.

"I've done all the research. The tuition's less than Middlebury—which you already agreed to. It's a lot less actually, which will more than make up for flights and any other extra costs. I won't need a car there so you can sell mine and put that toward living expenses too. I'll even get a job while I'm in school to cover extra expenses."

"Money isn't the issue, sweetie. You just can't go so far away. I would never see you. How will I be able to take of you—"

"I'll take care of myself! Here." I laid out the pages I'd printed with the all the information I'd gathered since New Year's. "I've established care with three doctors. I'll be able to get an appointment with all of them as soon as I get there." I pointed to the first sheet. "This is supposedly the best rheumatologist in California. She's only a ten-minute ride from campus. And Dr. Adler,"—I pointed to another sheet—"he's in the city, so I'll have to take the BART—that's the San Francisco train—but he's a world-renowned endocrinologist and happens to specialize in cortisol issues. Perfect, right?"

"There are more than enough schools to choose from in New England, honey. The answer's no. California is just way too far from home."

"This house is not a home. Not anymore. Not to me. It's a fucking prison."

"Ellie—"

"What? What other reasons could you possibly have for why I can't go? You said we have the money. I found all the doctors I could ever need. I'm not afraid to fly and you never have to come and visit me, okay? I don't even want you to." I was screaming, and my voice had become raspy with desperation. Years of pent-up hostility were manifesting themselves in this storm brewing in my kitchen "Their acceptance rate is fourteen percent. Fourteen! And *I* got in. So tell me. Why can't I go?"

"You can go." My dad's voice echoed through the room. "Just please stop yelling at your mother. You can go."

I was speechless. I hadn't even thought of going to Dad with this, considering he just deferred to Mom whenever I asked for something. He was trumping her for me? Gratitude trickled out of me. Before I could thank him, though, Mom cut in again.

"Joel, hold on a sec. She can't go to school in California," she repeated, acting like I wasn't even there. "And she lied to us about applying. We are not rewarding her for it."

"And why do you think she lied?" He turned back to me. "Sweet pea, I'm so proud of you. And I'm sorry you thought you couldn't tell us about this." He was getting choked up and it reminded me of when he told Theo about his scholarship.

Dad and I hadn't been close the last few years. He worked all the time, played golf every weekend. We didn't have the same kind of relationship we did when I was young. And every time I tried talking to him about colleges, he just repeated that we'd need to discuss it with my mother.

"I've obviously failed you as a parent if you were afraid to tell me you got in to a top-ten school," he continued. His eyes grew watery as he shuffled closer to me and held out his arms. "Is it too late to say congratulations?"

I hugged my dad tight enough that I felt the years we'd lost spark back to life. He was granting me freedom. In that moment, I felt like I had sprouted wings.

"We need to talk about this." Mom glared at him. "We have a sick child, or have you forgotten? How am I supposed to take care of our daughter when she's thousands of miles away?"

Dad kept one arm around me as he turned to her and spoke. "Well, she was pretty successful in this ambush." He gestured to all the papers I had spread out on the island: the doctor credentials and confirmations, the tuition budget I had prepared, the maps outlining how I would get to and from campus to each doctor and closest hospital. "I think she might be able take care of herself."

Mom's face fell as she walked around us and sank down into a chair at the dining table. I felt the zap of tension forming between her and Dad and hated being the cause, but I was finally getting something I wanted.

It wasn't the first time they'd fought about me. They were good at hiding it, usually keeping their voices hushed in the privacy of their room. But I always knew. Having a chronically ill kid was apparently tough on a marriage. This was something I understood so well that for years I strived to never be an inconvenience.

But with all thoughts of Theo being shoved out of my head, I had one singular goal, and this was it. I didn't care who it hurt or what I had to do. In that moment, I didn't care what it did to my parents' relationship or how they felt about me.

I couldn't even stop myself from asking for more.

"Dad?" He glanced down at me, a sad smile softening his features. "If I start classes this summer, I could catch up to kids my own age. With all the APs I've been taking, I could graduate in three years."

"All right," he said, directing us both into his home office. He grabbed his laptop and handed it to me. "Let's make this official."

Chapter Twenty-Five

Ellie

Now

"HE'S STARING AT YOU AGAIN," *Maya whispers, leaning across the table. She blows on her coffee so loudly I worry we'll be shushed while her eyes follow the man in question to the other side of the library.*

"*Don't look!*"

"*Why? He's cute. And clearly into you.*"

"*I know. We're sort of...dating.*" *I mumble the last part, but she hears me. And she's pissed.*

"*Eliana Klein, you have a* boyfriend? *And you didn't tell me? What the hell?*"

"*Be quiet,*" *I all but shriek, sinking into my chair and slumping my shoulders.* "*And he's not my boyfriend. We went out a few times. He's...nice.*"

Maya leans back against her cushioned seat and pins me with her Disney-princess-eyes. "*So why are you avoiding the perfectly nice not-boyfriend?*"

"*Can you please keep your voice down before he hears us?*"

"*No. Sorry. Can't do that.*" She crosses her arms over her chest. "*I am your best friend, and for the last six months, you have been pining over your long-lost love from high school. Nope. Do not interrupt me. You've been pining and you know it. It doesn't matter if you won't speak Satan's name, I always know when he's in your head.*"

"*He's not Satan.*"

"*Any man who makes my Ellie Belly cry is Satan. Say it.*"

"*Fine, he's Satan. Happy?*" I take a long sip of my peppermint tea and risk a glance at my not-boyfriend, Ben. Still here. Still hasn't seen us, I hope.

"*So, spill! Are you over Satan? And is this guy new-Satan? You still haven't explained why we're hiding.*"

"*Not new-Satan. His name is Ben, and he's very—*"

"*Nice. Yeah, sounds boring. What else is wrong with him?*" she asks.

"*Nothing's wrong with him. He's really—*"

"*If you even think the word nice again, I swear to god.*"

"*My, he's great. We're in the same econ class and had a few study dates, and we got dinner together last week. I was gonna tell you, but—*" Why didn't I tell her? I guess I've never had a friend to talk about boys with before. Or had a boy to talk about that wasn't a secret. I wanted to tell her when he first asked me out but there was this nagging sensation in my head, like once I told another person about him, it would be clear I was doing it again, making something bigger in my mind than it really was. "*I should have told you right away. I'm just sort of new at this stuff. I'm sorry.*"

"*You don't owe me an apology, El. It's your life. Can you tell me why you're avoiding him, though? Because if he hurt you, I will punch him in the balls.*"

I laugh at the serious expression on Maya's face. I've only known her for six months, but I'm confident she would do that for me. Like my own personal bodyguard.

"He didn't do anything wrong. It's just a little awkward because I was with him last night, and..."

"And? Did you guys hook up?"

"Yeah. But I didn't—"

"Finish?"

"What? No, I mean...no. But that's not what's making me feel awkward." Maya's eyes urge me to continue, and I think about how good it feels to be able to talk about this stuff. I lean across the table so I can lower my voice. "You know when you're with a guy you like, and you're kissing or...whatever."

Maya waggles her brows at my prudent "whatever," but I ignore her and continue. "You know how you start to feel all melty, like your limbs turn to honey and everything slows but also heats up, and it feels like your skin is covered in static, but like, the good kind? When you feel like you're floating, or flying, or just breathing a different kind of air? Or how you feel like your bones and blood and skin are all just magnets to each other and you can't think about anything else but getting closer and feeling more? I just—I didn't feel any of it."

She stares back at me for a few long moments as I listen to the murmurs around us in the library, but she doesn't respond. I wonder if I said too much. If I still have no idea how to talk about boys with my friends.

"Well, fuck." Maya scoffs, her bottom lip falling as she places both palms flat on the table between us. "I want some of that."

. . .

WHEN MORNING COMES, I wake to the feel of teeth scraping against my shoulder and a fingertip tracing circles around my nipple.

I gasp.

"Good, you're awake." Theo runs a hand down the length of my body and across my thigh, urging me to spread my legs. The teeth against my back morph into a tongue trailing up and down my spine. "How do you taste so good?"

I ignore the question and let myself enjoy every sensation he elicits as he slowly rolls on top of me.

"Again? Really?" I'm still sore from last night when he woke me up at two am. And from the shower before we went to bed. And our adventure on the snowmobile before that. Does he ever get tired?

"Ellie," he breathes, sucking on the hollow of my throat. "We're going to do this again"—kiss—"and again"—kiss—"and again." Teeth scrape along my collarbone. "Until you forget every other man that came between us." He perches himself between my thighs and settles his weight on me that's more soothing than any blanket. "Until I have every single first like I was always meant to. Do you understand?"

His words taste sour when they hit me. Why does Theo get to be jealous when I never had the chance?

But I'm stuck under his spell, unable to stop myself from opening my legs a little wider, looking up to meet his gaze.

"Make me forget." I'm not talking about other men. They're already forgotten, barely a blip in the world of my memories. But maybe if I can lose myself completely in this moment, he can wash away all the hurt that still lingers.

ANOTHER DAY PASSES and it becomes obvious that Theo and I both want to stay in bed, forever. The storm came back, but we still have heat, and I'm pretty sure we're both hoping that if we never leave this cocoon, the past cannot catch up. I tell myself not to think about it, about the last conversation we had, the text messages sent seven years ago that still burn like bile in my throat.

I tell myself not to think about it. But I'm not doing so well.

I wonder if at some point he's planning to apologize, to explain why he hurt me, why he lied.

In my imagination it happens randomly, a mused thought while lying in the dark. Theo admitting his mistakes in hushed whispers. *I should have told you about her. She never meant anything. I didn't know what I was doing.*

Would an apology matter? Or has time already erased his sins? I doubt my feelings would change, no matter his excuse. I think about the exercise from Dr. Green. If Theo gave me the most perfect apology, every word the one I want, would that be enough? I don't even know what the words would be.

Has Theo's betrayal ever lessened the love I have for him? Something in my head is telling me to let go of the past, but I'm not sure if I can. I don't know how to pretend all the hurt he caused hasn't left permanent scars.

So I try to keep ignoring it, the past. My focus is on now, here, this bed, this man, this version of us that exists only in this cabin.

But we can't hide in this pillow fort forever. It's been days, and we still have no idea when the power will be back, or when the generator will finally stop working.

I remind Theo as much when he starts reaching for me again, and he begrudgingly goes outside to check on it.

The storm has eased again, leaving a thick blanket of pure white in its wake. Each time I look out the window my breath catches. Nothing will ever be more beautiful than a landscape of fresh snow. Pines are scattered through the yard, each one frosted in glittering white crystals, dark green dots peeking through.

I can see the quiet, feel it. Serenity. No foxes or rabbits today, but still the most perfect view. The kind of view I could see every day and never tire of. The kind of view I used to dream about.

The power lines are still knocked down on the other side of the village. If the generator fails us, we'll have to escape. Just a few days ago I would have hoped for that very outcome, but now I can't imagine leaving this cabin willingly. I should probably be more scared of the storm, the power outage, the wild situation we're in. But I can't seem to feel fear when I'm with Theo. His comfort eclipses all my other senses.

Whatever sorcery Theo created with the generator that doesn't burn fuel, I hope he can keep it up a little longer.

"Still full." Theo walks through the door, kicking off snow from his boots. "It's fucking wild. The thing obviously isn't working. I have no clue how we have power right now. It doesn't make any sense. It's like—"

"Magic."

"Yeah, it is." He slides off his coat and boots and walks over to where I'm sitting on the couch. "I can't think of any other explanation."

We sit in companionable silence as Theo starts to rub my shoulders. When we're not naked and tangled in sheets, his hands have been on me in other ways. It feels like he's making up for all the years he couldn't touch me.

"Are we gonna talk about the tattoo?"

"Oh, you noticed it?" I was wondering when he'd say something.

"Do you really believe there is a single part of your body I haven't studied to the hilt in the last three days?" The first time he undressed me, I could feel his eyes on it, just before his lips. It's small, mostly hidden, marking the side of my ribcage.

"Do you like it?" I ask.

"I love it. Tell me about it."

"Well, after Maya and I became friends, I told her all about Mom and how big of a deal it was to leave home. And she said the first thing everyone should do after escaping an overbearing parent is to get a tattoo. So, I got one. Well, after I talked to my doctor and made sure it was safe, of course. Couldn't get rid of Mom in my head that easily."

"Ellie. I'm glad Maya encouraged you to do something adventurous, but you know what I'm asking."

"No, I don't."

"It's a flying penguin."

"It is."

"Is it for me?"

"No."

"El."

"It's for me." That was the truth. "I always felt like I had some kindred connection with penguins, the birds that couldn't fly. I used to dream of sprouting wings, flying away, seeing the world, escaping Mom, having a different life. I felt like a penguin trapped on land." His eyes glisten as they snag on my lips, hanging on each word, each breath. "So when I finally escaped, I don't know. I kind of felt like I had done the impossible. Dared to dream. Become a penguin that could fly. Wings are just a state of mind, right?"

Theo doesn't speak but his expression is filled with sadness. He takes my hand and rubs slow circles with his thumb, always comforting me.

"I guess it was for you too. There isn't much about me that's not about you."

I suck in a breath at what I just said, at what I gave away.

Theo's trying to school his features, but I don't miss the widening of his eyes. So I abruptly continue. "You sort of got me started on my penguin obsession. Cherry, Berry and Larry, remember?" He lets out a brief chuckle and nods. "But it's not like I was pining after you so hard that I had to get a tattoo about you or anything," I add. Because no matter how much has changed in the last three days, he's still the boy who stomped all over my heart and I refuse to give him that satisfaction.

"I almost did."

"What?" I ask.

"Get a tattoo for you. Because I was pining so hard."

I swallow every traitorous feeling that snakes its way into my heart. "What were you gonna get?"

"Your face on my ass."

"Theo!" I smack him on the shoulder, just light enough to be considered playful.

"Seriously, I thought about it. Not your face but—okay, it's really stupid. Please don't laugh. I was going to get a snow globe."

"On your ass?"

"On my heart."

Longing hits me like a brick. All the air in my lungs is gone, leaving nothing but pain in its void. Theo continues on like he didn't just drop that revelation.

"You don't even wanna know all the crazy things I thought about doing those first few months after you left me."

"Left you?" I recover the ability to speak because...how can he say that?

"Sorry. I know you didn't just leave me. I know it wasn't about me. Honestly, though? Sometimes it felt like it was. I was not in a good place."

"You weren't? Why?"

"Fuck, Ellie. You're seriously gonna ask me *why*? Maybe because I loved you? Maybe because the second you cut off contact with me, I couldn't think about anything else? Did you know I drove halfway to California one time?" I shake my head in utter disbelief. "Yeah, that was fucking stupid. I almost missed a game. I even asked coach if I could transfer to play at Cal. He was ready to kill me halfway through that season."

"Theo, I don't understand."

"Look, I don't blame you for going away for school. I was so happy for you, so excited that your parents actually let you go. And I shouldn't even be thinking about that shit year because you're here now and that's the only thing that matters. But just tell me why you cut me off. Why couldn't you tell me what you were doing?"

"I had no idea you were hurting like that. Really." Indignation takes over, and my next words are biting. How dare he put any blame on me for our separation. "But I was hurting too. When I found out about your girlfriend—"

"Ellie—" He tries to interrupt, but fuck that. He got to vent, so do I.

"I was devastated. I couldn't see straight. And Mom and Dad and Ezra, they were all just pitying me. Laughing at me, probably. Do you have any idea what that was like for me? I couldn't even tell them why I was so upset. They just thought I had this weird obsession with you."

"Ellie. What are you—"

"That was the lowest I've ever been. I had to get out and cut ties and honestly, I had no desire to talk to you after—"

"Ellie!" he yells, and I look at him for the first time since I started speaking. "What girlfriend?"

"What, you can't remember which one? Chloe! The girl my brother knew all about but somehow you never mentioned to me." My rage intensifies. It's wild to me that he's making me relive the worst moments of my life. That he's making me say her name after all this time. "The one you spent Christmas with instead of me."

"Ezra knew who? What are you talking about? I never had a girlfriend." His words settle over me. I have never known Theo to be anything but genuine, and his face is practically screaming it. "The only girl I ever had was you."

Chapter Twenty-Six

Theo

December 22, 2016

ELLIE

Ez just said he won't be back till Christmas Eve because you two are going to Stowe together. What's going on?

THEO

Yeah

He was kind of pissed last year that we didn't get to do much, just us

I'm a hot commodity with the Klein family ;)

ELLIE

I feel like I haven't seen you in forever between hockey and school. I was so excited for today

SHE WAS RIGHT, and I felt like shit about it. My schedule had gotten out of control this year and it felt like I was constantly being pulled in different directions. It was difficult enough having a secret relationship and trying to sneak around her parents, but between hockey and classes I hadn't seen Ellie in weeks.

In my defense, I hadn't seen Ezra since the summer. I was honored he came to so many of my games. And as much as I did want extra time with Ellie, I didn't want to neglect my other best friend. I was already lying to him every time we spoke.

I owed him this.

THEO

It's just an extra two days apart. Please don't give up on me

I'll be thinking about you the whole time

Gotta jump in the shower before he gets here. I'll see you soon, El

I turned on the shower, trying not to let the guilt swallow me whole. I hated disappointing her. Sometimes it felt like I was letting everyone down around me.

I was a bad friend to Ezra for lying, a bad boyfriend to Ellie because she couldn't even call me one. Fuck, I was drowning. And the only idea I had on how to fix things was completely absurd.

I turned off the faucet and grabbed a towel. When I opened the door into my room, I was met with a face full of revulsion.

"Are you fucking my little sister? What the hell is this?"

Ezra held out my phone in front of him and I saw Ellie's most recent text. It must have come in while I was in the bathroom.

ELLIE

As long as you'll be thinking about me in the shower...

Fuck. Time froze, or at least my mouth did. I had no idea what I could say to that, no idea how far back he had read.

"Well?" Ezra shouted.

"It's not like that. We're..." What the hell was I supposed to say? We're in love? I wasn't ready to have this conversation with him. I wasn't ready for her parents to know.

"How long?"

"What?" I asked.

"How long have you been fucking my little sister, you piece of shit?"

"Stop saying that! I'm not fucking her, okay? It's not like that." I took a cautious step forward to grab my phone, but he chucked it at the wall so hard I heard the glass shatter.

"What's it like then? All the times you stayed at my house, you were just trying to hook up with Ellie? After everything my family has done for you? My dad got you this fucking scholarship! This is how you thank him?"

Ezra was pacing around my room, eyes wild with fury. I wasn't sure if there was anything I could say to placate him. Fury was rolling off him in waves, his eyes darting left and right, fists clasping like he was picturing my throat. Every movement he made was erratic.

"Ezra, listen to me. You have been there for me like no one else has. I'm so grateful for everything you and your parents have done for me. I am. I just, I also like Ellie. It's not one or the other, okay? This doesn't change anything between you and me."

"The hell it does!" He shoved me. It caught me so off guard I almost hit the wall.

"Tell me what to do. How do I make this right?" My heart was beating so fast I thought it might explode out of my chest. I sat down on the edge of my bed, watching him think, wondering how I could possibly solve this.

"Here's what's going to happen. You're not coming over for break this year. I don't want you anywhere near my sister or my house." He paced some more, and I swore I could see steam coming out of his ears. "You have a hockey thing up in Canada that you can't get out of. I'll tell them for you, so you don't even have to lie."

I watched his head work as he continued to determine my punishment.

"I won't tell my parents about this. Because they would be devastated, and you know it." The blow hits me right in the chest. I'd only feared how they would react, but Ezra's words gave it legs. They would never approve. They would never understand how I feel about her.

If there was one thing that mattered to me in life, it was making sure I was the kind of person my parents would be proud of. Even before they left me, I was always trying to impress them, trying to follow their guidance to the best of my ability. But they were gone, and I found myself looking to my pseudo-adoptive parents—the Kleins—for the approval I sought.

Trying to reconcile that with my love for Ellie was tearing me apart. How could I get through this without disappointing someone? Ezra was already looking at me like a stranger. Was this it? Did I just lose my brother?

It felt like the time had come when I would have to choose between them: Ezra, Ellie, their parents. I wasn't ready.

"Okay. What about Ellie?"

"What *about* Ellie?" he yells. "I want you to leave her

alone. You're fucking pathetic, taking advantage of her like that."

"I didn't—"

"I'm still talking!" I shut up, knowing I wouldn't get anywhere trying to defend myself. "You're not coming to see her. You're not going to call her. She'll be going to college soon and she'll forget all about whatever this...this *thing* is anyway."

"Okay." He was wrong, but that was between me and Ellie. I wasn't going to let him make the decision for her. Her parents were controlling enough.

"Would we even be friends still? Or were you just hanging around trying to get your dick wet every Christmas?"

I flinched. How could he think of me like that? He was the closest thing I had to a brother, to a *family*. He really thought I would treat Ellie that way? Ezra was the one always sleeping around, not me.

"Ez. It's not *like* that. Can you just let me explain?"

"I can't even look at you anymore." He stalked toward the door. "I'm gonna hit Stowe by myself. So much for that boys' trip."

The door slammed in my face.

FOR TWO DAYS, I tortured myself.

Abandoning my shattered phone, I spent forty-eight hours in isolation down at Sugar Valley. I camped out among the trees, hoping I would feel a presence there, that I could somehow talk to my parents, have them tell me what to do. I was fucking lost and needed their guidance more than ever before.

No answers came to me, only more turmoil. *Should I show up on Christmas and watch everything blow up in my face? Stay away until Ezra cooled down? Say screw it all and go buy the ring?*

The only realization I had was that I needed to protect Ellie in this. Her relationship with her family was already strained, especially when it came to college. If they found out she'd been sneaking around with me all this time, they might rescind the little bit of freedom they were offering. It would kill me if Ellie couldn't go where she wanted or live in the dorms because of my stupidity.

As selfish as I wanted to be, I needed to be patient. For her. For the future I had planned for us.

> ELLIE
>
> Is it true? You're not coming?

The text came through on Christmas Eve while I was still at the store buying my new phone.

My heart shattered. Just a few words on the screen and I could sense her disappointment.

I so badly wanted to drive straight to her, but I had already made my decision. I would explain everything to Ellie once Ezra was back in Boston. He wouldn't be able to get involved once he was back at school, and Ellie and I could figure out the right way to tell her family about us. Together.

> THEO
>
> I'm so sorry Ellie
>
> Let's talk when I get back in town, okay?
>
> Happy birthday

A whole week and no response. She was obviously pissed at me for not coming. And not talking to her was killing me too. I ended up spending the break in Montreal with Raj, trying to distract myself. Unfortunately, just being there made me think of Ellie and the best birthday I'd ever had when she brought me to the Biôdome.

THEO

> Happy New Year! Hope you and Latke aren't having too much fun without me ☺

Stupid. Reckless. Ezra was with her and probably checking her fucking phone. I didn't even care. I missed her so much. This was the longest we'd gone in years without at least texting, and it felt like I had lost a limb. I was completely off balance without her presence.

Three more days and I knew he'd be back at school. Then I could call her.

I must have called a hundred times.

She never answered.

THEO

> Just got back from Montreal. Can we talk? I've tried calling you a few times but it just goes to voicemail

> Did Ezra say something to you?

> Please call me back? I really don't want to do this over text

> It's okay if Ez knows about us. I promise everything will be okay, just please talk to me. I need you, El

<<unable to deliver message>>

Fuck!

AN ENTIRE MONTH went by with no word from Ellie. Ezra still wasn't speaking to me, Ellie fucking blocked me. I used to think it was cool that Ellie was so anti social media, that she never got caught up in Instagram followers or taking a million selfies like other girls I knew. Now, I could only hate the fact that I was cut off from her completely, with not nearly enough saved photos of her on my phone.

My two best friends were suddenly gone, and I had no idea what to do. By February, I'd lost hope that I would hear from her again, so I called Ezra. I hadn't even attempted to reach out to him since the holidays. My last text said "I'm ready to talk whenever you are," and was met with nothing but crickets. So I called.

I called a dozen times, left three voicemails, didn't even mention Ellie in my attempt to force him to respond. Nothing.

Finally, desperately, I went straight to the source.

When I pulled up to the house and saw Ellie's car in the driveway, my heart started beating to a foreign rhythm. There was so much hope inside me—she was *right there*. Close enough I could taste her. But there was also a pit of dread. She was *right there*, and she had severed me from her life. Why?

"Well, this is a surprise." Mr. Klein greeted me at the door, reminding me yet again to call him Joel. "You're taller than me now. You can use my first name. What are you doing here?"

"I umm—" *haven't actually come up with an excuse to be here, other than basically stalking the love of my life, your daughter.* "Ez borrowed one of my hoodies at Stowe, said I could come grab it."

He looked a bit puzzled, and I didn't blame him. But he urged me to head upstairs anyway. I paused at Ellie's room.

The door was closed, and I held my ear to the door like a creep trying to hear what she was doing. Nothing.

I knocked. Nothing.

I opened the door ever so slowly. She wasn't there.

Grabbing a random VU sweatshirt from Ezra's closet, I made my way back downstairs.

"Oh, hi, Theo," said Mrs. Klein. "I didn't know you stopped by. Did you want to stay for dinner?"

Shit. Did I? Where the hell was Ellie? "Umm, I was actually just grabbing something Ez borrowed. I should get back to school."

"Oh, okay." She went back to stirring something on the stove, her face downturned. She looked disappointed.

"I was gonna say hey to Ellie. Is she in the basement?"

Mrs. Klein scoffed. "No, she's at the library." And then, under her breath, "Always at the library."

"She probably won't be back for a few hours, said she'd take care of her own dinner," Mr. Klein said, making his way into the kitchen.

"Oh, sorry. Just saw her car here and..."

"Chase picked her up."

"Chase?" What the hell kind of name was Chase? And why would Ellie's parents let her hang out with some guy who's name was one big red flag?

"One of her friends from school. He's been helping her finish some courses early."

Ellie's mom huffed at that and stormed out of the room. I had no idea what was going on, but it felt like my cue to leave, so I told Joel I had some studying to do too.

Ellie was one of the smartest people I knew. She didn't need a fucking tutor. Was she really at the library or was Chase just her newest secret she hid from her parents?

Yeah, I was spiraling.

I had to remind myself that this was my fault, no one else's. I was the reason we were a secret. But it didn't take the sting away at all.

I called her again. Still blocked.

The rest of that semester, I put every bit of frustration I had into hockey, and it paid off. Raj and I brought home the school's first frozen five championship in nine years.

Mr. Klein found me after the win, showering me with praise while I used all my willpower not to ask about Ellie. I failed.

"Did Ellie—or Ez—make it to the game too?" It wasn't a crazy question.

"Just me today. Ez had finals and Ellie left for California last week."

"California? What?" I knew I must have heard him wrong.

"Ezra didn't tell you? She's going to UC-Berkeley." His face was gleaming with pride. And I was in shock. I didn't even know she got in. Why didn't she tell me? He was still talking but I was struggling to hear the words. "...wanted to get started with summer classes so she could catch up to the kids her age... I'm sure Ez will fill you in soon...Go celebrate! Ice Bears!"

He slapped my back the way my coach did and left me standing there with my mouth agape. Ellie was in California? *How?*

Was that why she cut me off? She got the chance to leave Vermont and decided I wasn't even worth saying goodbye to?

The end of the school year whizzed by, and Raj convinced me to do summer with him in Montreal. After spending winter break with his whole family, I had no objections. They were extremely welcoming, even when I was at my grumpiest. Plus, I was able to work, teaching at a hockey camp for juniors.

He'd been an amazing friend to me. He spent half the summer trying to cheer me up, even when I was cagey as hell about what had happened. I never told him about my fight with Ezra, just that Ellie left me when she left for college.

I was constantly second-guessing how our relationship would look to outsiders. Her parents had taken me in like another son, helped me get into private school and then college. They had done so much for me, and I didn't know how I could live with myself if they thought I had somehow exploited them like Ezra suggested.

Plus, they had money, a lot of it. I had nothing, not yet. I always planned on making something for myself before telling her parents about us, wanting there to be zero questions about my intentions with her.

But maybe Ezra was right, and I did take advantage of Ellie, or at least her situation. It didn't mean my love for her wasn't real, but I wondered if she was only with me out of convenience. She wasn't allowed to date. Sneaking around with her brother's best friend who stayed in her basement was a lot easier than trying to go out with guys from her high school.

Looking at it from this new angle, Ellie going to California without as much as a goodbye...Maybe I never meant shit to her. Maybe I was just a placeholder until something better came along.

These thoughts were all-consuming, wrecking me the entire summer. It was the not knowing that was killing me. Did she really love me? Why didn't she tell me about school? Was she better off without me? Should I even keep trying to contact her?

By the time I got back to Burlington I'd fully lost it. I asked coach if I could transfer, to which he threw me out of his office. Then I almost missed our first game of the season after a spontaneous road trip to go find Ellie. I made it past Ohio when I realized how audacious I was being. If she had any desire to see me, she would answer my calls.

It wasn't until November that things changed. When Ezra called me about Christmas.

"Hey, how you been, man?" Ezra opened the conversation.

How you been? We hadn't spoken in almost a year, and he was acting like nothing had changed.

"Umm, okay, I guess? It's been a while, Ez."

"Look, I know things have been weird between us. But I'm not mad anymore. I was worried about Ellie, but she's great. She's loving Berkeley and has a ton of friends there and I realized that whatever your thing was with her wasn't really a big deal. I mean, I still don't like it and I don't think my parents should know, but it's all good, okay?"

I poured over his words, translating them like a mad scientist. Ellie was great? What did that mean? Why did he think it wasn't a big deal? Did she tell him that? Did they talk about me? Did she ever know Ezra found her texts?

The questions were fucking endless.

"Are we good?" Ezra asked, impatiently waiting for my response.

"Yeah, Z. Of course. We're good."

"Great. Then I hope you'll be back for Christmas. We all missed you last year."

I TRIED TEXTING Ellie before break, filled with hope that she unblocked me.

She had not.

I was terrified to see her again, not knowing how to talk to her with the little privacy we would be awarded. And without the chance to text, it would be even harder.

Since Ezra's phone call, I'd thought about what to say to her, never landing on anything useful. Then I decided to redirect my energy into finding the perfect snow globe for her birthday gift.

I already gave her one with penguins when she was eleven, but it felt like the right one anyway. I saw it at a small store near campus. This one had two penguins instead of three, and they were huddled together, molding themselves into one body. It reminded me of all the times Ellie snuggled up to me when she was cold, all the times I snuck into her room at night, all the times when it was just the two of us on the ice or in the snow.

I didn't know if she was going to laugh at me for the sentimental gift or even speak to me at all. I had never felt so fucking clueless in my life as I drove to their house on Christmas Eve.

The one thing I hadn't prepared for was for Ellie not to be there at all.

Chapter Twenty-Seven

Ellie

Now

"You really were mine. That whole time." The murmured words float from my mouth and land between us on the couch.

I'm still trying to unravel everything Theo just told me. *He never had a girlfriend. My brother made it up. He would have explained all of this if I had only answered my* fucking *phone.*

"What did you say?" he asks.

"All this time. I thought that—that maybe you were never really mine."

"I was yours, Ellie. Fuck, I still am."

His voice grows thick and guttural as he pulls me into a tight embrace. "Can you forgive me?"

"Forgive you? I should be asking you to forgive me. All this time..." Time we should never have spent apart. Time I thought my best friend had betrayed me. Time I spent mourning my love for Theo. "It kills me that you thought I would just leave like that, that you weren't worth saying goodbye to."

"I should have tried harder. Shouldn't have given up that

easily. I kept wanting to talk to your parents, but I was so scared about how they'd react. That was so fucking stupid. I should have asked them anyway; I should have done anything to be able to talk to you."

"Are you kidding me? None of this is your fault. You were all alone and I should have been there for you. I could have at least listened—"

"Screw that. It's not your fault either. Why the hell did Ezra lie to you? I don't..." He trails off, lost in thought about my brother. Why *did* Ezra lie to me, and not just to me but my parents? Was he trying to hurt me? Or Theo? Was there some reason he didn't want us together? My brother and I got along a lot better that year. And he was thrilled when I told him about Berkeley, he even visited me once before he started med school.

Was it all a façade? Maybe he just wanted me gone.

"You really thought I cheated on you?"

I'm taken aback by the sudden change in topic. And by Theo's wording. "No. I didn't think you cheated. I thought I was a joke. I mean, you were never my boyfriend."

"Ellie." He sighs, taking my face in his hands. "You were so much more to me than a girlfriend. I was wrong to not give you the label. I was wrong for keeping us a secret and I will probably never forgive myself for that mistake, but—" He squeezes his eyes shut and I spot a single tear caught in the corner, refusing to fall. "If there is one thing you need to know, in this whole fucking disaster, it's that you have always been it for me. From our first kiss on that ice, I never wanted anyone but you. I love you, El. I always have."

His words hit like snowflakes melting into my flesh, sending shivers through my veins. Words I needed to hear so badly to mend all the little cracks and gashes in my heart. Words I have heard in my dreams, stared up at the night sky and wished for.

Words that mean absolutely nothing to me unless they drop from Theo's lips.

"When Pete said that—" I pause to take a shaky breath. "My ex. When he told me he loved me, all I could think about was you. I ended things about five minutes after he said it. I didn't even feel guilty; I just knew it was all wrong. It made me wonder if it's even possible to love more than one person in a lifetime. Do you think we were doomed from the start to ever find someone else?"

All I ever wanted was that cozy kind of love. The gooey heart, curled toes, crinkled eyes kind of love. The kind that feels like hot cocoa warming my bones. Summer rain, fluffy socks, s'mores by the fire. That small kind of love you get lost in from too much happiness to ever wonder what else is out there.

I'm not sure why I was looking when I knew I had already found it.

"I think...I don't know," Theo answers. "I think you can love different people in different ways. But my mom always said you can only have one favorite, one person you want to spend every day with no matter what. You were always that person for me. You still are. I never even wondered if there could be someone else. I've just been waiting for you to come back to me."

Tears flood my vision before they begin their trek down my cheeks.

And Theo kisses every one of them away.

His lips sail across my face as he repeats the same words over and over again. "I'm yours. I've always been yours." Our bodies drift toward a full collision, until he picks me up off the couch and lays me down in our fort. "You own every piece of me that matters."

The moment he sets me down, I tug him closer until it's impossible for us not to be kissing. We may have spent the last three days making up for all the sex we never had, but in this moment, its significance has turned to dust.

It was a distraction, a physical response to the chemistry neither of us could deny.

Now, love surrounds us, infusing all the air we breathe. Every inch of my skin is coated in it.

It all happens swiftly. Our kisses turn molten. Our clothes disappear.

Hot skin.

Wet lips.

Slow hands.

A battle on bedsheets between who can tug the other closer. Everyone's a winner.

We move together in expert precision, reveling in the taste of each other's breath, like we've been doing this forever. Maybe we have, in a way. Finding our rhythm together for years on the ice.

He pushes into me with care, with passion, with seven years' worth of desire. And he doesn't stop until stars block my vision and I'm nothing but putty in his arms.

There is no pillow talk today. Just peace. No more questions rattle in my brain about the past, about his intentions or my escape plan. My head is quiet, just like the forest outside blanketed in fresh snow. Marshmallow fluff softening every edge of my anxiety.

I don't fall asleep; I'm just coasting in bliss when I feel him return to the fort. The sugary scent of peppermint hits my nose as his mouth brushes up against my side. He's kissing my tattoo.

He doesn't pick up his head, but his hand appears in front of me with a candy cane, offering a lick. I oblige before he pops it back between his own lips.

"What'd you name it?" he asks.

"I didn't."

"Liar." His tongue glides up the side of my ribcage, right over my flying penguin, and before I can respond to his accusation, he blows against the same spot. It sends an icy chill across my skin. I hear him suck on the candy before he repeats the same motion, and every part of my body tightens.

Lick. Blow. Repeat.

Lick. Blow. Repeat.

"What's its name, El?" His lips sail over my skin, teasing me again and again.

"Pancake," I exhale in what sounds like a single syllable. My brain isn't capable of holding anything in right now. All I can focus on is the feel of him, of what he's doing to me.

Laughter racks his body, sending shudders to my own. "Of course, it is."

The conversation seems to be over. Theo's intense concentration falls on his peppermint, and on me. He continues his assault on my skin, long licks followed by minty breaths. He does it again and again, up to my shoulder, across my breasts, down to my hip, against my thighs. He doesn't stop until the cooling sensation is everywhere, until I'm writhing against him, begging for some sort of relief.

Lick. Blow. Repeat.

Lick. Blow. Repeat.

"Theo," I beg.

"I'll give you what you want," he murmurs. "Just tell me you love me, Eliana. I need to hear it."

Have I not said it yet?

"I love you. I've always loved you. Since I was nine, remember?"

He wasn't lying. He gives me exactly what I want. More than that. The peppermint hasn't left his mouth and the sensation is overwhelming, sparking my most sensitive skin with prickles of pleasure I've never felt at the hands of anyone else. His lips, his tongue, his teeth; I feel everything in overdrive.

Within seconds, I'm close, panting with need for release.

"Tell me you're mine."

"Yours," I breathe.

"My Ellie," he continues, with a hot kiss to my core. "Then." A flick of his tongue. "Now." Another. "Forever."

Two more flicks and I shatter to pieces, breathless and sated, wondering how I ever went seven years without him, without this.

"Yours. Always."

"Why didn't you ever come home?"

I'm attempting to light the candles for the sixth night of Hanukkah when he asks. I can't believe it's been less than a week. I'm starting to feel like I've lived in this snowstorm my entire life. Or maybe I just never want to leave.

"You mean for the holidays?" I ask. Our sex-hazed afternoon turned into staying up all night and sleeping most of today away. Two days ago, I discovered the man who broke my heart never actually betrayed me, but we still have so much of the past to uncover. The questions we have for each other feel boundless.

"Yeah. That first year you were gone, I thought I would finally get to see you. It didn't feel real, you not being there."

I never planned on staying away this whole time. I had the ticket to go home for my birthday that first year. But the stress revolving around that trip had been eating me up inside. After Dad made Berkeley official, Mom and I barely spoke. She didn't even come with us to send me off to school. And that whole year, Dad would call and email to check in, but Mom never did. I knew she was just being passive aggressive, that she was hurt by my decision to leave home and my dad siding against her. But I was still so angry; there was nothing I wanted to apologize for.

"I was going to. I had my ticket. But when I thought about seeing Mom..." I trailed off, my mind back in that kitchen with her. "We hadn't talked since I left and...I just couldn't do it. Maya told me she was staying in the city for Christmas with her parents and invited me to join them, so I called Dad at the last minute and told him I was sick. I knew they wouldn't argue with that."

Being sick may have been a lie, but my entire body had been buzzing with anxiety.

"Your mom was a mess."

My eyes shoot to Theo. "What?"

"She lost it, El. She made this special cake for you and when your dad told her you weren't coming, she ran outside and threw the whole thing in the trash. I barely saw her after that." Thickness fills Theo's voice as his emotions take over. "Well, except once."

Our eyes meet and I just know that whatever he's about to tell me is not going to be easy to hear.

"I had been sitting in the sunroom all night. I'm not sure why but I liked looking at the stars—and I knew how you'd always lie in there when you couldn't sleep. So I just sat there, waiting for midnight I guess. I think I may have just been hoping you would miraculously appear. It felt so wrong to be apart for your birthday." He blows out a shaky breath. "And then your mom came down. She sat next to me and just started sobbing. She kept saying 'She's never coming back, is she?' and fuck, I started crying with her. I'd been wondering the same thing."

"Theo..."

"It sort of became our tradition," he murmurs.

"What?"

"I haven't missed your birthday since number nineteen. I went back every year hoping you would show up." He pauses to drag a hand across his face, trying to hide the tears that have slipped. "And every year on your birthday, your mom and I find each other at midnight in the sunroom. We've never discussed it. She probably thinks I'm just there to support her or something, but we just sit and cry for you."

Words escape me. The thought of my mother crying over me like that refuses to compute. I was her project, the kid that always needed fixing. There were never big feelings or emotions for us, we just didn't have that kind of relationship.

And the thought of Mom *and* Theo crying over me—together—makes me ache. I may have mixed up feelings about her, but they're both still the two people I have loved most in my life. I only ever wanted her to let me live unencumbered. I never wanted to hurt her.

I never wanted our relationship to end. I just couldn't find another solution.

And then, just when I'm feeling as guilty as can be, I remember why I decided not to come back for any birthdays after that.

"I was supposed to come home that summer too. But every time I saw her text, the last thing she sent me, my nerves about seeing her would skyrocket." I had one of my worst flares ever, stuck in bed for weeks. That's when I finally started seeing a therapist.

"What text?"

"From my birthday. Number twenty. It was the first time I had heard from her since I went to school." I replay that moment in my head, envisioning the photo she sent me. "She sent me a picture of you and Ez. All it said was 'Happy birthday. The boys missed you.'"

"Seriously?" Theo chides. "God, you mom's an idiot."

It feels good to laugh. To let the walls down and focus on anything other than regret. I've always loved how Theo can take something as complex as grief and winnow it down to a grilled cheese sandwich.

"AG?" I look up to meet his gaze, curious where this conversation is headed. A glimmer of a smile peeks through his lashes as he asks, "Wanna make latkes?"

We'd plowed through most of the fresh food in Theo's cabin already, but we had a few eggs left and I was happy to find potatoes and onions safely tucked away in the pantry. I grabbed the box grater and as many kitchen towels as I could find and got to work.

"What's that?" I ask, taking in the sight of Theo holding two large plastic bags.

"Frozen apples. I had them in the garage. I was saving them for the sanctuary, but I don't have any pre-made applesauce, so we'll use these."

"I don't wanna steal food from the animals!"

"I've got plenty, and it won't be up and running until March anyway. I know you won't eat a latke without applesauce. Show me how to make it?"

"I'll peel. You chop." I sidle up next to him at the island, spreading all our ingredients out in front of me. He casually drapes an arm around me before pressing a light kiss to the side of my neck.

A feeling comes over me, a flicker pulsing through my chest. This is how it was always supposed to be.

Theo and I didn't spend many Hanukkahs together growing up since it rarely fell as late as Christmas. But the first year it did, he fell in love with latkes, as well as my homemade applesauce. It used to be one of my favorite things to cook, mostly because of the aroma that would fill our entire home. After that first year, he started requesting them every Christmas after.

Brisket, pizza, latkes and waffles. Those were the typical treats served over the winter holidays. Sometimes birthday cake. We weren't exactly conventional, but the traditions were *ours*.

All the holidays blurred for us. Hanukkah, Christmas, my birthday, New Year's Eve. They were all irrelevant, yet crucial at the same time. They were what we grew up on. They forged us. They marked all the milestones that mattered.

They were the story of Theo and Ellie.

"Do you really need that much oil?" Theo asks as I begin the treacherous process of frying the latkes.

"Yes, Theo. It's Hanukkah. This whole week is about oil." He doesn't respond but the look on his face tells me he has no idea what I'm talking about. "Wait. Do you not know the story of Hanukkah?"

"Your mom always said all the Jewish holidays were the same. 'They tried to kill us. We survived. Let's eat.'" He shrugs.

"She's not wrong, but Hanukkah is a little different. Actually, no, her logic still stands. It's about a military victory."

"Seriously?"

"Yep. The Maccabees. My memory of the story's loose, but there was this decades long war, and after the Maccabees finally won, they took back some special temple in Jerusalem. They found a jar of oil there for lighting a menorah, but it was only enough for one night. And miraculously, it lasted for eight." I smile up at him, proud to share some knowledge of my heritage. "So, they did try to kill us—war—and we survived— yay!—and now we celebrate by eating delicious greasy food that reminds us of the oil miracle."

"Huh." Theo frowns, thoughtfully. "I had no idea it was about the oil. I thought there must have been a potato famine or something."

"Sorry, Theo. We can't all be Irish."

I finish the last batch of latkes and plate a few for us to eat. Theo starts devouring them before he even sits down. I bite down my grin at the moans he makes after each bite.

He finishes two latkes and then looks at me with a serious expression. "My people better watch out. The Jews know how to make a mean potato."

Chapter Twenty-Eight

Theo

Now

"I'M GONNA KILL YOUR BROTHER."

We've spent seventy-two hours unraveling seven years, combing through every detail of our last conversation together and everything that came after. We talked until there was no longer a single question or misunderstanding between us and eaten two days' worth of latkes.

I have felt every emotion known to man these last few days, but suddenly my fury has eclipsed them all. I knew Ezra was pissed when he saw the texts, but less than a year later we were back to normal. He treated me as though nothing had changed, just a minor blip in our lifelong friendship.

But he put Ellie through *misery*. She'd been hurt so badly, she fled to the other side of the country. How could he do that to her? The only thought that gives me any solace is that he didn't understand what we meant to each other, that he thought he was breaking up some casual hook-up-over-the-holidays relationship instead of fucking soulmates.

Because that's what she is to me. Anything less is fiction.

And yet I can't decide if I hate Ezra for what he did or if I just *want* to hate him. Maybe it's both. Or maybe I'm starting to realize that without his act of betrayal, Ellie never would have gone to California, never would have become the person she was meant to be, never would have had the chance to be independent from her family.

I've loved Ellie for half of my life, but this new version of her is incredible. The girl I grew up with who cared so much about pleasing everyone around her has finally chosen to prioritize herself. She needed that time away. Needed to make a friend like Maya, needed to travel the world and find her own limits when it came to her illness. No part of me wants to admit it, but maybe she also needed that time away from me.

There's a sick and twisted part of me that feels grateful for what Ezra did. He caused Ellie enough pain to make her desperate. And he caused me just enough to let her go without a stronger fight.

I hate him.

I hate him, and I love him. I love him, but I hate him. Is this what it feels like to have a biological sibling? Maybe he really was my brother all along.

"Do you think he did it to hurt us? Or just me, maybe? He hated me for a long time," Ellie says, interrupting my chaotic thoughts. "I don't know why else he would do something like that."

"He never hated you, El. I know you thought that, but it wasn't true. I think he may have taken his frustration out on you sometimes. He just wanted attention. But he was mad at your parents, not you."

I can see her considering what I said, looking back on all the memories, trying to see them from a different angle. It makes me wonder if I should be doing the same. Should I have known Ezra would do something like this? He'd made it clear he didn't like the idea of me and Ellie together, but I never even considered that he would be so careless, so selfish.

Our friendship was supposed to be bigger than that.

"Remember the last time we went to Reggae Night?" Ellie asks. "He was such a dick to me. How can you say he didn't hate me? I spent half the night wondering what I did to piss him off."

Fuck. There's still so much she doesn't know. "I knew."

"What?"

"Why he was being a dick. I knew." She narrows her gaze at me, and I know she wants answers. This isn't my story to tell but I'm so fucking sick of all the lies, all the secrets her family kept from her.

"Look, it was never your fault. But I knew why he was drinking so much, why he was so angry. That's why I gave him a pass that week."

"What are you talking about?"

"That fall," I reply. "He got sick, like *really* sick. I think it was food poisoning, but he was in the hospital for a few days. It was bad. And he asked your parents if they could come get him so he could stay at home for a while until he recovered." Ellie's brow furrows in confusion. Like she can't believe she didn't know about this. All the shit her parents kept from her; it was never right.

"He called me after all this happened, but basically, your parents said they didn't want him anywhere near the house, mainly you, in case he had a stomach bug or something else that you could catch. I don't know what they said to him exactly, but he was upset enough to tell me about it. I ended up spending a weekend down there to take care of him. He made me swear not to say anything."

Her lips part but nothing comes out. I hate being the one to tell her this, but I am through with all the secrets.

Finally, she murmurs, "I can't believe I never knew that. Any of it."

"I'm sorry, El. I should have told you. I just—I was already lying to Ezra about us, and I felt like I owed it to him to honor his wishes. And when he was yelling at your dad, I really felt for him in that moment."

Ellie's head sways side to side as she takes everything in, but she has to know this changes nothing. "You know none of this even comes close to a reason for what he did to you. To us."

"Maybe not. But I think I understand it more now. I think —" Her gaze is searching, everywhere but me. "I think he felt like I stole you from him. Like, first I stole Mom and Dad, and then you. He never wanted me anywhere near his friends, but he didn't really have a choice with you staying in our home. God, I hate that I did that to him."

"Ellie, don't you dare put this on yourself. It was never your—"

Sparks fly through the room accompanied by loud popping noises. Ellie jumps into my arms right before it all goes black. The sounds subside as we look around, our only form of light the eight votive candles in our makeshift menorah.

It's the last night of Hanukkah.

"Do you think the generator finally ran out of fuel?" Ellie asks.

"No idea. I'll go take a look."

"I'm coming with you." She grabs a quilt, already preparing for the lack of heat, and follows me outside.

The generator's empty, completely. I'm so fucking confused. This thing worked perfectly without ever using a drop of fuel. It should never have lasted more than twenty-four hours, and we got a full week. But now the fuel's gone. We're out of options.

I look at Ellie. "We're just like the Maccabees. It lasted for eight nights."

"Okay, let's not get dramatic. You didn't just win a war."

It feels like I did. A seven-year war. What could feel more like winning than having Ellie back in my life?

But without any power, we can't stay in this cabin.

This cannot be happening. I need more time. More time with Ellie before she goes back to California. More time to see if there's still a future with us. More time to show her that my feelings have never changed, that I still want the life for us we always dreamed about.

How do I keep her?

We may have realized that our tumultuous past was constructed by Ezra, but that doesn't change that a lot of good came out of it for her. She has a great life in San Francisco, a career, friends. She said she's only happy sometimes, but who am I to tell her she has to give all that up?

I need more fucking time.

Ellie's shivering, the loss of heat already tangible. So I say the only thing I can.

"We have to leave."

Chapter Twenty-Nine

Ellie

Now

I'M NOT READY.

I'm not ready to leave this cabin. I'm not ready to leave Theo. I'm not ready to go back to real life.

Because that life doesn't *feel* real anymore. My past, present, and future have all collided in this cabin and I have no idea what reality will look like when I leave it. It's like I'm trapped in a snow globe of my own creation, one made of all my favorite dreams and worst nightmares. Fear is something I left in my rearview seven years ago, but fear is all I can feel right now.

We step inside and my eyes immediately dart to the fireplace, still going strong. The only thing in this house that isn't electric. I remember seeing a huge pile of wood stacked in the garage. Theo follows my gaze and I wonder if he's thinking it too.

"Do you think we could last one more night?" I ask. "If we

stay by the fire?" It's not nearly as cold outside now that the storm is over.

The corners of his mouth hitch as he looks back at me. "Only if you stay really close so I can keep you warm."

We reposition the mattress closer to the hearth and wrap ourselves in all the blankets Theo owns. I'm actually a little warmer than necessary, but there's no way in hell I'm telling him that.

We spend the rest of the night tucked into each other, cuddling, kissing, enjoying the extra time we stole for ourselves. But the tension surrounding us won't go away. The fear, the guilt, the uncertainty—all these emotions refuse to let me sleep.

"How can we ever make up for the time we lost? How did this happen?" I whisper the question into the blankets, unsure of who I'm really asking.

"What do you mean?"

"I just keep thinking, what if I hadn't come to Vermont for work? Or what if the storm came a day later? Or what if—"

"El, stop. You can't focus on all the what-ifs, or you'll lose your mind. We got really unlucky seven years ago, so I think getting lucky this time was well-earned."

"Luck? You think it's just being lucky one day and not the next? Having good karma for a change?"

"No." Theo runs his hand along the side of my face before tucking a piece of loose hair behind my ear. "I think—I *know* we would have found our way back to each other. We just needed a little magic."

"Magic?" I scoff.

"Yeah. Our own little Hanukkah miracle. We were always meant to be together. Fate just decided to intervene. We were taking too long on our own."

. . .

WE'RE WOKEN up as the sun still sits low at the horizon, an indigo sky staring back at us through the window.

A loud gritty noise pours into the cabin, followed by even louder beeps.

"Is that the plow?" Theo jolts upright and runs to the window. "Finally! We'll be able to get your car out once they finish."

I walk into the kitchen and grab a glass of water. The time displayed on the oven tells me it's ten fifteen, but I know it's much earlier than that. He must not keep it set correctly. I'm about to tell Theo we should get some more sleep when—

"Theo..." I look back at the oven. At the time displayed there. Then it hits me that I'm only wearing a T-shirt and I'm not even shivering. "The power's back on!"

"It is?" He looks around before flicking a switch, watching the light dance a few times like he can't believe his eyes. "Holy shit."

He walks over to adjust the thermostat even though the temperature already seems perfect. It must have come back on in the middle of the night.

We don't have to leave now. *I* don't have to leave. Our gazes find each other, this revelation settling between us. It may be unspoken but we can read each other too well not to understand.

"El?"

"Yeah?"

"Got any plans for your birthday?"

A full-fledged grin lifts my cheeks. "What'd you have in mind?"

He glides by me to the other side of the kitchen where my purse has been all week, and to my actual shock, starts rummaging through it.

"What the—"

He pulls out my phone and presents it me.

"Un-fucking-block me, and I'll tell you."

ELLIE

Got a sec to chat?

MAYA

Calling you in five!

"Where the hell have you been?" Maya screams through the phone. She's trying to blow out an eardrum, but the sound of her voice still fills me with joy.

"I'm so sorry My. It's kind of a long story but we got snowed in and the power was out, and we were trying to conserve fuel for the generator, so we stopped charging phones. There was no service anyway." I blurt everything out as quickly as I can.

"Whoa, whoa, whoa. Back up, babe. You got snowed in? Where? Are you with your family?"

I give her the shortest version of the story that I can. She never knew many details about Theo—like his name—just that I had my heart crushed before I left for college.

"*Theodore Fox* is your first love? *Satan?* The guy you never got over? But he looks like Santa Claus!"

"Yeah, turns out the photo he was using is actually of his great grandfather, the original owner of the tree farm, and also the original Theodore Fox. Also, *my* Theodore Fox goes by Theo."

"Wait, wait, *wait*. Theo Fox? McFoxy? 2021 *playoff MVP* Theo Fox? Four goals in the third period of—"

"Yes!" I interrupt, because it sounds like she may never stop. "That's the one."

"Wait a second. Is he why you won't read any of the hockey

romances I've recommended? Because Briar U may be fake, but that series *slaps*."

"My, for the last time—"

"Wow. You're not coming back, are you? I'm like some long-distance matchmaker for our company. Jesus."

"I'm coming back, My..." Am I going back? I haven't really thought too much about what the future holds. I just know I want it to include Theo, no matter what. Maybe we could split our time? Shit. Something else we'll need to figure out.

"Hold that thought. I actually have some really good news."

"Yeah?" I ask, grateful for a change in subject.

"Remember the offer we got last month? From *Travel People*?"

"Of course I do."

"Well...they came back. And doubled it. More than doubled actually because they gave us much more favorable terms. We would both keep board seats."

"Holy shit. This is for real?" Maybe Theo was right about luck. All the years of not having it must have finally caught up.

"Yep. Obviously, we should discuss it. But I'm kind of inclined to—"

"Let's take it." This feels like a sign. Like Theo's right, and fate is still intervening, helping me follow the path I'm destined for, the path I'll get to share with the love of my life. "I mean, after the lawyers review it and everything. But, fuck. I'm in."

"Ahhh! I wish we were together so we could celebrate," Maya whines into my ear.

"What are you doing for New Year's?" I ask.

"Greg has to work. We fly back to SF on the twenty-ninth."

A giddy feeling takes over, so many things happening at once. So much to be excited about.

"Ever been to Vermont?"

· · ·

Theo came back from his loop around the village to find me squealing into the phone with Maya. She booked a flight from Barcelona to Montreal before we hung up, and I'd already worked out the details to go pick her up before returning my rental.

"I can't wait to meet her. I've never met one of your friends before."

His statement makes me inexplicably sad. Because I never had a friend like Maya for him to meet. It might take a while to adjust to our adult selves outside of the cabin bubble, but I'm ready for the opportunity.

"I should call Raj, see if he can come for New Year's too."

"Isn't he still playing for The Rangers?" I ask.

"Nah, he retired last season too. He's back in Montreal but we still see each other a decent amount." I laugh at the idea of two men in their twenties retiring, but I guess most people don't want to take hits like they did forever.

"It would be really nice to see him," I mention as Theo's phone starts to ring. When he looks at the caller, his entire expression freezes. I follow his line of sight to the photo of my big brother staring back at me.

"Are you gonna answer it?"

He doesn't respond, just keeps staring. Then his manner changes completely, wrath circling his features, and he picks up.

"Hey," Theo grunts. It's perhaps the least friendly "hey" that has ever been spoken.

"What's up man?" My brother's voice sounds through the speakerphone.

Theo doesn't say anything.

"Hello? Can you hear me?"

I urge Theo to respond, and he finally says, "Hey," again.

Like that's helpful. I wave my hand around, letting him know he needs to learn more words. "How's it going?"

"Good. I mean, you know, residency is crazy. But it's good. I'm actually heading up to Burlington in the morning, wanted to have a little extra time away from the city since I have to be back at work on the twenty-eighth. You still coming on Christmas Eve, or wanna hang sooner?"

I watch as Theo grinds his teeth, suppressing all the rage that wants out. He gives me a questioning look like I'm supposed to answer for him. I shake my head, absolutely not.

"Yeah man. I'll be there."

"Okay..." I can tell Ezra is perplexed by Theo's clipped tone, but he doesn't say anything else.

Theo utters a quick "see ya then," before hanging up the phone.

"No way. I'm not going." I finally got Theo back in my life. I am not ready to deal with my family just yet. Maybe after the holidays, after I know where I'll be living, or what's happening with *Wander*. It's all too much, too soon. Seven years and it still feels too soon. "We have plans! We can't just reschedule an entire day in bed."

He cups my face with his large hand, stroking softly in his Theo way, the way that shoves all my anxiety aside. He only says two words, but they're powerful enough to stop me from arguing.

"It's time."

Chapter Thirty

Ellie

Now

ON THE RIDE TO MY PARENTS' house, Theo's truck feels like a powder keg.

The tension, fear, and rage roll around us like waves at high tide, taking up more and more space as each minute passes. Stress has always been a demanding presence in my life, but today my anxiety is like a shadow, changing shape at will with each mile we get closer to my family. But that's the thing about anxiety. It's unpredictable. It's unforgiving. It's under my skin even after I think it's flown away.

The only thing stopping my nerves from causing a full-blown flare right now is the man beside me. I feel good about Theo. We haven't figured out our entire future together, but the unknown doesn't worry me. I trust him again, the way that I used to. The way that releases my uncertainty, knowing we will be together, no matter what.

But that doesn't stop the anxious energy about seeing my family from taking over. I have no idea what I'll say to my parents, to Ezra. From the look on Theo's face right now, I'm just as worried about him ripping out Ezra's throat.

We pull into the driveway, and I start to itch with panic.

"Are you sure this is a good idea? Maybe we should have told them I was coming," I say nervously, not wanting to get out of this truck. "Or maybe we just don't stay at all. Celebrating my birthday in the cabin sounds so nice all of a sudden. Think about how much sex we could have." He narrows his gaze at me as I bat my eyelashes.

"Ellie," Theo scolds. "We have to do this. It'll be okay, I promise. I'm with you." He folds my hand in his and sweeps his lips over my knuckles. "Always."

I stay firmly seated as Theo gets out of the truck and comes around to open my door. He practically yanks me down and holds my hand tightly enough to drag my whole weight up the front steps.

He knocks twice and I can't stop shaking. His thumb makes small circles across the back of my hand, trying his best to soothe me. I start to lean into him, wanting to feel more of his body against me, when the door swings open.

"Holy shit." Ezra gasps, wide-eyed and wobbly. He stumbles while he backs up to let us in, still tongue-tied, and that's when I turn to find Theo staring daggers at him. Ezra must be scared shitless.

"Ez? Is that Theo?" Dad's voice echoes from the kitchen and tears start to well in my eyes. The one person I'm not afraid to see today, but still feel so much guilt over leaving behind.

"Dad?" I squeak, making our way into the kitchen. Ezra is still at the door with his mouthing hanging open, but Theo hasn't left my side. Just like he promised.

"Ellie?" Dad yells. "Is that really you, sweet pea?"

He comes barreling toward us to give me a hug and I accept it with tears shining through both of our eyes. It feels so good to see him again. Theo drops my hand for only a moment and when Dad pulls away, he replaces it in an instant. He is determined to get me through this, and with him by my side, I think I can.

"Judy! Get over here!" Dad calls. "My California girl." He looks back at me, his face gleaming. "It's good to see you, honey."

"What is going on over here?" Mom shouts from the hallway.

My heart stops when I see her enter the room and our gazes meet. She blinks a few times, like she's not sure if I'm real or some apparition. Moments pass in utter silence before her gut-wrenching sob fills the space around us. Right before she falls to her knees.

Dad rushes to help her up, and I can barely make out the words she's speaking through her cries. When she finally stands up and composes herself, I track her eyes pointing directly at my and Theo's intertwined hands.

And then she whispers, "You brought her back," before rushing toward us both.

"You look—" Mom's eyes travel over me, noticing all the changes to my body. My nerves rattle under her perusal, wondering how she'll react, but she finishes, "—so healthy. You look amazing, Ellie."

The hugging feels endless, but I also appreciate how I haven't had to find my words yet. It finally hits me what Dr. Green was trying to puzzle out of me. I *would* like to move forward with my parents. It doesn't mean I have to forgive them, but having a relationship with them is still my choice. On my terms. The revelation feels good, a little bit of pressure releasing from my shoulders.

But Ezra is still missing from this equation, standing by the front door, nervous energy spilling from him.

Theo notices me noticing, and suddenly all his attention is back on Ezra.

"Will you be okay?" he whispers to me. I nod and he gives my knuckles another kiss. And then he lets go of my hand. He stalks toward Ezra and utters a terse, "Let's go," never stopping his movements before heading outside.

Ezra follows.

The door slams.

Mom and Dad are looking at me for answers that I do not know how to give them. Maybe it's being back in my childhood home, but my maturity level plummets, and I run to the window to watch the guys' interaction.

"What are they screaming about?" Mom asks from behind my ear. It's weird feeling her closeness to me, yet comforting in a way. A lot of anger still sits beneath my skin, but I can admit that I missed my mom, missed the constant presence in my life.

I can't hear anything, but it's easy to tell Theo is yelling. Ezra's hands stay up in a defensive position, but it doesn't look like he's getting many words out.

"Ellie?" Dad appeals for answers.

"I don't think it's my place to tell you. But maybe—"

"Jesus!" Dad yells as we all watch Theo punch Ezra directly in the nose. "What the hell does he think he's doing?" Dad moves toward the door, clearly planning to stop this altercation.

"Dad, stop. Let them handle this. Please?"

He looks at me with a thousand questions in his eyes, and then we're all focusing back on the window because Theo punches Ezra *again*.

Ez isn't fighting back. His face is stoic, his expression pooled in acceptance, even as blood trickles down from his nose.

I promised Theo I wouldn't intervene. We decided his fight

with Ezra and mine were separate battles. I just didn't realize how literal he was being.

The three of us keep watching as Theo goes back to using words instead of his fists. Mom comes up to my side and wraps an arm around me. I try not to flinch, but I can't help it and she pulls away with a sad smile. I want to apologize but I don't. I shouldn't. I need to set boundaries if this will ever work between us. Something about her expression tells me it's going to be a long road.

"So, you and Theo?"

"Me and Theo," I supply. There's not much else to it.

"I'm so sorry, sweetie." Her sniffles are audible as she turns away, and I notice my dad watching us with glistening eyes.

When I turn back to the window, I find Theo and Ezra hugging, something I was completely unprepared for. What could he possibly have said? Theo isn't smiling, but he gives Ezra's shoulder a tight squeeze.

As soon as the door opens, my dad charges toward the guys, demanding to know what the fight was about.

"It's fine, Dad. I deserved it," Ezra moans.

"Answers. Now."

"Joel," Theo starts. My dad looks back at him, his jaw working overtime while his eyes stay wide with questions. "Look, I'm sorry about hitting Ez. And that you had to see it. If he wants to tell you why, then I'll leave that up to him."

Dad huffs, looking around the room like someone should tell Theo he's insane. Then he turns to Ezra, but still gets nothing in response. "What the hell is going on here?"

"Can I talk to you and Judy?" Theo asks him. "Alone?"

For some reason, Dad's looking at me for answers now. I'm not sure what Theo wants to talk to them about. This wasn't part of our plan. But when I find Theo's eyes, he looks at me in a pleading way and I know he needs this.

"I should talk to Ez, so we'll leave you alone." I turn to my brother who's using his shirt to quelch the bleeding. "I'll grab you some ice. Let's talk in the basement."

"Did you do it to hurt me?"

"Ellie—"

"Theo said you didn't. He said you never hated me like I thought you did. But I just don't understand why else you would lie to me like that."

Ezra's eyes have been watering since we came down here and I can't tell if it's because of me or his bloody nose. We were able to stop the bleeding, but I can already see the bruises forming around his face. I feel a prick of guilt, knowing how important his job is to him. I doubt they'll be wanting him to see young patients and their families when he looks like he got in a bar fight.

"I never hated you. You really thought I hated you?"

I'm not sure how to respond so I just nod. Latke appears suddenly between us on the couch. I'm surprised the old cat is still so stealthy. She immediately paws at Ezra's bruised face sending scratch marks across his cheek. I guess karma really is a cat.

"Fuck," he groans. "I never meant to hurt you; I swear. That wasn't—" He pauses to sniff, which looks extremely painful. "I was just angry. When I found out about you and Theo, it felt like you were all just keeping secrets, talking behind my back. I know I acted irrationally and childish and...I just sort of went on the attack."

"But—"

"Look." He reaches toward me but seems to think better of the gesture and pulls his hands back to his lap. "I was pissed at

Theo. He was my closest friend and I felt like he was using me. Me, our parents, all because he was going after you. I was—" He sighs. "I was fucking jealous, Ellie. I'm a piece of shit and I was jealous and did a really horrible thing."

We fall into silence for a moment. I'm not sure how to respond since, well, I agree with him. Theo already punched him, and I don't feel like laying into him just to make him feel worse. But I still have so many questions.

"You never..." I take a second to compose my thoughts because they're everywhere. So many moments in our history skate through my mind, sparking all sorts of childhood memories I usually prefer not to think about. And the longer I let them linger, I realize that it's actually really fucking simple. "Liked me. You never liked me, Ez. I know it was tough when we were young. I know my lupus got in the way. But you were always avoiding me. Every time I was sick, I always hoped you would be there, but you never wanted anything to do with me. Maybe that's not what hate is, but it felt like it to me."

"You're wrong, El. I loved you. I just...fuck. I don't know. I always felt like I failed you. I'm your big brother. I was supposed to protect you, but I couldn't do shit. You were always stuck in bed, and you couldn't be with friends, and then I still resented you for taking all of Mom and Dad's attention. I was fucking useless. The only person I hated was myself."

This feels like a big revelation, and everything starts to click from the last five years. All the conversations we had centered around his medical school training, his residency, his patients. How passionate he was about pediatrics and emergency medicine. Like he was trying to prove to both of us that he learned how to help people.

People like eight-year-old me.

"And then Theo came along, and you finally had the sibling

you always wanted." I don't even mean to say this aloud, but it feels effortless to come to this conclusion.

"It wasn't like that; I never wanted to replace you. But you're right, he was like a brother to me. And sometimes I just needed to be away from Mom and Dad, and he was always there for me."

"And you never wanted to share him."

"No," he argues, but it's fucking weak. "Maybe," he admits. His eyes dart up like he's searching for the truth somewhere on our ceiling. Hell, it could be there. This ceiling, this basement holds all our secrets. "But I had no idea, Ellie. I promise you; I never knew what you meant to each other, not until five minutes ago. I didn't have a clue."

Time passes while I chew on his words. Latke is curled in my lap and actually letting me pet her. I guess she's gotten less discriminating in her old age.

"I believe you. We hid it pretty well. He was so scared about you finding out and hating him for it."

"But why didn't *you* tell me?" he pleads.

"Tell you? What, because we were so close? When did I ever talk to you about boys?"

"No. I mean that night—you wouldn't leave your room. I was planning to come clean. I felt horrible seeing you so upset. I was kind of shocked by your reaction, honestly. And I decided I was gonna eat the sword and tell you I lied." His eyes turn down, not willing to look at me. "And then you told me Theo didn't matter. I know I should have still told you the truth but— I knew I fucked up and I didn't want *you* to hate *me*. I figured if you really weren't that upset about him then it didn't matter. And then you were so focused on college and..."

"You thought you'd just get away with it?"

"Yeah, I guess." His eyes water some more. I don't relish making my brother cry, but it's hard to feel bad for him.

"What about after that though? It's been *years*. You really never thought you should tell me, or Theo? He's your best friend and you never considered you should be honest with him?"

"Of course I thought about it. But after you left for California, I thought it was all in the past." The tears start flowing down Ezra's cheeks. He's done trying to hold them back. "And I knew he'd hate me if I ever told him what I did. I was too afraid I'd lose my closest friend. I *never* knew how much you cared about each other, Ellie. I didn't know. I swear I didn't know."

"Is that why you told him how happy I was?"

"What?"

"Theo said you're always telling him and Mom and Dad how great I am, how happy. He figured we talk all the time. I didn't understand why you would do that, why you would lie about something like that."

"I just really wanted it to be true. I guess if I said it enough, it felt like it was."

I scooch closer to him on the couch and wrap my arms around him. I know it will take a lot more time to feel okay about him, but in this moment, I just want to hug my brother. I believe he made a mistake. And we have all made mistakes.

"It's okay. You only cost us seven years," I joke. But his sobs only grow louder. I pull back, place my hands on his shoulders, forcing him to look at me. "I forgive you, okay?"

"What? Why? You shouldn't." He wrenches himself out of my hold. "You should hate me."

I tuck my knees to my chest and lean back against the sofa, staring over at him. "Yeah. I should hate you. You did a really shitty thing. But you're my brother, and I don't want to hate you. I don't want hate to exist at all between us, whether it's real or in my head. I'm so over that word."

Ezra stares back at me with a blank expression, like he's

waiting for the chips to fall. I continue, "I think we both spent a lot of time not understanding each other, and we did *not* communicate well." He scoffs in agreement. "Let's fix it. Do better this time."

"You're really gonna forgive me?"

"Yeah, I'm gonna try. On one condition."

"I'll do anything, Ellie."

"Tell me what you said to Theo. Why did he hug you before?"

"I umm, I can't tell you that."

"You just said you'd do anything! Seriously?" I shove him lightly against the chest. I would go harder if it weren't for his bloody nose.

"All I can say is Theo asked me a question. And he liked my answer enough to hug me. I know he hasn't forgiven me and I'm not sure if he ever will. But I promise I will do whatever I can to earn your trust back."

"I like the sound of that." Theo's voice startles us both and we turn to find him coming down the stairs.

He strides over to the couch and sits down next to me, throwing an arm over my shoulder. He's back by my side, just like he promised.

"You good?" he asks quietly with a quick kiss to my hair.

"I'm good."

I pat Theo on the knee, three quick taps, the signal we came up with earlier. A way for me to let him know I want to stay the night, that I want to spend my birthday here with my family.

He squeezes me tighter, and I know he's pleased with this outcome. Neither of us want to hold on to our anger, not when we finally have each other in our lives again.

I look to Ezra and realize I have never seen him so uncomfortable, like he's not sure if he should be getting up to give us privacy, if Theo even plans on speaking to him. He's just... hovering. I think he's about to jump up and leave the basement when Theo speaks again.

"What do you think about bringing back the pillow fort? Are we too old to watch movies all night and sleep on the floor?" He throws me a quick wink but poses the question to my brother, and both sets of their eyes tell me it's an olive branch. The relief framing Ezra's face makes my heart sing.

"I think we can suffer for a night," Ezra replies. "I'll do an extra layer of cushions for our bad backs, just to be safe."

I start to laugh when Theo asks if he can talk to me alone. He says he wants to show me something upstairs before scooping Latke up to carry her on his shoulder.

"I'll get started on the pillow fort," Ezra says, already tearing the couch apart.

"Are you sure you're okay? Your talk with Ezra was...?"

"It was good. Much less eventful than yours." I smirk. "What did you talk to my parents about?"

"I had some things I needed to get off my chest. Maybe you and I can talk to them together at some point too? But there were a few things I just couldn't wait for. Sorry I didn't warn you ahead of time."

"I wasn't mad about it, only curious." We're about to reach my room when I remember what Ezra said. "What did you ask Ez—"

My words wither away as Theo opens the door to my room. It looks mostly the same, lavender coating the bed and carpet, my favorite books lining the walls. It's obvious my parents never touched it after I left.

But there are three new shelves on the wall next to my bed, and they're covered in snow globes.

Some I recognize, the menorah, the lobsters, the penguins—Cherry, Berry and Larry. But others are new.

I glide toward them as if they hold a siren song, vision hazy but feeling the need to touch each new piece of glass. I pick one up that has a bottle of champagne floating inside. Instead of snowflakes, it's filled with confetti.

"That one was for your twenty-first," Theo's voice sounds from behind me.

I'm not ready to confront what he's telling me, so I set it back on the shelf and grab another. This one has a dog inside that looks just like Noodle and I can't stop the sob from escaping me.

"I had that one made." Theo takes the crystal ball from my hands and flips it over to show me the bottom, etched with his name and life dates. "After he passed, I was sure you'd come home that year."

The bed catches my fall as I lose the ability to hold myself up. I try not think about Noodle Kugel too often. It's hurts too much when I do.

"Every year?" I ask.

"Yeah." He picks up another globe, this one with two penguins huddling together. "This was the one I brought for number twenty. I was so excited to finally see you."

"Theo," I choke out, unable to find any other words to express what I'm feeling.

"Every year, I hoped you'd be back. That it would finally be the year I would see you again. I never wanted to be empty-handed."

To be waited for, what a feeling. What a wonder.

"Do I get one this year?" As soon as I say it, I feel ridiculous. As if I really need a birthday present in the midst of everything happening between us and my family.

But Theo never lets me down. "Of course."

I hadn't realized he was keeping a hand behind his back until he reaches out to me, displaying my new gift.

"I had these made for the general store at the village. You're the first to have one though, since the store doesn't open until New Year's Eve."

I peek inside the crystal to find a miniaturized version of my favorite place in the world. The rink, the trees, even the festoon of lights. It's all an impeccable replica of Sugar Valley. On the base of the globe, seven words are printed in a whimsical script. *Magic in the Air - Sugar Valley Village.*

"It's perfect."

Theo walks over to my desk and opens the small drawer, pulling out a stack of envelopes. "Had to keep these hidden. I wasn't sure if your parents would read them."

"What?" I choke out.

"They're just birthday cards. You don't have to read th—"

His words are silenced as I launch across the bed and snatch the stack out of his hands. Each envelope has a number on it. I start with twenty.

#20

Happy Birthday AJ,

I can't believe it's been a year since I've seen you. It reminds me of your birthdays when we were kids, when I had to wait a whole year every time. It didn't seem as hard then.

I miss you, desperately. I'm sure you know that, but I needed to say it.

Can we talk, while you're home? I want to hear all about California.

-T

#21

Happy Birthday El,

Did you know I'm officially a Boston Bruin? I've seen a few people wearing my jersey and every time I wonder if you have one. Probably not.

If you're home this year, I'll get you one. I'll sign anything you want if I can just see you, one time.

I miss you.

-T

#22

Happy Birthday El,

Do you ever wonder about me? I feel like all I ever do is imagine where you are or who you're with. Sometimes when I lie awake at night, I ask Mom and Dad about you. If they watch over you since I can't anymore. I know it's ridiculous, but I can't get myself to stop.

Please be here this year.

-T

#23

Happy Birthday El,

I think I'm still in love with you. Will that ever go away? If you can't find another reason, just come home to tell me how you were able to do it. How were you able to forget about me when I'll never be able to forget about you?

-T

#24

Happy Birthday El,

These cards are stupid. I never gave you a card before you left me. Not sure why I keep writing them, but it's my only way to talk to you.

Do you still watch the stars at night when you can't sleep? Can you even see them where you live? I do all the time, but all I see is you.

-T

#25

Happy Birthday El,

I finally got the village back. I finally did what I've been trying to do since graduation. But I couldn't tell you. I couldn't take you skating

the second the papers were signed. And I'm
angry that you took that away from me.

I'm not sure how much you talk to your
parents, so I don't even know if they'll tell you.
Ezra says you're so happy with your new
boyfriend he doubts you'll ever come home. That
gutted me.

I keep telling myself this birthday will be the
last one. The last card, the last snow globe. I
can't tell if it's a lie or not. I want to give up,
but something keeps stopping me.

I don't expect to see you this time.
Prove me wrong.

-T

WE'VE DISCUSSED our missing years in depth this last week, but I hadn't *truly* realized Theo's pain until now. Anger reaches into my gut and tugs, wanting to resurface my feelings about Ezra, about my family. It's a potent mixture of rage and resentment, wanting to find some sort of vengeance through reparations.

The problem with anger though, is it only hurts those who hold on to it. It doesn't solve our problems; it can't change the past. And I've wasted a lot of time being angry. Angry, sad, resentful. I've spent years of therapy trying to move past these feelings, trying not to let them control me. It would be so easy to get lost in the hurt, to hate my brother, to avoid my family, but how does any of that benefit *me*?

There's a slew of new feelings to go over with Dr. Green, but outside of my work with him, I want to focus on the good in my life.

I take a deep, meditative breath and devote my attention to the man in front of me.

"I tried really hard to stop loving you, too. It just wouldn't take."

MOM MAKES brisket for dinner and a birthday cake for dessert. It has real sugar and icing, and she doesn't say a word when I ask for a second slice.

I decide to tell her about the doctors and dietician I have been working with in San Francisco, wanting her to know that I didn't just ignore everything she taught me. It's important to me that she knows I prioritize my health, that I can do it on my own successfully.

There's a small part of me that's searching for a sense of satisfaction, a smugness with how everything played out. *Look at me! Look at the man who's by my side, who loved me all along.*

But those thoughts feel false now. Maybe I leaned on Theo too much in my head, at least when I was younger. He's a part of me, but he's not all that I am. I can sit here with my family, proud of who I've become all on my own.

Mom asks about us staying for a few days, but I'm serious about drawing boundaries. After tonight, I'm going back to the cabin. The next time I'm with Mom, I want it to be in therapy.

Theo helps take some of the spotlight away from me by telling them how progress is coming along for the grand re-opening. And then, at my request, Ezra tells us stories from the hospital.

He's so passionate about treating children, and I feel a wave of pride knowing that he was motivated by me. That growing up with me drove him to a career of helping others. And I want to kick myself for not realizing that earlier.

As we finish eating, Dad asks us to stay upstairs until he can finish the last touches on the pillow fort. He was very excited to bring back the tradition that seemingly left when I did.

"We should get the movie line-up ready," I mention to the guys. And then to Ezra, "What do you wanna watch?" I grit my teeth over-dramatically, so he knows how much I do not want him to say *Die Hard*. I'll be very happy if he never makes us watch any of those again.

He looks at me thoughtfully, then at Theo with a rueful expression, at Mom busying herself with dishes in the kitchen, and finally back to me.

"Actually, I think it's time we let you choose, Ellie. What'll it be?"

Chapter Thirty-One

Theo

Now

TIME MOVES SLOWER TONIGHT.

Ellie and Ezra both fell asleep halfway through *The Holiday*. It was our second movie of the night chosen by El, who happens to enjoy romantic comedies more than she ever let on. But there won't be sleep for me this evening. I have been watching the minutes advance at the pace of melting snow.

Eleven fifteen.

Eleven nineteen.

Eleven twenty-three.

Eleven thirty-seven.

I can't wait any more. The nervous energy is eating me alive.

"El," I whisper, dragging my fingers through her hair.

She cracks a lid open to look at me. "What's going on?"

"Shh. Don't wake Ez. But I need you to get up." She eyes me quizzically but lets me offer an arm to help her stand. "Follow me."

Our hands stay clasped together as we walk upstairs, and I lead Ellie into the sunroom. For more than half a decade now, I have spent every one of her birthdays in this room, staring at the stars through the skylight, shedding tears with her mom. And yet, this room doesn't make me feel sad. No matter how rough each year was without Ellie, I always had hope.

"What's all this?" Ellie asks, noting the blanket and pillows I set up earlier on the floor.

"I wanted to watch the stars with you. It's almost midnight."

We lie down on the blanket and maneuver ourselves into a comfortable position, limbs entwined wherever we can fit them.

"So this is where you spent my birthday every year, huh?"

"Yeah. I think I'm ready for a new tradition. But I wanted the last time here to be with you."

She snuggles into me, and my nerves cease to exist. There isn't a doubt in my mind that this is what's right.

I reach into the pocket of my sweatpants, grabbing Ellie's final birthday gift and eye the clock. Three minutes till midnight.

I count every single second.

"Happy Birthday, Eliana." I brush my lips against hers as I slide the stone into her hand.

"What is this?"

I sit up, leaning back on my heels so I can collect my thoughts. It would've been smart to prepare for this, but my emotions are taking over. I have no idea what I want to say.

So I wing it.

"When you were nine, I let you fall on the ice. And you lied to me when you said it didn't hurt." Her mouth opens to correct me, but I cut her off. "The jig is up. I always knew." My lips twitch as the memories come flooding back. I was devastated then, and so focused on fixing my mistake. "I felt so bad about it that I begged my dad to help me find you a birthday present. He took me to the gift shop and said that I should pick out something sparkly, that girls love that."

Her brown eyes turn watery, catching the moonlight shining through the window.

"When you were ten, I was determined to show you a good time without any injuries. I promised myself I would never cause you pain again, and that goal has never changed."

"Theo, what—"

"When you were eighteen, I was so completely in love with you that I almost proposed."

"What?"

"I had it in my head that getting engaged was the only way I could tell your parents about us." Tears slide down my cheek as her shocked expression shines back at me. "There was never a doubt in my mind I would marry you one day. I had already picked out the ring when everything happened with your brother."

"I had no idea—"

"Can you stop interrupting?"

"Sorry." We share a quick smile and I kiss her because I can't not kiss her. Not when I finally have her back.

"When you were thirteen, I said you deserved more than a pebble." I squeeze her hand still holding on to the stone. The one I found lying in their front yard yesterday. Right after I hit Ezra for the second time. I swear it was glowing, a beacon calling out to me, telling me exactly what I needed to do.

In that moment, I forgot every single thing I was mad about, everything I had meant to say to Ezra. Instead, I asked him for his blessing.

I didn't need it, but I wanted it. I wanted a fresh start for all of us, without any obstacles like before. And I followed our conversation by asking his parents the same thing. They were probably perplexed by the suddenness of it all, but no one denied me what I wanted. Maybe deep down, they always knew.

"To be clear, you still deserve more than a pebble. Tattoo or not, you aren't actually a penguin. I'll get you something sparkly, anything you want." I blow out a breath, needing a moment to stop myself from rambling. "But this stone, it's a promise, my promise to you. I want to build a home for us, a whole life for us. I want to take care of you, to do everything I can to take away your pain. I want you with me for every Christmas and Hanukkah, every birthday and New Year's Eve. I want to spend every moment I have left with you by my side."

Tears glide down Ellie's face, but her smile is vibrant, her eyes sparkling like the stars gazing down upon us.

"Go on another adventure with me, AG. I promise it will be the best one yet. Will you marry me?"

Her grin spreads, cheeks flushed with emotion, but she doesn't respond.

My eyes plead with her, *say yes.*

She turns over the stone a few times in her hand, letting her thumb skim over the smooth side. Her gaze follows mine, watching her own movements, before she looks up again.

"Will you feed me, too?"

"Every day." Her lips twitch as she bites the inside of her cheek. "I'm sweating over here, El. Can you please answer the question?"

She slides toward me on the blanket and settles herself in my lap. "Yes." Her lips find mine in a kiss that feels like the warmth of a thousand suns. "Let's have an adventure."

Chapter Thirty-Two

Ellie

Now

"WELL," I turn to Mom, shutting the laptop. "What did you think of therapy?"

We just finished our first joint session with Dr. Green over zoom. I offered to meet with someone local, someone impartial who neither of us had met before, but she was adamant about meeting Dr. Green after I told her how much he's helped me these last six years.

It was a little strange, having a session in my parents' kitchen, but talking to him has become such a comfort to me that the awkwardness fell away after only a few minutes.

I did most of the talking today. He asked Mom not to focus on apologizing or trying to fix our past right away, but that he wanted her to listen. To stories I had told him about my childhood, stories from my time at college. He said she needed to re-learn me before we could start building our new relationship.

The way he phrased it—our *new* relationship—also gave me comfort. It meant I didn't have to go back, only forward. It made me wonder if I could do the same thing with my brother. I so badly wanted to.

And to my surprise, Mom really did listen. She also shed a lot of tears, many that are still streaming down her face even though we ended the call several minutes ago.

"It was something we should have done a long time ago," she finally responds. I'm so —"

"Let's not do that, okay? We can talk more about the past at our next session, but today is supposed to fun, remember?"

She sniffles a few times before getting up and moving around the kitchen. She's just tinkering with things, trying to distract us while she composes herself.

"Okay, sweetie." She takes a long breath. "I can't wait to meet Maya. Let me just go get cleaned up."

I texted Maya about the engagement hours after Theo popped the question. Her responding text included an appointment reminder she scheduled for us at the nicest bridal boutique in Burlington. Since she'd only be in town for a few days, I had to oblige. And when she asked if we should invite my mom, I couldn't say no to that either.

Introducing Theo and Maya when she got in yesterday was wild. It was so many firsts piled on top of each other. The first time ever introducing Theo as my boyfriend, only to be scolded by him since I didn't say fiancé. The first time Maya met anyone from my life before her. The first time Theo ever got to meet a friend of mine, someone who had knowledge of me that he didn't. He actually didn't love that part, and I imagine they're both still giving each other the third degree now.

Maya sprinted toward us across the baggage claim as soon as she spotted my waiving arm. She flung herself against me and picked me up to spin us around until I got dizzy and begged her to stop.

"You—" She pressed her pointer finger into the middle of Theo's chest. "—have a lot of explaining to do."

A very confused Theo tried to give her a hug, but she pulled back and crossed her arms. Then she made a slow perusal of him, eyes bouncing around in examination. She reminded me of a judge from the Westminster dog show. "Nice to finally meet you, Satan."

"Huh?" Theo asked, a frown forming on his handsome face. "I thought..." He looked at me for help.

"My, we've been over this. He didn't do anything wrong, remember?"

"Tell that to the excruciating six months of Barry's Boot Camp I had to endure." Her eyes focused back on Theo. "Do you have any idea how many brownie sundaes we ate because of you? My hips never fully recovered."

Theo and I both glanced at each other, wondering when Maya might stop the interrogation. Her serious expression never faded.

And still, Theo came through. "Well, it's a good thing you're gorgeous. Maybe we should make sundaes back at my cabin and keep the tradition alive?"

Maya couldn't keep up the act after that. She huffed out a breath, as dramatic as a toddler leaving a toy store. "Okay, fine. He's perfect." She threw her arm over my shoulders. "Let's go see this magical cabin of yours."

THE DRIVE HOME and the rest of the night were nothing short of perfect. It was the first time I got to be the glue. Growing up, I spent so much time and energy trying to be a part of Ezra's life; his interests, his friends, his availability. At school, I was always in the outer ring of the circle, friendly with many but crucial to no one. With Theo and Maya and me all together, I was finally a piece of the *core*.

Mom and I get in the car to head toward campus. We decided getting lunch together would be good before dress shopping. If I'm honest, my nerves are a little on edge remembering the last time we tried buying dresses together, but I have a good feeling that history won't be repeating itself.

When we park and walk into the restaurant, I'm hit with the revelation that another first is about to take place. My best friend is about to meet my mother.

"Hi, Mrs. Klein!" Maya jumps in for a hug right away and I'm filled with gratitude for her larger-than-life personality. I can just sit back and enjoy the show.

"It's nice to meet you, Maya. Ellie's told me so much about you," Mom starts in. It's not exactly true considering how little we've talked this week, but Maya did come up in a lot of stories I told in therapy. "Thank you for being such a good friend to her."

"Oh, please. I would be utterly lost without my Ellie Belly." Maya delivers the line with her signature flare. "She taught me about true love."

"I did?" Mom and I both frown in confusion.

"Umm, yeah! Why did you think I got so picky sophomore year? Your little rant about melting bones and magnetic skin and all the static." My jaw drops at her memory—albeit extremely inaccurate—of our conversation in the library. "You know what I mean. I thought you were this innocent girl that I could teach everything to about boys. And then out of nowhere you changed my whole perspective."

Mom's eyes shine as she watches us. I wonder if it hurts her as much as me that she never knew me like that, that a girl I met in college has this intimate knowledge of me that she never did.

Her sad expression morphs into a small smile. "Well, I guess we know who'll be toasting at the wedding."

THE GRAND RE-OPENING of Sugar Valley Village is in one hour, and Maya has already taken at least one thousand photos.

Theo and I keep catching each other's eyes as we watch her flit around the village taking charge of everything. First, she altered the window displays at Fox in the Snow and The Pizza Emporium. Then she made everyone pose for "candid" shots with the mini horses in front of our brand-new Moon River sign. In two days, she has somehow garnered the role of managing the village, while Theo and I just watch.

I'm going to miss working with her every day. We had a call with our lawyers when she first got in, and it sounds like the offer for *Wander* is exactly what we wanted. We'll be signing the papers by the end of January and taking a major step back from operating the business. She knows I'm planning to stay in Vermont, that I decided I want to help Theo grow the village into something even bigger and better than it was when we were kids. Now I'm wondering if she might want to help us.

Her current ask is a little more personal.

"Please," Maya begs. "It will be so gorgeous and magical and wonderful! Ever since Theo told me the story last night, I've been thinking about it. You need it captured on camera!"

She wants us to recreate our first kiss.

And she isn't the only one who's been thinking about it since he told the story last night. Hearing about that day from his perspective lit my skin on fire. It made me fall in love with him all over again. Especially the part about him feeling the presence of his mom, of her shouting in his head to "go for it!"

"But it already happened, My. You can't retroactively take a picture."

She folds her arms across her chest and pins me with a heavily raised eyebrow. "Try me."

"Come on, AG. Let's give the people what they want," Theo urges from my side. He's already handing me my skates.

"Are you sure you're okay that your family isn't here?" Theo asks. Maya snapped all her photos and even got me to do the perfect foot pop with my arms balanced over Theo's shoulders. Now we're just enjoying a few minutes alone on the ice before everything opens up.

"Yeah," I reply. "This day is about you. It was the right decision not to include them."

His lips find mine in the kind of simple intimacy we never had before. No secrets, no uncertainty, just easy love. The static-on-my-skin kind. I grin at the thought and Maya's words from yesterday.

"I wish my parents could be here," he murmurs.

"They are. I can feel them."

Theo's eyes crinkle as he smiles down at me. "You think so?"

"I know so. They've been with you the whole time." He might not realize how firmly I believe these words. Theo waited for me; he came back every year to give me my birthday present while I spent that whole time trying to forget him. Nothing has ever made me more of a believer than the hope he held in his heart.

"I really want you to be right," he whispers.

"I am. I also made a bunch of grilled cheese sandwiches

earlier when you were running around. Just in case we needed to get your dad's attention."

A few minutes later we're exiting the rink when I'm suddenly lifted out of the air and spun around in several circles.

"Ells Bells!"

"Oh my god, Raj! Put me down. Now!"

The former New York Ranger places me back on the ground before my skate takes out someone's eye.

"Mirage! You made it!" Theo chirps.

I quickly unlace my skates and slide my boots back on while Theo and Raj hug for a long moment. I notice Raj's confused face when he whispers to Theo, loudly enough for me to hear, "I thought we hated her," and Theo just responds, "Never."

"How about you say a proper hello to my fiancée?" Theo pats Raj on the back as he elongates his new favorite word. And then Raj scoops me up and I'm flailing in the air all over again.

RAJ AND MAYA become fast friends. I realize how much I love being the glue. Part of me wishes my brother could be here tonight, but there's something special about sharing the village with just Theo and our friends.

We try to make it to every corner of the village, checking in on each business as the crowd continues to grow. Everything will normally close at ten pm, but since it's New Year's Eve, the entire village will be lit up past midnight.

The four of us settle into a booth at Fox in the Snow just before we ring in the new year. Cindy opened another bakery in the main part of town when the village closed, but her daughter decided to work with Theo and reopen this location.

Theo loads up my mug with an abundance of marshmallows and his favorite peppermint whipped cream. I encourage

Maya to do the same, but she and Raj both opt for the adult version laced with schnapps and brandy.

"What do you think?" Theo asks me after a few warm sips.

"About what?"

"This. Could you really see yourself living here, at the village?"

"Theo Fox. I'd live in the trees as long as it's with you."

"In the trees? Really?"

I nod, smirking at him from behind my mug. "As long as we're together."

He wraps an arm around me until I'm halfway onto his lap, pulling me as close as he can. "This is all I've ever wanted. It feels unsettling to finally have it. Like it's the end of something.

"It's not. It's just the beginning."

He kisses me again, until Raj and Maya start to whine. And then Maya jumps up in her seat and points out the window.

"Look at the bunny! Damn, it's huge," she exclaims. Theo and I share a private smile. Why wouldn't I want to live out here surrounded by furry friends?

"Do you know what they're called?" she asks Theo. "El said you knew every collective animal noun."

Theo smirks and secretly pinches my thigh. "A fluffle."

"No way. You just have that kind of knowledge sitting around in your head?"

"Try me," he deadpans.

"Fine," she mimics. "Chipmunks."

"A scurry."

"Raccoons."

"A nursery."

"Jellyfish."

"A bloom."

"Bears," Raj chimes in, wanting to join the fun.

This time Theo raises an eyebrow and drags out the word. "A sloth."

Maya sits back in her chair, face full of wonder as we all laugh.

I turn to Theo and ask, "What about us?" I gesture from him to me. "What would our collective noun be?"

He kisses my nose and pulls me in close again. I can feel his smile stretch across my temple before he speaks. He says the words like he didn't even have to think about it, like it's just another fact he's had memorized for years. "That's easy." He smirks. "We're magic."

Author's Note

When I was in high school, I volunteered at the local Children's Hospital, specifically in their daycare unit for siblings of patients. This was an incredibly formative experience for me, seeing healthy children who were sometimes starved for attention, and spending all of their free time in a hospital while their parents were focused on their less healthy siblings. It was heartbreaking, humbling, and something I'll never forget.

As an only child with a chronic illness, it made me wonder what life would have been like for me if I had siblings. What would they have done every time Mom and Dad had to take me to the ER? Would they have blamed me when a vacation ended early? Or when there was a party I couldn't attend, so they couldn't either? Would they resent me? And if so, would they grow out of it?

Chronic illness affects so much more than just our physical and mental health, and I wanted to examine the complexity of that in this book. In how chronic illness can bring out the best and worst in us, how it can strain any type of relationship.

I'd like to clarify that Ellie's parents were in no way based off of my own. While writing her story, I found myself feeling more and more gratitude toward my own mother, and how she never let my physical limitations hold me back from experiencing everything I wanted to as a child. Even when she let me go to slumber parties, knowing there was a fifty percent chance she'd be picking me up in the middle of the night and rushing me to the hospital.

I hope I did justice to the Klein family in this story. I hope that you empathized with Ellie, but also her parents and brother as well. And I hope you agree that Theo is a national treasure who must be protected at all costs.

Acknowledgments

First and foremost, I need to thank every person who read, reviewed, and recommended Speechless. I wasn't sure if I would continue writing after my first novel, but seeing how well it was received in the book community gave me so much motivation to keep writing.

The idea for A Little Magic came to me one day last December. I thought, "what about a story with a Jewish girl who goes to Vermont for Christmas and gets stranded in a blizzard with her first love?" So, I built on that. But I have to thank my husband, Erik, for always talking about Vermont, for wanting so badly for me to love it there, that it was basically all I could think about over the holidays. I also need to thank him for inspiring so much of Theo. From his love of animals to his overtly kind and caring demeanor and his excellence in sports, I feel so lucky to be married to someone worthy of book boyfriend status.

Britt, thank you again for being the *best* editor. From offering to read my very first, *very* rough draft, to helping me polish this story enough to make it shine, you are a true gem. Working with you feels like a partnership and I am beyond proud of what we've accomplished together. I'm committed to meeting in person one day even if I have to travel halfway around the world. And when it does happen, we'll draw those diagrams ;)

A huge thank you to all of my beta readers: Taylor, Carissa,

Amanda (both of you!), Kathrin, Steph & Jenna. Your feedback is so valuable and truly made this book a million times better. Thank you for reading a very rough draft and donating your time to help me create something worthy of all your beautiful bookshelves.

A special shout out is needed for my beta and sensitivity reader, Erin, who not only fact checked every lupus mention, but also shared in my love for Taylor Swift references and gave me some solid one-liners! Sharing our experiences with prednisone within the comments of my draft was honestly something I treasured. You are a lupus warrior!

Sam. I feel so lucky to have stumbled across your Instagram page last year, because your covers are just dreamy. Thank you for taking the chaos in my head and turning it into something worthy of a frame.

Lastly, thank you to my parents for so much support and encouragement. Being an indie author is hard and having you in my corner means the world to me. Sorry about the candy cane scene.

About the Author

Lindsey Lanza is a book lover and romance author currently residing in New England. She is a tech start-up enthusiast by day, a voracious reader by early mornings, nights and weekends, and now writes love stories when she gets a spare moment. You can most often find her laughing about nothing with her husband Erik, perusing a dessert menu, consulting clients on zoom calls or obsessing over her Sheepadoodle Wally. A Little Magic is her second novel.

For more books and updates:
lindseylanza.com

 instagram.com/readwithli

Printed in Great Britain
by Amazon

31627129R00200